What's Left Between Us

A Pearl Girls Novel

☆☽☆

The answer is always love!

Gina Heron

ISBN-13: 9781790320455

For Eddie, and for Rob and Rachel, for Ryan, and for John, for Hernandez, and for all the others finding their way back home.

And always, with love and gratitude, for Z.

ACKNOWLEDGMENTS

I've been writing this book in one form or another for six years. That said, many eyes have seen it, and many hands have touched some version of it. I'm grateful for each and every person who has read, critiqued, helped research, or supported me in one way or another in this effort, whether named here or not. There are so many, I'd need to write a whole other book to acknowledge you all.

First and most of all, thank you to all of the service members who inspired me, helped me research, allowed interviews, and read these pages for accuracy. I am humbled by your courage and hope the end result makes you proud.

Caleb and Aislyn, I can't begin to tell you all the ways you inspire me. You make me a better human, and you are the reason I wake up earlier than God to do this. I hope you will be as proud of me as I am of you. I love you with a fierceness.

My mama, Irene. Thank you for loving me anyway.

My sister, Angel. I still want to be like you when I grow up, because you have the most beautiful heart of anyone I know. No one inspired me to write Bay more than you did.

Melissa Freeman, my editor, thank you for reading every crap word I've ever written, for laughing and crying with me all the way through it, and for being one of the very best friends I've ever had. Thank you for all you did to make this book sing!

And Jennie Shaw… I hope you didn't think I was kidding when I told you this would say that I can't do anything without you. I can't. You are the best critique partner in the whole world, and you have made me a better writer, and this story more than I hoped it could be. Thank you for all the hours you've spent on it with me. Also, no one has ever taught me more about my value as a human than you have, and I am eternally grateful for how you believe in me, personally and professionally. Thank you most of all for your friendship, because it has changed my life. You are a rainbow-glitter-love-bomb badass amazing human. Also thank you for slowing my roll when I really need you to. Because I really need you to.

Special thanks to Kristy Woodson Harvey, Kimberly Belle, Kathryn Craft, Heather Bell Adams, Kimberly Brock, and Suzanne Palmieri for offering up your kind blurbs for What's Left Between Us. Your thoughtful reads and feedback helped get it ready for the world, and I am forever grateful! I am so lucky that you are not only authors I look up to, but also ones I consider friends.

My #5amwritersclub crew, thanks for giving me other early-bird creatives to hang out with in the morning! Y'all have been making my mornings more productive for so many years. I appreciate you! Jay, J-Ro, Tif, Karma, Kip, Lori… much love to you!

And all of you who have read and offered feedback over the many drafts of this novel, THANK YOU!! I know this isn't a comprehensive list, but I'm going to try:

Denise Bruce, Cathy Bruce, Leigh Labbo Hewitt, Gina Evans, Carol Brown, Tif Marcelo, Vicki June, Tommy Fennel, SFC Hernandez, Paige Burris, Pam Klein, Wade Poston, Tee Jae Nettles, Connie Vincent, and Ellie Hicks. Thank you all!

Kasey Corbit, Kris Kisska Mehigan, and Terry Lynn Thomas… I love you so.

Patti Callahan Henry, for your gracious encouragement and support. The right words at the right time mean everything.

Erin Niumata, thank you for your tireless efforts on my behalf. Your editorial input has helped make this book shine. Thank you for seeing something in it, and in me.

Michael Krajewski, thank you for lending your gift to make the outside of this book something I need to live up to on the inside. She's beautiful, like your heart. I love you.

And to all of you reading these words, thank you for taking a chance on me and Bay. It means the world to me.

To love or have loved, that is enough. Ask nothing further. There is no other pearl to be found in the dark folds of life.

—Victor Hugo, Les Miserables

CHAPTER 1

"What do you mean, he's missing?" Bay's voice cracked on the last word.

She shouldn't have taken the phone call from her daddy two minutes before walking on stage for the biggest performance of her life. But he'd called twice, back-to-back. She figured he'd wish her good luck real quick and she'd be on her way.

That's not why he'd called, though.

"There was some sort of ambush…" Mel answered, the words getting mangled, his deep voice straining with the weight of them. Bay could barely make out what he said with all the noise backstage and the sound of her own heart pounding in her ears.

"Daddy, you're not making any sense," she said, white knuckles gripping the phone. "Who told you that?"

"A warrant officer was here just now."

"Well, they must have got something wrong," Bay said. "Scott wouldn't have—"

"Bay, you got thirty seconds," Warren, the stage manager at Smokey's, said. He made a grab for her phone, but she bent forward and knelt close to the curtain where he couldn't reach it.

"Gimme a minute," Bay said to Warren through gritted teeth.

"Oh, Bay, I'm sorry, hon. You've got that show tonight. With all of this we just—I wasn't thinking."

"I don't understand. How—how is Scott missing? Who took him where?"

"They said—Lord, they think it was the Taliban. Kedrick and Simpson were out with him. Kedrick is dead. Simpson's been taken to a hospital somewhere in Germany. And Scott—they can't find him. The warrant officer said he hadn't been located and had likely been taken somewhere and—he's gone."

"Bay, now!"

Before she knew what was happening, her phone was out of her hands and Sally, her guitar, was in them. Warren shoved her forward and she stumbled onto the stage.

Bay stood beneath the twinkling lights strung in layers above her, alone in front of the rich red velvet curtain, her mouth hovering ever so close to the microphone. She didn't make a sound.

The boozed-up crowd had been rowdy before, but the longer Bay was up there—her heart now still and heavy as a stone in her chest, bearing down on her lungs so she couldn't take a deep breath—the quieter they became. With the spotlight on her, she couldn't see past the first row of tables.

Bay positioned Sally in her arms, willing her autopilot to take over, but nothing seemed right about it. Her fingers moved on the strings, but all she felt was discord. The sound couldn't reach her through the ringing in her ears, Mel's words rewinding, playing back, rewinding again.

They can't find him?

Bay's arms gave way and Sally slid from them, landing on the floor. She blinked back tears. Brandt Thoreau was out there somewhere in the crowd. He'd wanted to hear her sing live himself before signing her to his label.

She'd been dreaming of this moment for a decade, working hard for it, playing every bar gig she could talk herself into, making a name for herself in the trenches of Nashville.

He's missing?

Bay had dreaded that moment for as long as she'd dreamed of this one, and now here they both were, the biggest moment of her life and the worst moment, crashing into each other on this stage in front of a room full of people who didn't realize her soul lay in a shattered heap at her feet.

Shoving her hand into the pocket of her jeans, Bay wrapped her fingers around the ring Scott had given her when they graduated high school, before he left for basic training. He'd said it was a promise ring, a promise that he would always come home to her. It was cheap—all he could afford at the time—and when Bay developed an allergy to the metal, she'd given it to him to carry on his deployments as a reminder of his promise.

But before his last deployment, when Bay had insisted they were over, he'd given it back. She'd spent hours looking for it over the last couple of days, needing it with her on this night.

She needed him with her. Underneath it all, that had been the reason she walked away. She needed him to stay, but he couldn't let go of his duty. This never-ending war.

She squeezed the ring so hard she thought the one rough, pitted cultured pearl it held might pop off the tarnished band. Bile rose up the back of her throat as sweat beaded on her neck beneath her hair.

Shouts started coming at her from the dark, urging her to sing.

"Bay, you okay?"

Warren was beside Bay now, gathering Sally from the floor.

She wasn't okay. Scott was missing. He could be dead, or maybe worse. Which was worse? Someone had him. What had he suffered? What might he be suffering as she stood here, grasping at her shot at fame like any of this was important?

None of this meant anything to her without him.

Bay backed away from Warren and the microphone, then bolted to the stage exit as the shouts from the audience got louder.

"What the—" Warren followed her toward the exit, but she didn't stop. She pushed herself through the heavy metal door into the dark alley and kept running, not caring which direction she took, as long as it was away from that stage, away from that phone call, away from the endless refrain...

He's gone.

Whatever tattered shreds of hope Bay had been clinging to were as lost as the promise of the ring she gripped in her shaking fingers. Scott was gone, and every dream she'd ever had was gone with him.

CHAPTER 2

☆☽☆

83 Days Later

Bay knew something about last times. Her life had been full of them, after all. They were wild, reckless things. Violent, unpredictable. Especially the ones you didn't see coming.

Too many years had come and gone since the last time Bay was in New Hope, and nothing was the same. She realized it then, standing in the dark on the cracked dirt path, watching her family move in bursts and flurries on the other side of the broad windows of Blossom Hill. The constants in her life, the compass points, shifted and weathered, degree by degree, in ways she never expected.

Even the house she'd grown up in was different, the shutters freshly painted, the old iron porch rails replaced with more modern white columns. It wasn't just the paint and porch rails that had changed, though. Looking up at Blossom Hill, she saw past the impeccable upkeep to the sorrow that must have surely seeped into the walls of every room in the house. The last Christmas she was home, the porch had glittered with white lights strung over heavy garland, an enormous wreath had hung on the door, and poinsettias of every variety had lined the steps up to the porch.

This year, though, there was a single candle in the window by the front door, a lone yellow ribbon tied around a column. The candle had stopped Bay in her tracks when she spotted it. She didn't know how she could move past it, that candle flickering there, the loss it signified. The cold seeped up through her boots and her skin prickled as she considered whether she could walk through the door of Blossom Hill, knowing it would feel as empty as her own heart without Scott there beside her.

But she'd have to go in eventually. There was nowhere else left to go.

The increasingly familiar anxiety of having run out of options welled up to form a lump in her throat, and she had no one to blame but herself. It was as if she'd lined everything that meant anything to her up on a fence and played target practice. And Bay was a damn good shot. Every single one of her dreams lay in pieces on the ground. Amazing, she thought, how far and how fast you could fall when you had nothing left to hold on to.

"You gonna stand outside all night contemplating the paint, or are you coming in?" The rich bass of her daddy's voice washed over Bay as he grinned at her from the porch and let the screen door bang shut behind him.

"Well, it is a mighty fine paint job," Bay said with the brightest smile she could muster. She bent to pick up her weathered guitar case from where she'd dropped it at her feet. Mel shook his head and chuckled while she struggled up the front walk. Bay had trained him well. He'd given up helping her carry things years ago. Her "do it myself" tantrums were legendary at Blossom Hill. The duffel bag and one small suitcase she dragged behind her held all she had left to her name, besides Sally. She'd pawned or sold everything she could in Nashville.

"Your mama was expecting you hours ago."

"And as usual, I disappoint," Bay said, puffing out a breath. She dragged her bag up the steps, sat the guitar down again, straightened to her full five feet two inches and looked up to take in the comforting sight of her daddy's face.

Mel stood a full foot taller than her, and even more than that in her mind's eye. He was the kind of man who took up all kinds of space and held your attention, from the shock of his dark hair and the sparkling blue of his eyes, to the boom of his voice, right down to his surprisingly graceful size thirteen feet. They stood apart, sizing each other up. Mel's hair was a little more silver at the temples, his middle a tad thicker than she remembered, but his eyes danced with joy at the sight of her just the same.

"If you hadn't come home in the next few days, she had plans to go find you and drag you back." Mel pulled Bay into a hug, and she breathed in the wood-smoked scent of his old flannel shirt, pressing her cheek against it. "And you rarely answer that dang phone of yours. I don't even know why you have it."

"Missed you, Daddy," she said, straining to contain the emotion that shook her voice.

"And I missed you, baby girl," Mel whispered into her hair before pressing his lips to the top of her head.

Bay stepped back, swiped at her eyes, and looked around the porch. "It does look nice out here, even though you didn't decorate yet."

Mel shrugged. "Not much in the mood." He waved off her attempt at a response and bent to get her guitar. "You go on and get the heavy one. My back's not what it used to be."

As Mel continued through the foyer and up the staircase, Bay forced herself to take the last few steps through the door. She dropped her duffel and paused, expecting the sights, sounds, and smells of the LaFleur house at Christmas to assault her senses. But there was no Christmas music in the air to greet her, no hint of Murphy's Oil Soap blending with the wood from the fireplace and cinnamon and nutmeg from the kitchen. The house was quiet, subdued. She imagined her words would echo back to her if she spoke.

"Bay Laurel, is that you coming through the front door like a stranger?" Violet leaned around the doorway to the formal dining room to get a look at her.

Bay froze, her hand resting on a crystal tumbler sitting out on the wet bar by a bottle of Mel's favorite bourbon. She wasn't actually going to pour a drink, but she knew what her mama must think. Not the start she was hoping for. She stepped away and tucked her hands behind her back, twisting her fingers together in a tight knot. "Hey, Mama."

Violet threw the dish towel she was carrying over her shoulder and shook her head. "Lord, you need a drink time as you come through the door? Count it good fortune if anything's left in that bottle. Your daddy's been nippin' all day. Better get in here before

Leigh Anne combusts," she said, already headed to the kitchen, the heart of Blossom Hill.

Breathe in. Breathe out.

Bay steeled herself against the sharp edges of Violet's voice and ordered her heart to its proper place in her chest. "Well, that's not like Daddy. Y'all must be running him crazy," she said, not sure whether Violet could hear her. She drifted through the empty formal rooms of her parents' home, letting her hands run over the cool velvet back of the antique sofa, the soft lace of the curtains, the brass edges of framed school pictures of herself, her brother, and her sister.

She hesitated near the door to the kitchen and counted to ten before rounding the corner and entering the fray.

"Well, finally!" Leigh Anne, Ethan's wife, put her hands on her plump hips and smirked at Bay. Leigh Anne wasn't a large woman, but her consistently overdone hair and makeup and bright, layered outfits gave her a puffed-up appearance that sat well with her overbearing personality. She examined a manicured nail—candy cane striped—and tilted her chin up. "Right in time to miss yet another family dinner prepared just for you."

"Now, Leigh," Violet interjected, "no need making a fuss. I fixed you a plate, Bay. You can heat it if you're hungry."

Bay grabbed her sister-in-law's face and kissed her hard on the cheek. "Good to see you too, Leigh."

Leigh Anne pushed Bay off, her face twisted with a look of disgust. "You smell like an ashtray."

"I smell like I've been on a bus for hours,'" Bay said, mirroring Leigh Anne's aggressive stance. They faced off like two prize fighters weighing in for a match.

"Gross. No wonder," Leigh Anne said, waving a hand in front of her.

"Your attitude's the only thing smellin' up the place."

"Girls!" Violet banged her hand hard on the counter. "Can we not be civilized for five minutes?"

They fell silent at Violet's outburst. Bay shrugged and Leigh Anne rolled her dark eyes as she worked the pearl hanging around her neck back and forth on its chain.

Leigh's pendant was simple, much like Violet's, with one small diamond suspended with the pearl on a thin gold chain that she could wear every day—and she made sure to pull it out from her collar and call attention to it when Bay was there to see. Leigh didn't have to say how much she enjoyed getting to be a part of The Pearl Girls while Bay sat out, waiting her turn to join the ranks of the married women in Violet's family, which was a coveted position in their little town.

But when Ethan had married Leigh Anne (too young, in Bay's opinion), Bay decided she didn't care if she ever became part of that particular club. In spite of a difficult upbringing, Leigh was smart, pretty, and hungry for better things by the time she was a teenager—all things Bay respected about her until she realized they came coupled with a cunning streak wide as the Edisto River. Leigh set her sights on Ethan in ninth grade and made sure he married her straight out of high school, urged forward by a faux pregnancy. Even if she was only a kid herself at the time, Bay was the only one in the family brazen enough to call Leigh out on her deception. They'd been at odds since.

Bay turned her back on Leigh and offered Violet an awkward hug.

"Whew!" Violet said as she shrugged out of Bay's grasp. "You do smell like an ashtray."

"Sorry," Bay said, twisting her hands in a knot behind her back as she walked to the far side of the kitchen island. "The renovation looks amazing, Mama." She was surrounded by classic white marble countertops, high end professional grade appliances, and beautiful whitewashed cabinetry. But the old rough-hewn heart of pine floors shone the same as before, and were somehow a perfect fit.

"Well, thank you, Bay," Violet said. She wiped over the sparkling countertop with the dish towel she carried. "Glad you finally got home to see it. We were disappointed that you didn't come sooner, with the news and all."

Bay froze where she stood, her breath catching in her throat as her chest squeezed. She pressed her palms against the cool marble surface of the island, searching for a way to explain. "I know. I'm sorry, Mama," she choked out, falling short.

"I guess you stay busy with your music, but…"

"Let's not talk about it. Please," Bay whispered, closing her eyes, "It's hard enough to be here without him. I can't talk about it."

Violet lifted a hand as if to reach for Bay, then let it drop to her side. "I was hoping maybe being home for the holiday would be a comfort. I don't—"

"Bay, the girls are waiting for you in there," Mel said, walking through just in time to change the subject. "Leigh had all our old VHS tapes put on DVD. They want to watch them, but they've been waiting for you."

Violet rolled her eyes and sighed. "Lord, I know she meant well, but..."

"What's on them?" Bay asked, peeking into the next room.

"Mostly some old stuff from when y'all were still kids, birthdays and Christmases and such," Violet answered. "We hadn't watched those tapes in ages. Leigh took them months ago to have them transferred to the DVDs. Lucky us, they came back just in time for the holiday."

Bay groaned. "Oh, great. Memory lane, just what I wasn't hoping for."

Ethan got up to greet Bay with a smile and a hug when the girls spotted her, announcing her arrival with shrieks of "Aunt Bay!" He bent to lift her up and squeezed her before dropping her hard on her feet, his caramel brown eyes squinting over a bright smile. Bay reached up and patted his scruffy cheeks. "Hey there, handsome," she said.

"Girl, you're wasting away. I got a ten-year-old bigger than you," Ethan said, resting a hand on Lucy's head as she wrapped her arms around Bay's middle. Lucy and Bree were ten and seven, the eldest a quiet kid like her father, the youngest a spitfire after her mother's own heart. "You still haven't learned how to cook?"

"Who knows when she eats, or what? How on God's earth Violet raised a daughter that refuses to cook," Leigh Anne chimed in. She flipped through the case of DVDs that sat on the coffee table.

"I don't eat, Leigh. I live on whiskey and cigarettes." Bay plopped down beside her sister-in-law, smirking at the bitter bite of truth in her own words. "What's on these besides Christmases?" she asked, squinting to read the labels on the DVDs. Leigh flipped a page, and Bay found an unlabeled one. She plucked it from its sleeve.

"Probably just a blank," Leigh said, flipping another page.

"Or it could be a mystery DVD," Bay whispered to Lucy and Bree. They rewarded her with a round of conspiratorial giggles.

Leigh snatched the DVD from Bay's fingers, leaving them stinging, and slid it into the player. Ethan pushed in between the two of them and winked at Bay. In a matter of seconds, the static on the TV screen was replaced by a grainy image of the New Hope Raiders football field. The camera panned from the field to the players standing along the edge of the field.

"Look at you, Daddy," Bay said, leaning in to watch a young Mel lined up with the rest of the offense, waiting for their turn on the field. "You're so handsome. I bet you had all the ladies chasing you, mister star quarterback."

Mel laughed as he moved in closer. "I only had eyes for Violet, I swear it."

They watched as Mel jogged from the sidelines, strapping on his helmet.

"I thought you played quarterback," Ethan said as Mel lined up at running back.

"Yeah," Bay said, "what's with this?"

Mel's brow furrowed. "We switched it up here and there. Unless this is senior year..."

"Who is that at quarterback?" Bay asked, dropping to the floor and scooting close to the TV. "The way he moves...it's..."

Her breath hitched when, at the end of the third down play, the quarterback took his helmet off and looked almost directly at the camera as he jogged back toward the bench. Another player punched his arm, and his smile showed a dimple she'd recognize anywhere.

Maybe the guy's hair was darker, and skin, but that dimple, those eyes, even the way he moved beneath all the padding...

"Enough of my old glory days," Mel said in a rush, grabbing up the remote to stop the DVD.

"Dad, wait—"

"It's time to put these away for the night, I believe," Mel continued, talking over her, pulling the DVD out and turning just in time to nearly knock Violet for a loop.

"What in the world, Mel?" Violet grabbed his arm to steady herself.

"There was a guy on that one," Bay said, getting to her feet to face her parents. "He reminded me so much of..."

A look passed between Mel and Violet that Bay couldn't discern, the kind of look shared by two people who'd been together so long they could practically read each other's thoughts.

"What? What is it?"

"Oh, sweetie, that's hardly possible. I'm so sorry. I bet you see him everywhere you go," Mel said, moving to squeeze Bay's shoulders in a half hug.

She shook her head. "No, not really."

Except that day at the grocery store, and on the corner of Union and 6th, and that night I nearly pulled that poor guy off his stool at the bar..."

"I mean, sometimes, but—"

"You do have a history of seeing things that aren't really there," Violet said with a shrug. Leigh snorted from where she sat beside Ethan.

"Leigh, quit it." Ethan gave his wife a cutting glance.

"Geez, sorry," Leigh huffed.

It had taken Bay years to learn to keep her encounters with her dead twin sister to herself, but when her parents threatened to have her committed, she gave up the ghost, so to speak. They'd hauled her to therapy every week for two years after Lillie died, which she found cruel at the time. She understood a little better now, though, how hard it must be to try and help someone recover from an unbearable loss when you're suffering through it yourself. Even after the years of therapy, and after Bay moved off to Nashville, she'd still find Lillie hanging around Blossom Hill whenever she returned. Bay didn't believe in ghosts—not really—but she knew in her heart that Lillie would always be a part of her.

She wished she could find her now.

Her fingers found the delicate silver butterfly resting on a chain around her neck. Lillie had worn it every day until the day she died. She'd left it hanging on the lamp in their bedroom at the beach house that last night. Bay found it the next morning, put it on, and had never taken it off again. It was tarnished now and had lost all its shine, but she loved it just the same. Scott's ring hung on the same chain as Lillie's butterfly now. It was some solace, at least, having these little reminders of them resting together near her heart.

"It's hard to believe it's been over two months already," Ethan said

"Eighty-three days," Bay squeezed out between gritted teeth.

Scott had been missing in action in Afghanistan for eighty-three days. Bay didn't need a calendar to keep count. His absence was as palpable for her as his presence. It brought her heart—her whole life—to a standstill, the lack of him, the not knowing if he was hurt, or suffering, or afraid…or if he would ever come home to her again.

"Maybe I am seeing things. I know I still feel him. I know he can't be…"

A heavy silence fell around the family, and Bay shrank a little further into herself as they all cast cautious glances at her, like they were waiting for her to unravel, to dissolve into a puddle of tears in the middle of the floor. She twisted her hands until finally Mel reached for her.

"Bay, honey, we all want him back, too," he said. "We're all praying every day he'll make it home."

"I don't—I need some air," Bay choked.

Bay pushed past her parents and through the kitchen to the front of the house, where she paused long enough to grab her purse. She heard Mel tell Violet to let her go, to give her a little space before the door shut behind her.

She took the steps two at a time and jogged down the front lane, stopping about halfway, her breath coming in gasps as the tears she'd been holding back for months spilled over. Leaning against the low white fence that bordered the driveway, she wiped her face with the back of her hands, then dug through her purse until she found the old photograph she carried with her.

The picture was so faded now, it could have been a black and white. It used to be full of color, just as they had been full of life. Their little trio, Bay, Scott, and Lillie, faces pressed together, Scott in the middle of the two girls. Bay and Lillie weren't identical twins, though they were obviously sisters. Lillie was darker—her hair, the deeper blue of her eyes, her skin. She was delicate like the flower she was named after, a hothouse bloom next to Bay's fierce face and wild hair. Bay carried her strength like an invisible fortress, never minding her petite frame.

It had been taken the summer Lillie died. They'd been invincible right up to that moment. That's how it felt to Bay, spending their weeks out of school on Edisto. They ran miles over that sand, explored the forests and marshes, swam laps in the pool, raced sand sharks in the waves, and took turns diving from their sailboat to see who could stay under longest. Bay usually won, except the occasions when Scott forgot to watch out for Lillie. He was the one who watched out for her. Bay was jealous of the way he seemed to like Lillie a little more than her when they were younger. It took her years to understand that he didn't think Bay needed protecting, with her impossibly strong limbs and lungs, her fearlessness. Lillie was dealt the weaker hand at birth, asthma and that delicate beauty that leant itself to frailty.

Bay wasn't thinking of Lillie the night they lost her. She didn't know—couldn't remember—what she had been thinking. She remembered running as fast as she could from the beach house, her body jarring with each footfall against the hard-packed sand of the shoreline. She'd heard Lillie calling for her as she stripped off her shirt and shorts, and it had irritated her.

"Why do you always have to follow me?" she'd shouted back at her.

"Bay, the current—"

Bay had laughed, had stuck her tongue out at Lillie, and at Scott running up behind her.

"You can't catch me in the water!" she'd shouted as she dove in.

The shame Bay felt over her actions that night was almost unbearable. She'd noticed Lillie's shallow breathing as they stood there on the sand. She noticed, and it irritated her even further. Bay couldn't remember why she was so angry, but she was angry at all of them—Lillie, Scott, her parents—all of them. She told Lillie to get lost.

The undertow was stronger than she thought it would be. She swam out anyway, ignoring the shoreline until Scott caught up to her.

"Lillie."

It took a few seconds for Bay to register what was happening as he scanned the water and the shore, a few seconds for the panic to rise in her throat.

"Lillie!"

She would have turned back, gone to the house. She wasn't a strong swimmer. But they called for her anyway, for a minute, then two, until Bay felt something shift, break away from her. Something essential. She knew as they swam hard to shore, the salt of her tears let loose in the waves, seeking her sister, the better half of their whole. Lillie would not be on the shore, or in the house. Lillie was gone, and the best part of Bay was gone along with her. She couldn't remember what happened after, what happened for days or weeks after. The last time she ever saw her sister alive changed her, defined her. It broke her, that last.

Her selfishness caused Lillie's death. The same selfishness pushed Scott away when he was trying so hard to fix things between them. And now he had gone missing in a barren desert country, thousands of miles away from home, lost in a war that should have been over, that he should have been done with. But even though he was so far away, out of reach, he was always there in the back of her mind. The reason she breathed. The reason she couldn't breathe. The lost thing she'd be trying to find for the rest of her life, the love she could never replace. Bay convinced herself she would have felt him breaking loose from her, too, like she had with Lillie. She and Scott were so close, surely she would feel it if he were really gone…

And yet she worried, as much as she wanted him to come back to her, how much he was suffering. She hoped, and she tried to pray, but she couldn't bear the thought of what her answered prayers would mean he was going through.

She turned back to the house and watched the candle flickering in the window, its light reflecting the uncertainty of what hope she had left. If Bay had known she'd might not ever see Scott again, she would have told him that last time—was it really a few months ago?—that she loved him, that she forgave him, when he asked her to give it one more try. Instead, she dug her heels in, made demands that she knew he couldn't meet, insisted on being right even when she knew she was wrong.

Every breath she struggled to take since was a prayer for one more chance to change, because in all the uncertainty of the future, there was only one thing she could know for sure: without him, nothing would ever be the same again.

CAPTIVITY: DAY 83

Scott Jackson Murphy.
Sergeant First Class, United States Army.
Serial Number 224278972.
Last known loc: Korengal Valley, Afghanistan.
Coordinates: 34.8812° N, 70.9052° E.
83rd day in captivity.

These are facts. These are things I know.

But I don't know what hell's coming for me in the darkest hours.

Water, fire, blood, or bone?

It doesn't matter. I'll do what I need to do to survive.

But I won't talk.

The voices outside the door disorient me, the scrape of the key in the rusted-out lock. The one that would be so easy to bust through if I wasn't chained to the damn wall.

When they come, I state the required facts. Then they can do their best to break me. It won't happen.

Bone.

They tie the cloth sack around my neck, come at me with boots, fists, rubber hoses. I close my eyes and search out the space inside my mind where I can hide, where I can imagine anything happening but what's actually happening. That's when she visits me. Lillie.

I don't know why she comes, how she found her way here from the grave, but I'm damn grateful. Bay could always sense her around home, even said that they talked sometimes. I figured that was part of her grief working itself out.

Maybe it was her mind's way of surviving the loss. Anyway, Lillie, she takes me home, in my mind. She gets me out of this, at least for a few minutes. I keep thinking maybe this time it'll be forever, the real deal. That it'll be over. Whatever happens when you die, it's got to be better than this.

She holds her hands out, palms up. When she blows into them, butterflies scatter. Some land in her hair, like when we were kids. Butterflies chased Lillie—not the other way around. It was the damnedest thing.

I close my eyes and the memory Lillie delivers pushes through the pain.

I'm on the high school football field for the first time, but I'm not in high school yet. It's fifth grade, and our rec league team is scrimmaging some of the school's alumni at half time.

My gran isn't there. She's too sick to be out in the fall air. The LaFleurs aren't coming, either, even though Ethan's here too. I'm disappointed, watching all the other kids get pictures with their dads who are gonna play against them. I'm scanning the crowd at the sidelines, and I see her.

Bay's there. Somehow, she found a way to come. Her cheeks are pink from the cold, and that crazy curly hair falls out of the nest on top of her head. The way those blue eyes spark when she smiles at me. My heart does a little flip, and I smile back.

That's the day I realized that Bay would always be there for me, no matter what.

She was even there at my last deployment ceremony, after everything had fallen apart.

She held back tears. And for the first time, so did I. There was so much hurt between us, and I didn't know how to fix it. Well, scratch that—I knew. She told me how to fix it. I didn't listen.

For so long she was there for me, by my side, and that day, I just let her go. I'd forgotten what she meant to me.

But I remember now.

```
Scott Jackson Murphy.
Sergeant First Class, United States Army.
Serial Number 224278972.
```

God, please don't let that be the last time.

CHAPTER 3

Sunday morning at Blossom Hill revolved around two pressing issues: what Bay was wearing to church, and what Violet was cooking for dinner. The menu was a less complicated fix than Bay's wardrobe.

"Bay Laurel, you are not—I repeat, not—wearing those God-awful tight pants to Unity Baptist. You've got dresses still hanging in that closet upstairs that you will not lie to me and say you can't fit into. Now get your butt up there and change. For the sake of all things holy, stop behaving like a four-year-old," Violet said, clipping her words like a drill sergeant giving the day's marching orders.

Bay muttered a few choice words under her breath before responding. "Mama, please, join us in this decade, or at least this century. Nobody gives one holy hot damn about my pants, which are actually leggings, that I'm only wearing beneath this dress because you think it's a shirt. You do know lots of churches these days you just walk in wearing whatever you want? The Lord is fine with it."

"Bay Laurel LaFleur!" Violet shouted.

"Jesus, I know my own name!" Bay shouted back.

I am four years old in this house, she thought, frustrated that she and Violet had already fallen into the same old pattern of butting heads over every little thing. Bay trudged up the stairs and down the hall to her bedroom, twisted the old glass knob and threw herself inside. The sarcastic missives she'd been forming in her mind to shout down at Violet sputtered and died in her mouth, her senses all at once overwhelmed, abruptly confronted with the remnants of her youth. She'd meant to keep out of this space, had been so careful not to open this door, afraid she might get lost in the memories made here.

The bright light of the winter morning stormed the room. The shades had been left up, and the butter yellow ruffles of the curtains magnified the natural light to an unnatural frequency. Bay heard it buzzing in the air like static from an old radio, the crackle and hiss of the memories locked away in this room, the recognition of all these ordinary things that had become something out of a fairytale, a story written about another girl, polished in her mind to something perfect, something more than what was lived out here in reality.

Everything stood as it had when she'd been in high school. Her antique jewelry box with the broken latch sat in the center of the dresser, still holding some old costume pieces, one door half open. A few of her notebooks were stacked on the desk and a decorated soup can that she made in grade school held pencils and pens. Grandma LaFleur's old handmade quilt, a gift to Bay when she turned fifteen, covered her twin bed.

And Lillie's bed, the one closest to the window, still made up with her own quilt, as if one day she'd come back in and curl up on her side and chatter at Bay until they both drifted off to sleep.

Bay wandered to the dresser and picked up a framed picture of the girl she had been, one Scott had taken of her in the boathouse down at the pond. She'd been laying in one of the boats, legs dangling over the lip, her face turned away from him, the sun shining in her hair. Most likely lost in a daydream. What would that girl think of the woman she'd become? She'd likely be let down right along with everyone else, but she'd be the only one who could understand how lost in the world her grownup self was, now that the tether to Scott, the one person who'd always kept her anchored, was broken.

"You sure went and did it this time, didn't you?"

Lillie spoke to her from the window seat. She sat like a golden shadow in a stream of sunlight, butterflies resting in her hair. It was as if she brought their last summer with her, too, when she visited.

Bay studied her sister, who would forever be the same, locked in at twelve years old, her tangled waves a darker, tamer version of Bay's wild strawberry blonde curls. "Lillie," she whispered, her throat tightening. She sat across from Lillie—the idea of Lillie—close enough that their knees might touch if it had been possible. She reached a hand out, but let it drop to her lap as tears threatened to spill down her cheeks.

She closed her eyes and breathed in the warm saltwater and bubblegum smell that filled the room. Lillie's little appearances left Bay flooded with an odd mix of relief at her presence and sadness over her loss. Bay wanted so much to wrap her arms around Lillie one more time, but she knew that was one wish that would never come true. "I was worried you weren't—that maybe you wouldn't be back again. It's been so long."

"Oh, Bay," Lillie said. She leaned forward, cupping her hands together. The butterflies gathered in her palms. "I missed you, too."

"Who said I missed you?" Bay asked with a wink.

Lillie laughed, the sound like wind chimes filling the air around them. Her butterflies scattered.

"Not everything needs to be said."

"But some things do," Bay said. "You're right, Lillie. I really went and blew it all to hell this time. And now…"

"Now you know what's worth fighting for. But you've always known that Scott is worth fighting for, haven't you? Maybe if you stop fighting with yourself so hard, you'll win the next round."

Bay threw up her hands. "I don't know what fight I've got left in me now," she said, her voice giving way to her pain. "I don't—if he doesn't come back, I don't know how to go on. And if he does, I don't know if he'll ever forgive me for what I did. I don't know how I'll ever make it up to him."

"You will. And you'll mend fences with Mama, too. Already would have if you weren't both so mule-headed."

Bay rolled her eyes. "Lord knows, she's driving me crazy already, Lillie."

"She's got her own cross to carry," Lillie half-whispered, twirling a strand of hair around her finger, sending the butterflies fluttering. "It's hard for her, too. Try and understand."

Bay sighed. “I do, Lillie. And I know it’s all my fault. One day maybe she’ll be able to forgive me.”

Lillie stared off past Bay, her brow furrowed. “First she has to forgive herself.”

“Forgive herself for what?” Bay’s voice twisted as her mind worked over Lillie’s statement.

“You both carry such a heavy burden for something neither one of you could have done a thing to change. Scott, too. Bay, you’re going to have to help him find his way home.” Lillie wavered, faded.

“How am I supposed to do that?” Bay asked, reaching for her sister, knowing she was about to slip away again.

“Keep your eyes open, Bay, and your heart. Trust them both.”

“Find something?”

Bay jumped at the sound of Violet’s voice close behind her. She squeezed her eyes shut and took her time catching her breath. When she looked at the window seat again, Lillie was gone.

“No, I didn’t,” Bay answered quietly, getting up and rushing to the door without considering the contents of her old closet. “I’m wearing my clothes, the ones I have on. I can stay here with Daddy if you’re embarrassed by my perfectly appropriate black leggings.”

Violet put a hand on one hip and the other to her temple. “Leigh Anne’s already told all your friends from school that you’ll be there for the Women’s Union breakfast. You’re coming, pants and all, if you insist on ’em.”

“I don’t mind staying behind. Really.”

Violet hefted Bay’s guitar from the bed and walked past her and across the hall to the guest room where she dropped it on the white chenille spread.

“I guess you want this in here, since you’re not staying in your own room for whatever reason,” Violet said flatly. Bay could feel the irritation rolling off of her in waves.

“Less memories floating around in here to keep me up at night.” Bay watched from a distance as Violet stood over her old guitar case, her fingers trailing along its seams, tracing the decals, the dents and scratches.

“This is the case your daddy got you for your sixteenth birthday.”

Bay crossed her arms over her chest. "Yes, and I know, it was expensive."

"Too expensive," Violet said. "He's so indulgent of your whims."

"Whims, Mama? Are you serious?" Bay tried and failed to keep the defensive edge from her voice.

Violet rapped her knuckles against the case. "Yes, Bay, your whims. He insists on encouraging you to chase your dreams, to follow your star, whatever that means."

"Because he understands what it means to me."

Violet shook her head. "No, Bay, not because he understands. He doesn't understand, and you certainly don't understand or care how hard it is for me. Ethan, he's so solid. He finished school, started a family, he and Leigh work normal jobs—"

"And landed a few minutes from your doorstep, where you can keep them right under your thumb, just how you like it," Bay broke in.

Violet didn't have to say how much she resented Bay for leaving New Hope, especially after they lost Lillie. The LaFleurs were a tight circle, and Violet was the axis, her love the centripetal force at the center that kept them all within reach of each other. Bay had betrayed her when she floated away, out of orbit. And now here she was, crashing down on Violet's manicured life like a falling star, burning out and breaking apart in the atmosphere, her and this guitar case full of scars, full of hurts, full of wrongs that she could never make right.

"I guess you've got me pegged, Bay. I like my family close, so we can take care of each other. Anyway, I can't protect you from yourself, can I? I can't undo the damage that's done. It seems like you'd understand at some point that we've already lost enough," Violet said wearily, as if she were too tired of this argument to close any distance between herself and her daughter.

Bay studied her mother from the doorway. "I'll stay here with Daddy this morning. I can help finish up dinner."

"Fine," Violet said, not turning to face her.

"Fine," Bay said. She turned away, then hesitated, her frustration bubbling over. Lillie's words rang in her ears. "You know, Mama, I've lost a lot, too. Everything, pretty much, and it was a hard thing for me to do, dragging myself back here with nothing but all these regrets. I came home, though, and not just because I didn't have anywhere else left to go. I don't know how to fix this, but I want to. And I needed you, Mama. I need you."

Bay hurried down the stairs too fast to hear her mother whisper, "Oh Bay, I need you, too."

CAPTIVITY: DAY 84

Scott Jackson Murphy.
Sergeant First Class, United States Army.
Serial Number 224278972.
84th day in captivity.

I make these mental notes as soon as I wake up, every time I wake up. I can't afford to lose track of real things, real time.

I've lost eighty-four days of my life in these Taliban shitholes, three so far.

Is this even real?

It's hard to move, and not because of the chains. Bruised ribs, maybe cracked. The right side of my face throbs.

I check for weather conditions, or what I can determine about them through the small wired-over slit that provides ventilation into the mud-walled room that's been my whole world for the last twenty-three days.

I'm pretty sure of the date. December 18th. Close to Christmas. Not that it makes a damn to me now. My dreams, my memories, they don't make a damn either. But it all seems so real when Lillie comes, like she has this morning, with butterflies in her hands. She blows them toward me, and I'm a kid again. For however long the memory lasts, I'm home.

Fifteen. It's the anniversary of Lillie's death, and Bay's still drowning. Drowning in her hurt, in the guilt I don't quite understand. It's my fault. I was supposed to keep an eye out for

Lillie in the water. It was my job, not Bay's.

When I tell Bay I love her, she laughs. *"Oh, you do? Then what color are my eyes?"* she asks, turning to me with her eyes closed.

Why do girls like to play these games?

"What do you mean, what color are your eyes?"

She crosses her arms over her chest. "You don't even know. If you loved me, you'd know."

"C'mon, Bay, you're bein' dense."

"You're the dense one, Scott. You don't know a thing about love."

"Fine. They're blue. Carolina Bay blue. But gray like a storm cloud when you're mad. They're green in places, more in the right than the left. You happy?"

She grins at me. *"Yeah, I guess."*

I close my eyes as she opens hers. *"Now, what color are mine?"*

"Green, deep green, like the forest. So dark you think they're brown until you look really close. I could roam around in them forever and not get bored," she says.

"Careful, now," I whisper, my lips almost touching hers. *"You might get lost."*

She stares up at me and touches the silver chain around her neck, her eyes going dark, like deep tidal pools. Like sorrow. *"I already am."*

I jerk to attention when the door swings open—the memory locked up so they can't take it. It's not them, though, it's an Afghani boy, barely a teenager himself, coming through the door with breakfast.

Focus, Murphy. Smile at the kid. Look him in the eye. Be trustworthy. It might be wrong, but sometimes you use whatever you've got, even if what you've got is bruised and bloodied to hell and back. I might lull him to get close enough eventually to grab him and search out a weapon.

He studies me. With my beard, my dark skin, I could be this boy's father. Maybe I'm Middle Eastern, at least part. It's hard to tell. That's been an advantage in this war before.

"Thank you," I say, then in Pashto, evenly. "Dera manana."

"Good morning, soldier Murphy," he whispers in hesitant English.

"Good morning to you," I say. "I'm sorry, I don't know your name."

"Behnam," he replies. "My name is Behnam."

There are voices outside, and he shoves the tray at me and runs to the door. I struggle not to let fear or frustration show on my face. His rush of movement kicks dust onto my plate. It'll have to do, anyway. Not like I can send it back to the kitchen. And eating a bit of Behnam's dust is a small price to pay for a little hope.

He pauses at the door and nods. I hold my breath and try to catch pieces of the conversation outside, but nothing is clear. Finally, they move on.

I blow at the fruit and breads on the plate, careful not to let the lukewarm milk slosh in its small cup. I try to focus on my meal, but it's hard to fight the jolt of adrenaline my short interaction with Behnam injected into my veins. Here's an opportunity, if I avoid the mistake of forging any real bond with the boy. It's not a mistake I can afford a second time. Not that I had much of a chance to bond with the girl who attempted to help me before. But when you watch somebody die…when their eyes lock onto yours at the moment…

Don't think about the girl. You make opportunities any way you can. Use what you can, who you have to.

Given present circumstances, I don't have the luxury of being above much.

CHAPTER 4

Bay slid into Scott's old Dodge truck, the one he'd bought from Mel with money he'd saved cutting grass and taking odd jobs their first year of high school. The smell of ancient vinyl and tobacco settled in around her right along with the memories flooding in. She used to joke that he loved that truck more than he did her. "*It's close. Argue your case,*" he'd say, pulling her close.

When he was deployed, Mel would drive the truck a couple of time every week. Now that she was home, and without her own wheels, Bay figured it was something she could do. Running her fingers over the steering wheel, she could imagine his hands, the left dangling on the wheel at twelve, the right skimming her hair as it flew in her face with the windows rolled down. It was always a fight, getting him to let her drive, and she usually lost. He'd fight about damn near anything, for the hell of it.

Her eyes closed, she whispered the only prayer she could muster. "Please, God, let him still have that fight in him. Please."

She opened the glove box and grabbed the keys, then took out the pack of Marlboros she knew would be there, his old red lighter tucked in with them. She cracked her window and lit a stale cigarette, took a long drag and left it dangling between her lips. She didn't smoke anymore, not much, anyway. But she needed something to take the edge off all the feelings being in New Hope stirred up for her. The absence of Scott, the skirmishes with her mama...maybe it was all too much, coming back here, trying to fix things.

She leaned hard on the clutch while her right hand fiddled with the floor-mounted stick shift. Her mind wandering, she turned the key in the ignition and the truck roared down the drive. The old familiar feel of it eased Bay as she made her way to town. She'd only been back home a few days, but the restlessness that plagued her through high school was already bubbling in her veins.

She parked in front of the New Hope Public Library, an impressive new landmark on the corner of Main Street. The sign on the door announced it didn't open until 9am. Bay stood on the sidewalk out front kicking the heel of her boot against the bottom step. She figured she'd get a new library card while she was out, along with a stack of books to keep her mind occupied, and maybe check out one or two of those Christmas romances Violet loved as a sort of peace offering. No such luck, unless she found a way to kill a whole hour. And she only had one errand to run for her mama that day.

Bay made her way down Main Street toward The Owl's Roost. The palmetto trees lining the center median were studded with huge colored lights for Christmas, still on in the morning light, and the storefronts that weren't vacant were decorated with a mish-mash of gaudy décor.

A bell chimed when Bay entered the café, signaling her arrival. The Owl's Roost had been redecorated since Bay had been home, but the changes served to make it appear even older than it was. It was all black and white—the checkerboard floor, striped walls, tablecloths on the three small tables—with pops of red scattered about. The L-shaped display cases were half empty, the early morning crowd having cleared out. There'd be nothing left after lunch. No matter the décor, the food was great. Amelia Patterson, who was Violet's first cousin, had been running the place since Bay could remember. She was the only woman Bay knew whose cooking rivaled Violet's.

"Well, Bay, aren't you a sight for sore eyes," Reva Patterson called across the tiny space, a smile lighting her face as she came around the counter for a hug. "Still pretty as a picture, I see. We missed you at church yesterday."

"Hey, Reva," Bay called back with a smile. "You're a beautiful sight for sore eyes yourself. How have you been?"

Reva yanked at the net that covered the tight bun on top of her head. "Hot as hell in here at the moment. I took a day off from work today to help Amelia get these cakes ready to sell at the festival, and we've been at it since the crack of dawn."

Bay laughed. "I'm sure Amelia appreciates the help. She'll sell a truckload for sure."

"I sure hope so," Reva said conspiratorially, casting a glance toward the kitchen.

Reva had been married to Amelia's son, Tommy, for six or seven years by now. Bay had heard from Violet that there was some kind of drama at their wedding that resulted in Reva being the first woman ever to have married into the family without receiving a pearl. She didn't know the whole story, but she could relate to what an uncomfortable place that was for Reva—on the outside looking in. Bay couldn't imagine what might have happened. She'd never known Reva to be anything but kind, and Amelia for her part wasn't prone to being petty. In any case, it was obvious from her raw hands and pink cheeks that Reva was still working hard at making amends for whatever had happened, all these years later.

"Bay!" Amelia came from the kitchen wiping her hands on a towel. "How you holding up, darlin'?"

Bay felt the turmoil of her emotions twisting her face and shrugged her response, unable to find an answer to that question.

"I can't imagine. I cannot imagine," Amelia said, pulling her in for a hug. "What can I get you? A cup of cocoa?" she asked.

Bay searched her pockets for the ticket Mel had given her. "I'm supposed to be picking up a cake for somebody's birthday at the bank."

"Reva decorated that one for me last night. She's quite talented, you know. Let me go get it."

Reva beamed at the praise from her mother-in-law as she handed a mug of cocoa over to Bay. "Oh! I didn't do the writing on that cake yet. Let me go finish it." She hustled back to the kitchen.

Bay sipped her cocoa, watching what little traffic moved by the windows for a minute, then wandered around the room. The black, white, and red Amelia had used decorating matched New Hope's school colors, and the shelves were lined with pictures from high school teams through the years—football, baseball, softball, cheerleaders. She stopped at one photo she recognized as Mel in his football uniform, kneeling, one hand on his helmet, the other cradling a football. Next to Mel's picture was a black and white of the team from the same year. She leaned in closer, looking for Mel in the three rows of players, her eyes found another familiar face first—the face from the DVD that reminded her so much of Scott.

"Who is that guy?" Bay sat her mug on the nearest table and snatched the picture from the shelf. Her heart skipped several beats. She studied the young man's face again in parts—the full lips, square jaw, prominent nose, piercing eyes. The similarities were clear, even though this face was a little harder at the edges than Scott's.

"Amelia?" she called, not even hesitating as she stepped behind the display case and into the small kitchen. Amelia turned from the counter where Reva worked, eyes wide.

"What is it, Bay?" Amelia asked, concern furrowing her brow at the urgency in Bay's tone.

Bay held the picture up in front of her. "Who is this?" she asked, tapping her finger against the number—13—on the young man's chest.

Amelia leaned in to study the photo. "Hmmm…the face is sure familiar, isn't it?"

"You don't know who it might be?"

Amelia rolled off her gloves and took the frame from Bay's hands, turning it over on the counter. "Can't say as I do, but I believe we can find out." She pried at the back of the frame until it popped open, making her jump. "A lot of these old pictures from the high school year book have the list of players at the bottom, but the frame might be hiding it. And here it is."

She ran her finger over the list until she found number 13, then handed the unframed picture to Bay with a smile. "Marco Ramirez. Seems like the Ramirezes were only around a year, maybe two." Amelia shook her head. "Haven't heard that name in ages."

Bay leaned against the counter to steady herself as she stared at the name. "Marco Ramirez," she whispered. "What do you remember about him?" Bay asked without looking up from the picture.

Amelia let loose a sigh and shook her head. "Well, let's see...Marco's parents moved here when he was already in high school. I believe they came all the way from New York by way of Puerto Rico—or was it the Dominican Republic by way of New York? Lord, my memory is shot. Anyway, he came to work for your granddaddy, down at the Edisto place first, and then back here."

"So, they knew our family?" Bay asked, her eyes going wide.

Amelia nodded. "I don't think you can live around New Hope and avoid it, honey. Anyway, like I said, I believe it was tenth, maybe eleventh grade. He was quiet, I remember that. At least until he got on the football field. Everybody said he was the best dang quarterback this town ever saw. But don't tell your daddy," Amelia said with a wink.

"What about the girls?" Bay asked, raising an eyebrow. "He's pretty hot."

Amelia raised a hand to her cheek and dropped her eyes to the counter. "I don't—he—I suppose he kept to himself, from what I recall. He worked at the farm with his parents when we weren't in school, and they pretty much kept to themselves, too. They all left town after he graduated, moved back up north where they had family. Can't say I've seen or heard a thing about any of them since. Couldn't tell you after that."

Bay set the photo down on the counter. "It's just—the smile, and the eyes. He reminds me of..." she whispered.

Amelia turned the picture and stared. "Oh, Bay, you think he looks like Scott? Well, I guess there's a little resemblance. I wouldn't have seen it if you hadn't mentioned. The Ramirezes weren't from around here, and they were long gone before y'all came along. Just a coincidence, if I had to guess. No way they were related."

Bay nodded. "It's weird is all. I'm pretty sure I saw him on an old video Mama and Daddy had, too."

"Did you ask them about him, if they remembered him?"

"No, not really. They just figure I'm seeing things that aren't there again. Not dealing with my grief and all that."

"Honey," Amelia said, reaching out to squeeze Bay's hand. "Not knowing, it's got to be so hard."

"You see it, though, don't you? The resemblance?"

"Well, yes, but I wouldn't read in to it much. Here, let me just put this picture away in the back, and—"

"Do you mind if I hang on to it?" Bay snatched the picture up and held it to her chest. "I just want to show my folks—"

Amelia twisted her mouth into a grimace. "I don't know if that's the best idea."

"Why not?" Bay asked, her stomach knotting. There was something Amelia wasn't telling her. Something she—and maybe her parents—didn't want her to know about Marco Ramirez.

"It's just—I mean, they're already concerned, you said. About you seeing Scott and all? If you come home dragging this picture…"

"But they'd have to see it, right?"

"Sure, they would, but, like I said, it's just a coincidence. I wouldn't go making too much of it. It's a worry enough for them, too, with Scott missing, I imagine."

Bay winced. "I see your point. No need giving them something else to worry over. But do you mind if I hang on to this anyway? I promise I'll keep it to myself."

Amelia nodded her head, and without another word between them, Bay headed out the door with the picture, the cake, and the edges of an idea, a connection forming in her mind.

"Who are you, Marco Ramircz?" shc muttered as she headed back to Scott's truck. "And why doesn't anybody seem to want me to find out?"

CAPTIVITY: DAY 85

```
Scott Jackson Murphy.
Sergeant First Class, United States Army.
Serial Number 224278972.
```

The man with glasses comes in, looking like Pastor Weaver at Unity. But this bastard sure as shit ain't no pastor. It's gonna be a bad night for me.

Water.

He brings water when he comes. I'm convinced I'll drown every time, but then I don't. Lillie doesn't let me.

Ain't that a pain in the ass? I let her drown, but she won't let me. And I'm pretty sure that's the only reason I don't, because these assholes failed waterboarding 101. I've never done it myself, but I know this isn't how you do it. As soon as I think I won't be able to catch another clear breath, push the water out of my lungs, she's there in front of me, blocking the light. She shakes her head, scattering butterflies, and points behind me. I guess I'm not done here.

I hope to God I'm not done, that Lillie wouldn't keep me suffering in this hellhole to end up dying here anyway.

```
Scott Jackson Murphy.
Sergeant First Class, United States Army.
Serial Number 224278972.
```

He wants to know what we were after, the man with the glasses. I laugh because we didn't really know. I want to say, "You tell me." But I don't because that would be a small victory for him. That would be a reason to push harder. I keep my eyes shut tight and my mouth shut tighter. Remember when to breathe, when not to breathe.

Remember how to breathe.

Lillie's butterflies surround me, and then Bay's coming down the stairs the night of senior prom, and I can't catch my breath. That red strapless dress sets off her hair just right. She wears it down, a crazy tumble of curls, the way I love it. And that devil of a grin she gives me…I know she must be up to something.

We dance under red, white, and blue balloons, eat at tables with American flags for centerpieces. We even wave sparklers like it's the Fourth of July. Just a few years after 9/11, the world's reeling around us. Nothing's the same. I'm not the same.

Even though we're seniors a few weeks from graduation, and it's prom night, Bay still has a curfew. I'm disappointed when she says goodnight without mentioning sneaking out and down to the pond with me. We keep a bag with blankets stashed in a corner of the boathouse, and sometimes we stay down there 'til damn near dawn, kissing and talking and…well, always almost.

Until tonight.

I go home and leave my rented tux in a pile at the end of my bed. I lay there for I don't know how long, staring at the ceiling, trying to figure out when to tell Bay what I've done. I'd planned to after prom, but…well, guess not. And then a little tap-tap-tap on my window changes things up in a hurry.

"Bay Blue, what the hell are you doing?" I whisper as I push up the window.

"Sneakin' you out of the house for a change," she says. *"Put your pants on and hurry up!"* She looks me up and down, then adds with a wink, *"Or don't put your pants on."*

I climb out and follow when she takes off running. In the moonlight, I can see her hand held out behind her for me to take, her hair whipping around her face. Her laughter carries in the wind as we run hand in hand down the dirt road past Blossom Hill, the barn, and a stretch of fields before rounding the corner to the pond. She draws up short of the boathouse and I lurch to a stop behind her, my momentum almost knocking her over. She ties a bandana over my eyes.

"What are you doing?" I ask again. She shushes me and ties a tight knot behind my head.

"No talking. Not one more word. Okay?"

I grin and nod blindly, then let her lead me forward. She leaves for a minute and I hear the doors to the boathouse close behind me. She unties the bandana, and I open my eyes. Candles are lit everywhere, even in the boats that sway with the motion of the water, pulling against their ties. The light reflects from the tin onto the water's surface. The air even seems to glow. Our old blankets are piled up in our regular spot on the edge of the landing, with a few extra added.

"Wow, this is something else, but we're gonna burn the place down, girl," I tease. When she walks around me and takes a step back, so I can see her in the black lace next-to-nothings she's stripped down to, I lose my breath. She holds a finger to her lips and shakes her head, that wicked little grin lighting a gleam in her eyes again.

"No more talking." She steps closer and leans against me, and I run my hands up her back, beneath her hair.

"Bay Laurel, are you—"

This time she holds her finger against my lips. *"Close your eyes and kiss me."*

So, I do. I forget everything but the taste of her mouth, the taste of her skin, the heat of her hair tangled in my fingers. I forget how to breathe.

And I pray that she'll forgive me, somehow, when I tell her that I've enlisted in the army. I hold my breath through the days after that she won't talk to me, days when she wears shades in school to hide her swollen eyes, days I think maybe I've really lost her.

On the fourth night, she taps on my window again. She climbs in and curls up beside me, and we promise to hold onto each other, no matter what.

```
Scott Jackson Murphy.
Sergeant First Class, United States Army.
Serial Number 224278972.
```

God, please let me hold on. Please let her hold on.

CHAPTER 5

Bay plundered like a common criminal through the cabinets and drawers and closets at Blossom Hill, looking for the box of DVDs they'd been watching the night she came home. She'd had to wait for both of her parents to leave the house that morning so she could hunt them down and get another look at Marco Ramirez on the football field.

"Jackpot!" She raised her fist in the air but kept her voice to a whisper, even though she was home alone. It had taken her almost an hour to find the DVDs shoved to the very back of the top shelf of Mel's closet, and she had no idea when Violet would come strolling back in. Bay took the whole box with her to the upstairs rec area that was open to the den below, so she'd be able to hear if anyone came in.

Flipping her way through the box looking for the unmarked DVD, she tried to figure why her parents wouldn't want her making a connection between Marco Ramirez and Scott. It could have something to do with how she saw Lillie around Blossom Hill, like her mama pointed out the other night. They couldn't force her to therapy if she suddenly started conjuring Scott, too.

But it felt like something more, and she had nothing but time on her hands, so...

Bay snagged the first blank DVD she found in the case and loaded it into the player. She scooted back across the carpet so she could see the screen better, chewing a nail as she waited impatiently with the remote in her other hand so she could fast forward to the parts she wanted.

The picture cleared and, after several seconds of the camera being jostled, the screen went white. Then it zoomed out, and Bay could see that the white had been from Violet's wedding dress.

It was her parents' wedding video.

Her mother was standing in the middle of a circle of women—Amelia, Grandma Olivia, Amelia's mother, Cora, and several others Bay recognized but couldn't quite name—all wearing chiffon dresses in an array of tasteful pastel colors. Bay's grandmother stood before Violet with a blue velvet box from The Palmetto Tree, where all the Pearl Girls' pendants were made, in hand. As the camera focused on Violet and her mother, Bay could see that Violet was fighting back tears.

"Aw, Mama," Bay said, "you were so beautiful in that dress."

"My sweet Violet," Grandma Olivia said, "as you step forward into your future as a wife today, you become a Pearl Girl. One thing we Pearls know for certain is that, as important as it is to always keep moving forward, it's also important to understand where you came from.

"The Pearl Girls descend—or, rather, ascend—from a long line of survivors, including our founder, Willa Pearl Honeycutt." Olivia paused and reached for Violet's hand. Violet dabbed at her eyes. "You look so much like her, more than any of the rest of us."

Bay recalled the portrait of Willa Pearl that hung in the foyer, her midnight hair, dark eyes, and skin so much like Violet's, the cocked brow and mischievous curve of her mouth hinting at why Violet always said Bay was Willa's spitting image in all the ways that counted.

Willa Pearl Lowry Honeycutt's rise from a hardscrabble upbringing in a still-unrecognized Native American tribe into the area's cotillion crowd was a legend in the Lowcountry of South Carolina.

Grandma Pearl launched into the familiar telling of Willa's story. Willa's father had been a raging alcoholic after his wife died. He barely showed up to work the turpentine stills at Honey Hill, the longleaf pine plantation owned by Jefferson Honeycutt, a young farmer who'd inherited the plantation and owned the falling-down shack Willa and her father occupied. At sixteen,

Willa was smart enough to know that her father was squandering what little he earned, and that, when rent came due, he'd have to trade whatever they had left of value to keep a roof over their heads. And what they had was pearls, natural freshwater pearls harvested generations ago from the Edisto River by their Native American ancestors. Determined to protect the only inheritance she had, Willa began sewing pockets into the hem of her skirt at night, slipping a few pearls in each one.

Willa wasn't able to hide all the pearls before Jefferson came to collect a rent payment, and as she'd feared, her father tore through the house searching for them. Jefferson watched Willa calm her father, then square her shoulders and retrieve the cigar box half full of pearls from beneath her bed, a simple feather mattress laid in a corner. She'd tipped up her chin and held his gaze as she brought him the offering with tears in her eyes. Jefferson took the pearls, but promised to hold them until the Lowrys could pay the back rent in cash.

Over the following weeks, Jefferson stopped in more and more often, bringing produce and cooking supplies at first, then flowers and combs for Willa's raven hair, and finally a delicate sapphire ring set in white gold carved with butterflies, since he'd noticed that they seemed to follow Willa when they went out for walks. She didn't hesitate when he asked for her hand, and on their wedding day, when he returned her pearls to her, strung together with diamonds and a beautiful handmade butterfly brooch, she knew she'd never regret it, and that she'd spend her life making sure he never did, either. From the day they were married, Jefferson called Willa his Pearl, and he'd cherished her their whole lives.

Jefferson and Willa had three daughters together, and when each girl got married, Willa had a single pearl set in a pendant for the bride from those she'd kept sewn in her skirt all those years ago. Her daughters continued the tradition with their daughters and daughters-in-law, dubbing themselves The Pearl Girls.

As Olivia opened the blue box with Violet's pearl pendant inside, Violet pressed a hand to her mouth and turned away.

"Violet, what's the matter?" Amelia asked, following behind her as Violet rushed to the little bathroom that stood just off the bridal suite at Unity Baptist. Violet slammed the door, and Amelia pushed close to it, cupping a hand to her ear.

"What in the world?" Olivia scampered over. "Baby, are you alright?" she called through the door.

"Sounds like maybe her nerves are getting to her," Amelia offered, standing back with wide eyes.

Olivia looked toward the camera and smiled sheepishly. "The child has always had a nervous stomach."

Cora rolled her eyes. "I told you to get her something for that this morning."

"She said she didn't want anything," Olivia said, irritation threading her words.

"Well, you shouldn't have listened. You could have at least slipped her a little nip of brandy," Cora retorted.

Violet emerged from the bathroom then, looking meek and pale.

"Oh honey," Olivia said, putting an arm around her, "are you going to be able to make it through the ceremony?"

Bay watched with concern as her mama nodded in response. Violet was overcome with emotion, that was obvious, but it didn't look like happiness or nerves to Bay. What she saw in Violet's face was pain and confusion. Maybe even terror.

"It's just…" Violet began, placing her hand lightly on the jewelry box that Olivia was holding between them.

"What is it?" Cora asked, placing a comforting hand on Violet's shoulder.

"I don't deserve all of this, not any of it." Violet's voice was broken, almost inaudible.

Olivia laughed, her big, outrageous, rambling laugh that Bay missed so much it brought tears to her eyes. "Don't be silly. No one deserves it more than you. You've been nothing short of a wonderful daughter, and you're going to be a wonderful wife to Mel. He's lucky you stuck by him—"

"No," Violet said, shaking her head so hard her veil nearly came loose, "I'm the lucky one."

"Ladies, it's almost time," Cora said, nodding pointedly at the jewelry box still unopened in Olivia's hands.

"Violet Grace," Oliva said, pulling open the lid of the box, "my only daughter, my only child, it is my joy to welcome you as a Pearl Girl today. May your future be as bright as the shine on this pearl, and may you be reminded every time you wear it of where you come from, and where you belong."

The camera zoomed in disjointedly as Olivia hooked the pendant around Violet's neck. Bay leaned in to study it, letting herself wonder for a moment what kind of setting Violet would choose for her pearl, if she ever got married. They'd talked about it once, when a proposal from Scott seemed a certainty, but Violet had been determined to keep her plans for Bay's necklace secret. And when she and Scott ended, Bay went right back to insisting she didn't care if she ever got that pearl or not.

She worked hard at believing her own lie. Resting her fingers on the cool metal of Lillie's butterfly and Scott's ring, she thought she'd rather have them anyway.

Bay checked the time and knew she should look for the other DVD if she wanted to study it before Violet came back, so she fast forwarded and watched bits and pieces of her parents' wedding ceremony and reception. At the end, she watched as her parents descended the steps of Hampton Hall, her grandparents' home, to cheers and fistfuls of rice raining down on them.

As they said their goodbyes and Mel opened the car door for Violet, Bay saw him. Marco Ramirez stood in the shadows of the wraparound porch, hands in his pockets, eyes hard, mouth clamped shut in a tight line. It was harder to see him in the fading light, but she didn't understand how everyone else could deny his resemblance to Scott.

Bay watched as Marco mouthed something to Violet, shaking his head. Whatever Marco was trying to communicate to her, it had stopped Violet in her tracks. She stood frozen by the car door for a long moment, then turned quickly and climbed in. As Mel closed the door behind her and jogged to the driver's side, smiling and waving to their friends and family, Violet smiled through fresh tears, her eyes darting back toward Marco. When the camera panned to the porch again, Marco was gone.

"What in the world…" Bay muttered to herself as the video ended.

If she hadn't been certain there was more to the story with Marco Ramirez before, his appearance at her parents' wedding convinced Bay she was on to something. Only now, she wasn't entirely sure she wanted to know what.

CAPTIVITY: DAY 86

```
Scott Jackson Murphy.
Sergeant First Class, United States Army.
Serial Number 224278972.
```

Everything is quiet today. I'm not much conscious, thank God. My eyes, I can't keep open. Lungs burning. I am so heavy, so full of regret.

Lillie is here, and the butterflies. I sleep, I dream. I can't help myself. And Bay is the one dream I have left.

I hate how easy it is for my work to slip into my personal life. The skills I've learned, like lying by omission. Keeping shit to myself is part of my job. But Bay could sense it, even from a distance.

"I met someone in Afghanistan, a woman." I blurt it out over dessert at her favorite restaurant in Nashville. We were deciding to try again. And I couldn't do that without telling her the truth. All of it.

Bay freezes, staring at me while ice cream drips from her spoon. *"A woman? What woman?"*

I run a hand over my hair and avert my gaze. *"Emerson. Emerson Davies is her name. She's an aid worker with an organization in England."*

"Emerson?" Bay asks. *"You haven't mentioned her before. What kinda name is Emerson?"*

"She's British Indian. Her parents are both writers. They named her after Ralph Waldo Emerson."

"Yeah? Your favorite poet. Huh."

"Yeah, funny, the first time I met her I quoted from ol' Ralph before she told me her name. 'Finish every day and be done with it,' you know. Anyway, we worked together on some outreach programs. The organization she works for and my team, I mean." I ramble when I'm nervous. And the way Bay's watching me makes me nervous.

"And this woman, Emerson, she's what to you? Were you sleeping with her?"

My mouth won't make words. My mind scrambles, but I'm too late to reassess the situation, to figure out the right approach to reach the desired outcome. Bay throws her spoon down and pushes away from the table.

"So, this transfer, this move so you can go back...you're leaving me for another woman? That's what you're telling me? You're telling me you're leaving again, taking this risk when I have asked you—practically begged you—to –so you can be with this woman, Emerson? You're risking everything—your life, our life together, our future—you're risking it for another woman?"

"No, I wouldn't—"

She's on her feet, backing away. *"Don't tell me you wouldn't when you already did."*

It takes me a while to catch up to her, to try to explain. God, the fight we have. All I can see is hurt in her eyes.

She begs me not to leave again, to back out of the transfer. I tell her I have to go, try to convince her I wouldn't break her trust, ever. That I had to let her know about Emerson, even though Bay and I weren't together when it happened. I couldn't have that secret between us. And I tell her the transfer's a done deal. I have to go.

I assume she'll forgive me. So, I leave.

But something breaks in her. She tells me to go, to get lost. I run with that and forget everything else she said. I forget how she was on her knees, begging me to stay. Begging me not to leave her again.

She begged me to stay, and I left anyway. And now I can't get home to her.

CHAPTER 6

Maybe it really was some crazy coincidence, like Amelia said. One of those weird doppelganger situations. Scott just somehow happened to look a whole lot like Marco Ramirez. And maybe she misinterpreted what she'd seen on that wedding video. It could have been something innocent, or nothing at all.

That's what Bay kept telling herself as she made her way mindlessly through the list of chores Violet left for her the next day. She repeated it in her head like a mantra through dinner, *just a coincidence*, as she half listened to her daddy going on about one of the tellers at the bank, and as she loaded the dishwasher, wiped down every surface of the kitchen, and wandered around the house, aimless. She said it out loud in the car as she drove to the Sugar Shack, *just a coincidence*, and one last time before she stepped out and into Will's friendly hug in the parking lot.

"What's up, girl?" Will asked, giving her a quick shake by the shoulders as he grinned at her.

"Not me, Willis, not me. This girl is down," Bay answered, taking his hands and squeezing them.

If Bay, Lillie, and Scott had been a trio, Will was the extra body who had often made them a quartet. And after Lillie was gone, he became more of a fixture, a solid, good thing Bay knew she could lean on. He was Scott's best friend, through thick and thin. When Bay and Scott headed off to Nashville and the army, Will stayed behind to study welding at the local technical college. He'd known all his life that nowhere in the world would suit him like New Hope. Bay used to feel sorry for him, but now she was a little jealous that he'd known where he belonged, without ever seeming to question it.

Will hooked an arm over her shoulders and pulled her toward the door. "Well, nothing beats being down like gettin' down, so let's get to it!"

"Oh, you plan to shake it for me tonight, do ya?" Bay asked, laughing for what felt like the first time since she got back to town. Will was one of the tallest people she knew, and one of the least coordinated. Even at his size, he still looked like a teenager with his innocent hazel eyes, spattering of freckles across his nose and cheeks, and dark, wavy hair that stuck out in every direction from under his Braves hat. Bay couldn't resist reaching out to push a stray piece behind his ear.

She'd been feeling so out of sorts she almost canceled their plans, but by their second round, she was grateful that Will had pushed her to come out for a while. It had been a long time since she'd been to a bar when she wasn't playing, and longer still since she'd been anywhere like the Shack. The best way to describe the place was dirty. It wasn't much more than an old barn converted to a bar, its uneven cement floor covered in cheap faux parquet linoleum that didn't appear to have seen a mop since it was laid, rickety laminate tables and folding chairs, an ancient jukebox, and a bar constructed of varnished plywood.

There were a handful of men at the bar, a few more scattered at the tables around Will and Bay, and one other woman—the waitress—wandering in and out from the back room. The music from the jukebox played low as they reminisced over their drinks. Bay drank fast, washing the bitter taste of unanswered questions from her mouth with sweet memories and Southern Comfort.

"Hey, do you remember in high school, senior year, it must have been January because your folks gave you that little Mazda for Christmas?" Will asked.

Bay grinned. "Yeah, and you and…"

"Scott," Will said. "Me and Scott."

Bay shook her head. "Y'all pushed that car all the way down the lane in the middle of the night and we hauled ass to Myrtle Beach…"

"It was freezing cold, but we had the windows rolled down, and you were singing at the top of your lungs. God, even when you tried to sing off-key you couldn't…"

"And you were driving like a maniac down 378. I still don't know how I squeezed into his lap, even as little as I was…"

"Still are. We were lucky to make it there in one piece, all jammed in that two-seater, shiverin' and shakin'…"

"Only to find that the boulevard was near abandoned when we got there."

"And none of us had the good sense to check the gas gauge."

"Of course not. I mean, how else would we end up stranded in my shiny new car in the middle of the night at the Park & Blow without a cell phone between us?" They laughed even harder then, leaning their heads close across the table.

"Who names a convenience store the Park & Blow anyway?" Will's shoulders shook as he leaned back on two legs of the chair.

"We sat there trying to figure out what to do, and all I could say was how my daddy might come get us, but then my mama would kill us all…"

"Yeah, but Scott came to the rescue, that fearless son-of-a-bitch. I still can't believe he had the balls back then to wake up that store owner to get gas in the middle of the night. Thank God that's who even lived in the house down that dirt road."

"That's just like him, though, isn't it? He always makes a way."

"Yeah, he does, Bay." Their laughter faded away and they couldn't look at each other for a moment. The pain of missing Scott infused the air around them, making it heavy, hard to breathe. Will reached across the table and took Bay's hands in his.

"I know how hard this is for you." He dropped his eyes to their joined hands and squeezed Bay's fingers.

"I challenge you, dear Willis. Please, allow me to run the table on you." She pulled her hands from his and pressed the heels of them against her eyes, then stood up and made her way to the lone pool table at the far end of the bar. The table was open, so Bay fished quarters from her bag, pushed and pulled hard on the feeder, and grinned as the balls dropped at the end of the table. "I rack, you break."

Will chose the least crooked cue and chalked it, grinned across the expanse of stained green felt between them. "What are we playing for, Bay Blue?"

"Shots."

"Shots? One of us has got to drive outta here tonight, girl."

"Yeah, that would be you. One game, one shot for every miss. Now break, dammit!"

A few shots later, Bay stood against the wall and glanced sideways at Will. "How many was that?"

"One for me. Lost count for you." She grinned, pushed herself off the wall, and felt the floor sway a little beneath her.

"Hey now, it's not time for the room to start moving." Will's hands were at her waist steadying her as she dug for more quarters. A couple of the guys from the bar had come over and were waiting to play.

"Let's let these boys have the table," Will said, nodding in their direction. Bay turned to speak to them.

"Oh, you guys want to play with us?"

"Nah, that's okay. We'll wait if you ain't done," the closest one said. Bay noted his grungy white tee beneath his unbuttoned uniform shirt, the grease-stained hat he wore pulled down so far you could barely see his beady eyes. When she tried to find them, they seemed to skitter right and left at the same time, but she thought maybe that was the liquor.

The other guy, a short, red-faced balding man wearing the same kind of uniform shirt, with a paunchy belly and bulbous nose, sneered at her. She had a flash of recognition. It was the sneer—she'd seen it on his face before. He wasn't the kind of man who'd take to a strong-willed woman like her, she imagined, regardless of the fact that he didn't actually know her.

"You're…what's your name? From the club? The quail club? I've seen you there a time or two when I've been out with Daddy," Bay asked him, trying for her friendliest tone to ease the weird tension she felt building.

"Don't have to ask who you are, little miss Bay from up on Blossom Hill, one of them Pearl Girls or whatever y'all like to call yourselves. Figured you'd be too fancy for this kind'a place, but I reckon after all these years you spent slummin' with that traitor…"

Will pulled at Bay, trying to ease her away through the tables.

"Come on, Bay."

"Wait, no. What do you mean by that?" Bay hissed. She shook Will off and stepped closer to the man.

"I mean ain't nobody in here interested in seeing your uppity ass around. Get lost like that boyfriend o' yours did, will ya? Everybody actin' like he's some kinda hero. Boy wasn't nothin' but a bastard kid of a junkie your daddy took pity on. He probably walked off and defected like that other piece of shit did over there. What was his name?"

Bay's ears rang, blood rushing to her face. There had been rumors at first that maybe Scott wasn't taken—maybe he went willingly—but as details of the mission he was on emerged, those rumors had been quickly dispelled. It had taken a while for the media to even catch up to the activity that was still ongoing in Afghanistan. After the last election cycle, the whole country damn near forgot the war, and the soldiers still caught up in it.

She'd always supported Scott's service, even when she didn't necessarily agree with the decisions the government was making. But she'd been exhausted with the worry, and ready for what was next for them before their relationship imploded. Hearing what people were saying after he first went missing nearly gutted her. It was one of the reasons she'd dropped out of sight, unplugged from everything.

And now here was this guy… All the frustration, the guilt, the anger that had been creeping up on Bay consolidated into her fist, and her thumb curled over her tight knuckles as she stared him down. The next thing she felt was the crunch of his nose against her clinched hand, the shock of seeing the sudden stream of blood running to his mouth when his head snapped back, the vibration of pain that ran from her fingers to her shoulder. He hadn't anticipated how hard she could hit, and neither had she. They stared at each other in disbelief as he sputtered at her.

Then her feet were off the floor and she was dragged across the room, her slack legs banging against tables, knocking over chairs that fell with tinny clangs to the floor. The night air burst into her face before she was stuffed into the passenger side of Will's truck, and they were bouncing out of the parking lot.

"Jesus Christ, Bay!" he finally managed. "Where in hell did that come from?"

"You heard what he said. Why didn't you hit him?" Bay shouted.

"You didn't give me a chance!" Will yelled back at her.

"No, you were pulling me out before I even had time to defend..." Her eyes flashed with renewed intensity, and Will cringed.

"Scott. His name is Scott. Now get hold'a yourself," he said, his tone softening as he checked the rear-view mirrors behind him. "Seemed like you did a decent job of defending him to me. It won't do you any good is all. Idiots like that, they don't know what they don't know. Heard one story with one theory one damn time, and that's as much as his mind can hold. Jealous redneck, wants to believe the worst so he can feel better than somebody. And that guy's mean as a snake when he drinks. You're making yourself an easy target reacting like that. What he thinks he knows about Scott, or about you, it don't mean shit."

"Well, you don't know shit either."

Will grunted, checked the mirrors again, and then scratched at the hives blooming on his neck. "You're right, I don't. Scott wouldn't talk about what happened between y'all, what ended it, and you wouldn't even answer your damn phone or a text. So why don't you fill me in, Bay. Tell me what happened, so I can tell you that none of this is your fault. Because I can see the guilt all over you, and I can't stand it. It's like it was with Lillie all over again. Scott wouldn't want you torturing yourself—"

"No!" Bay shouted, shaking her head violently as her hands slammed down against the dashboard of the truck. She sucked in a breath as pain shot through her right hand, then slammed it hard against the dashboard a second time. Tears stung her eyes and clouded her vision. "Torture is exactly what I deserve for letting him go the way did. I deserve to hurt, not him."

"He wouldn't want—"

"Don't, Will, please," she said, her voice cracking with her plea. "I can't hear how he wouldn't want me to suffer, or grieve, or...God, I just can't hear it anymore."

Will parked in front of Blossom Hill. He reached a hand out and rested it against her shoulder. "Bay, if there was anything I could do—"

Bay flinched under Will's touch, pushing the door of the truck open and spilling out. She heard him cuss when she fell, landing hard on her knees and palms. He rushed around to help, but she held up a hand and waved him off.

"I'm good," she said, using the step of the truck to pull herself up. "Wow, my hand hurts."

"Let's hope you didn't break a digit, Rocky," Will said, shutting the passenger door as Bay wandered out into the yard. "Where are you going now?"

Bay made her way to the weeping willow that stood watch over the south end of Blossom Hill, its bare branches providing no shelter from the bitter cold that seemed to have settled in around her heart. She tested the rope of the old swing hanging from a low branch before settling onto it. She gave it a half-hearted push and let the toes of her boots drag through the dirt. "There's nowhere to go," she said as Will took Scott's old place behind her, giving, her a gentle shove. "Everywhere I go here is everywhere he should be, and he's not." Her shoulders shook as she cried quietly, leaning her head against her good hand on the rope.

"I wish..." Will started, then hesitated. He held the swing, stopping it, and moved in front of Bay, kneeling in front of her, concern etching lines into his face. "What can I do, Bay?"

Bay rested her hands on his shoulders. "There's nothing anybody can do. There's nothing I can do," she choked out through her tears.

Will pulled her closer and she let her head drop against his shoulder. "I can't even speak his name. I try to pray for him, but how do I do that, because what do I ask for? I want him here, I want him to come home to me, but if I beg God to bring him back...what does that mean he's going through right now? I can't bear the thought of someone hurting him, breaking...breaking him down, his spirit. I want him back, but whether he's alive or—God, no matter what, that's never going to happen. He's never coming back to us the way he was. But if he's not coming home...I can't face that, either."

"Hey," he said, gently, tipping her chin up with a gentle finger so that she met his gaze. "I want him back, too. Every damn day. And I believe somehow he'll make it home. Since I got the call from Ethan that he was missing, I've been waiting on the call that he's on his way back. No way he won't make it back."

"I can't imagine the rest of my life without him."

"I can't imagine the rest of mine without a Bay and Scott." Will wiped her cheeks with his thumbs. "Any day now, he's gonna come flying up that lane, blowing the horn and squinting up at your bedroom window, hollerin' at you to get your ass out here and go for a drive so y'all can work this thing out. He'll come back to you. He will," Will said, trying to sound more confident than he was.

Bay took a deep, steadying breath and nodded. "He'll come back to me," she said. "Scott—Scott's coming home again. And we'll forgive and forget. He's coming home again."

One corner of Will's mouth lifted in half a smile. "Atta girl. Now, let's get you inside before we both freeze our asses off."

"It ain't that cold," Bay said, leaning into Will as they walked to the porch and up the front steps. "You wouldn't last through October in Nashville."

"I wouldn't want to try," he said, laughing. "You gonna be okay?"

"Mmmhmm," Bay muttered, trying and failing to get her key in the lock.

"Here, let me." Will took the keys and opened the door. He laughed as she tumbled inside. "Good luck sleeping that off. I'll bring Scott's truck before work tomorrow."

"Ycah, g'night, Willis."

Bay climbed the stairs, swaying all the way. She opened her old bedroom door enough to reach in and flip the light on and off twice, like she used to when he'd drive by and blow the horn. She waited for the sound to burst up to her, reassurance that maybe somehow, some way, they'd both get an answer to their prayers, and their lives could go back to what they'd been before. Maybe, just maybe, all was not lost.

CAPTIVITY: DAY 87

Scott Jackson Murphy.
Sergeant First Class, United States Army.
Serial Number 224278972.

It's way too quiet. Everything's off schedule. Even the sun hesitated to rise this morning. They talk outside the door, but they whisper so I can't hear. They're planning something. What are they up to? Maybe they're gonna move me again, trade me off to another cell.

Or maybe my number's up.

I hate this godforsaken valley I got lost in. The contrasts are stark—stoic mountains, expanses of desert, rich riverbeds—they are light and dark, hot and cold, like war. Brutal and unforgiving. This valley was made for war, for death. The way every type of terrain seems to merge into one thing, one place here...it feels like the end. Like the last place on earth. And, for me, this place symbolizes the end of everything I ever loved. This place was the end of us, of me and Bay.

And the end of who I was, before I saw the very worst in people…and the worst in myself. That's the thing about war, you see both sides. The best in a man is drawn out at times, the will to sacrifice for your brother beside you, or the scared kid wandering down the wrong street. But at other times, it brings out the worst in us. You learn things about yourself in war that you never wanted to know.

I watch a bee crawling over the screen of the small window. Another is outside, about to make its way in. There are hives nearby, a constant hum. We brought them here, taught the locals beekeeping, tried to give them an alternative to growing poppies. Someone somewhere higher up thought it was a great idea. Like opium's going anywhere.

I don't know how many times I've been stung by now. Seems like the little terrorists are always finding a way in. Every good thing we've done in this shithole gets turned around on us. What we give as a gift, they turn into weapons. Even the damn bees are attacking me.

But I guess that's how life works. A good thing can go bad in a hurry. Even love.

When I close my eyes, Lillie returns to me. She gets close enough that I think I can touch her before she releases the butterflies and dances away. I'm starting to wish she'd take me with her.

It's late summer. We're maybe ten years old, me and Bay, best friends, thick and thin. Today it's hide and seek in the fields around Blossom Hill. Everybody else is inside, ducking the heat. I tell her we're too old for it, but she says I can kiss her on the cheek if I find her.

I want that kiss. Like it or not, I'm playing her game.

It's a bright day, high sun, not a cloud in the sky. I jog between the rows of tobacco, brushing against the thick leaves that smell like moist earth and something a little sweeter sent straight from heaven. It's the first ring of hell, though, the space between them. Hot and humid, air so thick you could choke on it. I'm wiping my face with the tail of my t-shirt when I hear it—a weird panting sound. I think it must be the dog until I hear the moaning.

I scan the rows and see Bay on her ass, gripping at her chest with one hand and swatting around her head with the other. *"Bee,"* she wheezes.

The only weakness in Bay is her allergy to bees. I'm running to the house with her in my arms before she can blink. I've always been quick to act.

"Help!" I yell as I sprint toward Blossom Hill. I don't even

feel her weight, or the sand spurs pricking the soles of my bare feet. *"Get help!"* I yell again.

```
Scott Jackson Murphy.
Sergeant First Class, United States Army.
Serial Number 224278972.
```

I watch the bee land on my arm, try not to flinch when the stinger sinks in. I imagine the terror Bay must have felt that day, the sting of terror as her very breath was slipping away.

And I wonder why, right now, I feel nothing at all.

CHAPTER 7

The water transitioned from steaming hot to hot, warm to lukewarm, and finally to tepid before Bay hauled her stiff body out of the bath, teeth chattering. She grabbed the folded towel from the floor, the one Violet must have slipped under her head sometime during the night, dried off quickly and wrapped up in the blanket that she'd slept under. The small kindness from her mama brought fresh tears to her eyes.

Once, when Bay was miserably sick with the stomach flu, Violet set up camp in the bathroom, coming up with every little way she could find to make her more comfortable, keeping vigil on the floor all night, wiping her forehead with a cool washcloth, holding back her hair, singing her favorite songs. Bay could pinpoint the exact moment those times had come to an end—the moment they'd lost Lillie—and she couldn't really blame Violet for that, but in her weakened state she ached for her mother's love.

Her right hand also ached, the swollen knuckles throbbing in unison with each heartbeat. She recalled with surprising clarity the punch that resulted in her injury and hoped that the bastard's nose hurt worse than her knuckles. She shuffled down the hall to the guest room in search of pajamas. The scrapes on her palms and her bruised knees were as yet a mystery, but she supposed Will would laugh his way through whatever the story was behind those later.

"Thank you for managing to make it up the stairs and to the bathroom without vomiting on the rugs, dear." Violet greeted Bay in the kitchen with a smirk and a cup of coffee that smelled like heaven.

"You're quite welcome. Thanks for the coffee, and the towel and blanket," Bay answered sheepishly.

"You still smell like a distillery. I hope you aren't planning to leave the house today."

Bay looked pointedly at her pajamas and slipper socks. "It would appear I'm down for the count."

"We didn't get to talk last night after dinner. I'm almost afraid to ask how your outing with Will went, considering the state I found you in after."

"It was fine, for a night out in New Hope. I just don't feel much up to people these days."

Violet propped her chin in her hand. "Listen, I pushed you on Sunday, and I realize I shouldn't have. I don't want you to feel like your private life has to be on parade here. You've been through enough. But really, the hiding out isn't helping you. Get into town a bit, see some of your old friends. It might do you good. But for the love of all things holy, stay out of the bars and quit the drinking."

"I did come home, Mama. I'm not trying to hide. And I'll drink less." Bay raised her hands, let them drop to the table, and winced when her sore knuckles banged against the surface.

"What in the world did you do to that hand?" Violet asked, her voice hitching with concern as she reached for Bay's injured hand.

Bay hesitated, squinting at Violet. "I may or may not have punched a guy in the face for saying Scott defected."

Violet's eyes widened. "You did what?"

"Maybe I punched him. It's a little fuzzy. It feels more like I hit the wall," she hedged, hoping to dodge an argument.

"Bay Laurel LaFleur." Violet dropped her head back and stared up at the ceiling. "I wish I could say I'm surprised. If it was Leigh Anne, I would be."

"Oh, come on, no kicking me when I'm down!" Bay let a whine curl up in her voice. "Leigh Anne's mean as hell. She'd have shot him, especially when he started insulting the Pearl Girls, too."

"In that case, maybe, but Leigh Anne is underhanded about these things," Violet replied. "She'd talk somebody else into doing the shooting. You should take a lesson in covert operations from your sister-in-law, if Scott never taught you anything." Violet got a pack of frozen peas from the freezer and wrapped them in a hand towel. "Truth be told, if I'd have been there, I would have socked him good myself for disrespecting Scott, and then one more time for disrespecting us Pearls. Keep that iced down a little while. Do you need some aspirin?" she asked, already on her way to the pantry and her stock of medicine.

"Might be helpful. Thanks, Mama."

"Oh, Donna Stephens called this morning, from the Festival Planning Committee? I told her you'd be thrilled to sing at the Christmas Festival, since you're in town and all. I wrote her number down. She needs to know how many songs you want to do."

"Oh good Lord, I can't sing at the Christmas Festival." Bay blew out a breath and leaned her forehead against her good hand. Things had been going so well this morning with Violet. How was she going to get out of this without telling her Mama she hadn't worked since the day Scott went missing? Hell was about to break loose.

"Well, that was before I knew you were out sucker punching people. Maybe we should protect the public from your tiny fists of fury, keep you out of the spotlight?"

"It wasn't a sucker punch. He was looking right at me. But no spotlight. I'm not up for a public display right now."

"Isn't that what you do for a living, honey?" Violet clipped out, the pace of her words making clear the limits of her patience.

"Not since—I haven't played since he's been gone," Bay answered, her voice barely above a whisper. Her gaze dropped to her hands to avoid the disappointment and pity she knew she'd find in her mother's eyes.

Violet stilled. "Oh, Bay, I didn't know. I don't suppose you're obligated to do it, but—maybe it would be a good thing, a chance to get your feet back under you here at home. Pays three hundred bucks. I'm trying to take it easy on you, but I have to say, this might be a good time for you to consider some more reasonable, stable options for your future. You're thirty-two years old. Being dang near destitute loses its charm by now. Your daddy and I are happy to have you for a while, but you need to get to work with him at the bank after the holiday and earn your keep."

Bay gave a resigned laugh. "Thanks, Ma. I'm working up a plan, though. I'll be outta here in no time."

Violet sighed. "Well, if performing is something you still want to do, you gotta get back on that horse sometime. Might as well do it now. And it'll mean something, you know? Think about it. And now I'll drop it because your daddy did ask me not to push."

"Thank you. I will think about it, Mama." Bay watched Violet move around the kitchen, mentally sorting out dinner for the night, opening and closing drawers and cabinets. She decided now was as good a time as any to catch her with her guard down—though her guard was rarely ever really down. "Hey, how well did you know Janice Murphy?"

Violet froze for a second, then shrugged dismissively. "I knew her in passing, like you'd know somebody five or six years younger who grew up here. She didn't stick around long enough after Scott was born for us to have really spent time together as mothers with children the same age."

"And they didn't have any other family around, outside of his Grandma Aggie?"

"No. Why the questions about Janice?"

"I guess it's something that's always been in the back of my mind, but the other night, when we were watching those DVDs, there was this guy on Daddy's football team and he reminded me so much of Scott. And then I was at The Owl's Roost and Amelia has some old team pictures scattered around, and there he was again. It's just got me thinking about his family, you know? What if we could somehow find out something about his dad's family?"

Violet cut her eyes at Bay. "Scott has us. He has New Hope. And, from what I gather, he hoped he would have you, too."

"I don't mean that. Of course, he has our family, and friends…I can't help but wonder if anybody has a clue, you know, who his dad might be? This Marco Ramirez guy could be a dead end, but—"

"Marco Ramirez? How'd you find out his name?" Violet's words came out clipped, and she raised a hand to her lips.

"His name was with the rest of the team names on the picture at Owl's Roost."

"What else did you hear? What did Amelia say about him?" Violet asked, fumbling with a dish towel, then turning away from Bay to wipe over the clean counter.

Bay's eyes went wide. "Nothing, really, except that he was only in New Hope a year or two and hasn't been heard from since. Why, Mama?"

"Some things are best left alone, Bay. This is one of them," Mel said from the doorway.

"Hey Daddy. I was just telling Mama—"

"I heard enough of it. Now's not the time to go digging around Scott's family history. Nobody's heard from Janice in so long, she obviously doesn't want to be found. She may not even be alive, considering how hard she was living when she left. She never seemed interested in telling anyone who his father might be. And like Amelia told you, the Ramirezes came and went. End of story."

"Never mind that. You don't think he might want to know more about his family?"

Mel gave a frustrated grunt. "Can't say I ever heard him talk about it. Anyway, now's not the time to get focused on that. You need to focus on getting your own life back together."

Bay dropped her head and stared at her hands. "This just felt like something I could do for him, you know? I need to do something."

"There's something I need to give you, Bay," Violet said. She strode out of the kitchen and returned a moment later, an extra-large, padded and sealed envelope in hand. She placed it on the table between them and sat down. "These are some things I think you should have. Mel and I were listed as Scott's next of kin. What he had in Afghanistan they sent here."

Scott's things.

It took Bay a minute to catch her breath—it felt like a bucket of iced water had been thrown in her face. She wasn't ready to deal with his things. Nobody prepared her for that.

"Do you want to tell me what's in here?" Bay said apprehensively, her throat constricting around the words.

"No. You should go through it when you're ready. There is one thing, though, a song or a poem. At first, I thought it must have been one you wrote, but it's Scott's handwriting, I think. I've never known him to be a writer, but it's very pretty. If it is a song, it might be a good one for you to sing at the festival. That's something you can do."

"What? He doesn't—he never wrote anything that I knew of."

"Well, it was folded up in his ID wallet. Maybe it's one of yours he copied. Anyway, it's in there, and…I don't know. It might be a nice way for you to honor him, if it meant something to him."

Bay got up from the table, taking the envelope with her, and paused at the door. "I'll take a look at it, Mama. I don't know about performing, though. I'm not sure I can."

Another one of those looks passed between Mel and Violet, one Bay couldn't quite read.

Violet gave Bay a look over her glasses. "Well, dear, no better time to find out."

She couldn't say no, but she didn't say yes, either.

That's what Bay told herself all the way up the stairs. She opened the door to her old room, sat down in the middle of her bed, placed the heavy envelope in front of her, and ran a finger over the sealed lip. It was an easy game, guessing at its contents. There would be pictures of her and Scott, ones that she only had to close her eyes to see. She could feel the shape of a couple of paperback books, but couldn't be sure which ones they might be. Probably a few handwritten letters she'd sent Scott during training and deployments were there. And this song, or poem…she told herself that it could be anything, any old song that reminded him of her, or one that he thought she'd like to try out. Scott made a habit of doing things like that. He was thinking of her all the time. That fact was heavy in her hands, ticking in time with the beat of her heart, an unpinned grenade.

"Dammit, Scott! Damn you for doing this to me!" she said, choking back tears.

She almost hurled the envelope across the room. Her anger was irrational, she knew, but that didn't stop it from welling up. It wasn't fair. He left her here alone, to deal with the aftermath of their breakup, and her fractured family. Without another thought, she snatched the envelope from the bed and flipped it upside down, letting its contents spill out in front of her.

She picked up each item she recognized and set them in careful stacks around her. Once those were sorted, she studied them all, one by one, collecting memories from each. There was a small knife, Army green. Bay smiled to herself as she eased it open and placed a finger against the butterfly emblem on the blade. Lillie had picked it out for Scott's birthday one year when they were kids and hounded Mel until he bought it. A Tim O'Brien novel—*Going After Cacciato*—that was highlighted here and there. Bay flipped through it a second time, noticing the neatly written notes in some of the margins. She closed her eyes and put the book down. Scott didn't read much fiction, and those weren't his notes. The book must have been mixed in with his things from someone else's. And the guys passed books back and forth all the time. Another book, this one of poetry…Ralph Waldo Emerson.

Emerson. She opened it and flipped through. Same handwriting in the margins. She closed it and pushed it away, as if the pages singed her fingers. She didn't want to consider that they were from her—that it was possible he'd still been carrying gifts with him from the woman he'd had an affair with.

Okay, not an affair. She and Scott had broken up before he met Emerson. But it still felt so much like a betrayal when he told her about his involvement with some mysterious, angelic-sounding woman overseas. Bay hadn't been able to let it go. So she'd let him go instead.

Bay shook herself and turned her attention back to the contents of the envelope. There were two pictures from Afghanistan she hadn't seen before: Scott smiling at the camera, a thick beard shadowing his face, machine gun at the ready, ammunition bearer slung over his combat gear; and another one with a few of his teammates, all in plain clothes, posing by a newly plowed field with two women. In the second picture, Scott was leaning in to whisper something to one of the women. She was almost as tall as Scott, dark-skinned, dark eyes, strands of black hair blowing around her face as she broke into laughter. Studying the photo, Bay had to admit she was beautiful.

So many moments had been captured between Bay and Scott like the one in that photo. He loved to catch her right before the flash popped, so that she had her mouth open and head thrown back in almost every picture of them together. She wanted to erase the image of another woman beside him from her mind, but it would always be there. And it would always be her—Emerson, the one who seemed to have awakened something new in him, something foreign to Bay in the man she'd loved her whole life.

Or maybe that was some weird, out of character insecurity talking. Still, even though Scott told her about Emerson, and assured her that the relationship had been short-lived and well over before he came home, before they'd determined to work things out, it shook Bay's confidence in what they had. Scott had formed a bond with another woman, had still considered Emerson a good friend. Bay hadn't been able to accept it.

When they'd broken up, she went on a handful of dates herself, but the effort was half-hearted at best. As odd as it was this day and age, Bay had never doubted who she belonged with. No matter how chaotic and unstable other aspects of her life had been, Scott had been true north for her. She'd just assumed that would always be the case.

She stuffed the picture into the O'Brien novel. The only thing left to contend with was the worn, folded sheet of paper lying on the bedspread. She picked it up, unfolded it halfway, and let her fingers run over the creases and wrinkles where it had been folded, unfolded, and refolded many times, by Scott's own hands. It was a single lined sheet, and the writing was Scott's. She read through the lines—a poem she'd never read, or a song she'd never heard—until the meaning, the deep feeling implied by those words, tore like shrapnel into her heart. Because she knew they weren't meant for her.

He wrote something beautiful for someone else. For Emerson.

Bay felt her head start to pound, her blood pressure rising. She balled up the paper and squeezed it tight in her fist, hurled it across the room, and pushed herself off the bed. The neat stacks from the envelope scattered, some pieces tumbling to the floor as she crossed the room and slammed the door behind her. She didn't care what Violet or anybody else wanted. Bay decided then and there, she'd rot in hell before she ever put what Scott had written to music. Whatever it was, it wasn't hers.

And maybe he wasn't hers anymore, either.

☆ ☽ ☆

Hours passed before Bay found her way out of the guest room bed. She sat on the edge, working her swollen hand, opening and closing her stiff fingers against the tightness in her knuckles. Her mouth was dry and her empty stomach churned. *Eat, shower, and then figure it out,* she thought. She padded down the stairs, into the kitchen, and rummaged the pantry for peanut butter and jelly. The house was still and quiet. Mel would be at work all day, managing a loyal staff that remained mostly intact even through the uncertain years, and Violet was most likely holiday shopping with one of the ladies from church. Bay stared off into space and let her mind go blank as she took small bites of her sandwich and chugged two bottles of water.

The solitude was a refreshing change from navigating the tense threads of her relationships with her family members the last few days. Social skills weren't exactly her strong suit, and the demands and attention left her feeling drained. She needed time to herself, to think things through, find the quiet space at her core so she could clear a path to move forward.

Back in her old room, Bay carefully picked up the strewn contents of the envelope Violet had given her, placing each item on her bed with renewed reverence. Scott had read these books, flipped the pages himself, used that small knife in the field, looked at these pictures as many times as she had, maybe more. She retrieved the crumpled sheet of paper last, took it to her desk and smoothed it out, then placed her old dictionary on top of it. She would salvage it for Scott, regardless of the ache it stirred in her chest. But she vowed she would forget it, clear it from her memory, as soon as it was tucked away with the other things. She'd figure out something else for the festival on Saturday, but she wouldn't be turning that into a song.

Bay wandered around the house and finally made her way outside, trying to gather her thoughts. The day unfolded into winter blues and grays, the dark earth, quiet roads, and cloud-spattered sky presenting their first real display of winter. She shivered inside her thin pajamas and tapped her foot on the floor of the front porch. Lillie wandered up the steps by the fourth tap.

"I didn't think you'd be up so early," she teased.

"Oh, you were watching from the bushes last night, were you?" Bay asked.

"From the hammock, yeah." Lillie perched on the top step, tilted her head back, and stretched her bare legs in front of her. It made Bay even colder just looking at her, although she realized Lillie wouldn't notice the temperature. "You and Will sure had a late night."

"Yeah, we did," Bay answered, sitting down herself. "He got me drunk. Or I got him drunk."

"That much was obvious. I'd worry I'd missed out on the drinking and stuff, but Lord, you look awful."

"Ha! Well, I feel it. As far as that's concerned, you didn't miss much."

Lillie laughed, and Bay felt the warmth of it in her soul. There was something healing in it, something that soothed her. She held a breath and let it wrap around her. Lillie never stayed with her long enough.

"I miss you," Bay said. "I do. It's cold here without you. Lonely."

"Me, too," Lillie said. She held out her hand, palm up, and the butterflies gathered there. She pursed her lips and blew at them, and they scattered again. "But I'm always warm. Something to look forward to."

Bay smiled. "So, apparently I'm playing Saturday at the Christmas festival."

"Really? How'd that happen?"

"Mama asked me to do this song she found in Scott's stuff. Although I think it was a poem he wrote, not a song. And I got the distinct impression that she and Daddy were trying to distract me. It worked."

Lillie turned to face her. "Scott wrote a poem? That rhymed? For you?"

Bay laughed. "I'm surprised at the things you don't know. Are you not peering over my shoulder day and night?"

"I can't be everywhere all at once, and I don't get to know everything, either. I already told you that." Lillie shrugged. "But things I know, I know."

Bay took a minute to think on that. "It wasn't for me, it was for

Emerson. And I don't ever want to see it again. I definitely won't be putting it to music. I'll have to come up with something else. If I can even do it."

"Of course, you can do it. Just do what you do. Do it for Scott. Sing it so he hears you…so he feels you, in his soul. Try."

"It's not going to bring him home, is it, Lillie?"

Lillie closed her eyes again, tilted her head as if she was listening for something. She didn't respond.

"Nothing I do can bring him home. It feels like a useless effort," Bay said.

"No effort made from love is ever wasted." Lillie got up and twirled down the steps, pirouetting down the front walk in her bare feet.

"I guess I better pull it together. I think I'll go write something, like, now."

"I know you will," Lillie answered. "And it will be perfect. I love you, Bay Laurel."

"I love you, Lillie Belle," Bay whispered to the empty air around her. "Thank you."

After a hot shower and a change into fresh clothes, Bay focused on clearing her mind of its present-day clutter. She'd made her decision. She would honor Violet's request with a song for Scott, a new song, one she would write over the next couple of days. It was a huge risk, as new songs tended to be. The endeavor was fraught with emotional landmines, but she determined she would make it happen, make it through it, and then leave it all on the stage behind her when she was done. It was one night, one song, one time. She cleared her old desk in her bedroom, moved all her things into the space where they belonged, and opened her guitar case for the first time since she arrived.

"Okay, Sally," she said, easing her old friend out and settling in around her, gently thrumming her aching fingers over the strings. "Let's see what we've got."

CAPTIVITY: DAY 88

Fire. Oh God. Too much fire.
Please forgive me, Bay. I can't hold on anymore.
God help me. Please let it end.

CHAPTER 8

"Bay!" Violet called up the stairs early the morning of the festival. "Honey, your daddy made you waffles!" She started toward the kitchen, stopped, and then came back to the stairs. "Bay Laurel!"

"Okay, Mama!" Bay yelled back, laying her guitar on the bed. She hustled down the stairs and followed Violet to the kitchen.

"She up?" Mel didn't turn his focus from the old waffle iron. Saturday morning waffles were his specialty, and if one wasn't absolutely perfect when it came off the iron, he'd throw it out and start again.

"I wonder how many vats of batter you waste in a given year," Bay teased.

"She's been up," Violet said, patting his shoulder as she moved by him to start the bacon. "I don't know how much she's slept at all the last couple of days. Guess she's a tad nervous about tonight."

"Hello," Bay said, waving her hands at Violet. "Standing here."

"Come here, princess, give your pa a hug," Mel said after scraping an unacceptable waffle into the trash. Bay walked into Mel's outspread arms and laid her ear against his heart.

"Don't worry about me so much, okay? Tonight's gonna be fine. I'm ready for it, I think."

He let her go and turned his attention to the waffles. "I know you are, baby, but are the rest of us?"

"Honest answer? No. Nobody's ever been ready for me when I happen."

"Ain't that the truth," Ethan said as he strolled in with the Lucy and Bree trailing him. "I thought we were going to the range this week, little lady."

"I did too, but something came up."

"Your sister is singing at the festival tonight," Violet said. "She's been shut up in her room for two days straight learning a song."

"Writing a song, you mean."

"You did something new? I thought—"

"I wanted to do one of my own. I know it's not the one you thought, but…well, it's the one I want," Bay explained, giving Violet a little squeeze to soften her delivery. "And I'm not being selfish, so don't start. If I was I wouldn't do this at all. I can't do the other one. It's not even a song, so if I'm writing music, I'm writing my own."

"Either way, I guess I better warn Will we're on guard duty tonight. Somebody has to keep the crowd safe from our little slugger, else half the town will end up with bloody noses and black eyes." Ethan grinned at her, his eyes sparkling.

Bay ducked her head and covered her eyes with her hands. "Guess there wasn't any chance you wouldn't get wind of that."

"Not a chance in hell. All the guys at the club applaud you. Harry's a shit."

"Ethan, language!" Violet broke in.

"Well, then, I suppose I won't feel like I bruised my little finger bones for nothing," Bay said over Ethan's laughter, flexing her still-sore digits.

The family settled in as early morning wore on through breakfast. For the first time since she'd come home, Bay found herself almost at ease. The morning with her family felt normal, when she shut out everything else and let herself enjoy it for a moment. Her brother, his wife and kids, her parents, moved about in their familiar patterns. Leigh Anne was being damn near pleasant. The girls were buzzing with excitement over the town's big yearly event before Santa's arrival, rushing through breakfast and obliging their grandmother's orders to get on hats and gloves and jackets before tumbling over each other into the front yard.

The expansive lawn in front of the house began to fill with people preparing for the morning parade, which started at Blossom Hill, for as long as Bay remembered, anyway. There were convertibles with beauty pageant winners riding perched on top of them, their teeth chattering beneath heavy crowns that slid this way or that. Trucks pulling floats with Christmas scenes from the local churches—a classic manger, the Grinch, a farm-themed affair—idled down the road and around the curve. The high school marching band and cheerleaders in their red, white, and black uniforms were busy socializing rather than getting into formation. The Junior ROTC drill team members stood together, fussing over their uniforms and flags. Bay turned from the window and trudged toward the stairs.

"You should bundle up for the parade," Violet said from the door of the kitchen. "I can't believe how cold it's gotten the last couple of days."

"I'm staying here, Mama. I need to finish up and run through a couple of things for tonight."

"Honey, if you're thinking of backing out—"

"No, it's not that." Bay felt her face twist under the effort she made at a smile. "I don't usually write a song and perform it in the span of three days. It still needs work. I want to get it right. Believe it or not, it's important to me to get this right."

Violet nodded, folded and unfolded the dish towel she held in her hands. "Well, I'm sure it's going to be wonderful. We'll come home after lunch. I'll bring you some barbeque from The Red Caboose."

"Thanks." Bay turned to the stairs, focused on one foot, then the other, until she was in her room, the door closed behind her. She laid the sheets of music out, forming a neat line across the bed.

Bay wouldn't admit it to Violet, but her mind was busy searching for plausible escape routes. It was bad enough working through her nerves to perform on any stage. But here, in front of a hometown crowd with high expectations, she felt almost certain she would collapse on the spot without a drink—or three—to get her through it.

Bay climbed into bed with the music she'd written and gathered the pages together. She rested them on her chest and closed her eyes, running through the lyrics and notes in her mind. She let herself drift into the melody, working her way through each line. Somewhere in the middle the memories overtook her and she drifted off.

The smell of a campfire at her parents' old barn blew around her, and she and Scott sat trading stories with their high school friends, just weeks before Scott would leave for Afghanistan the first time. He'd already been to Iraq, and he'd been confident that he knew what was ahead of him. He sat behind her, and she snuggled into the warmth of his body, shivered at his breath against her ear. They were so close…

Until somehow they drifted apart. And then Emerson happened. Scott swore to her they'd get past it, if she would—

Her eyes burst open at the sound of her phone ringing, her mind racing back through the memory-turned-fantasy. She fumbled around for it, knocked it off the bed along with the crumpled sheets of her song, and then dove for it. "What time is it?" she half shouted when she answered.

"Lunchtime, thereabouts," Will answered. She could hear the smile in his voice.

"Oh, great, I fell asleep," Bay groaned. "I was dreaming about nighttime—that night we had the last party at the barn."

"Great night. Not one I can say I've dreamt about, but it was fun."

"Well, maybe it was better for some of us than others."

Will laughed. "I don't wanna know. Come eat with me. Caboose has a booth. You know you want a barbeque samich."

"I would like a samich, but it's gonna have to wait," Bay answered, yawning. "And Mama's bringing me a plate, anyway. I need to finish up with this song. I must have dozed off earlier because all I managed so far today was rolling around in it."

"Um, I'm not sure what that means."

"It means that I want to avoid this evening's festivities so badly on a subconscious level that my body is trying to shut down and render me incompetent to stand trial. Or whatever."

"Bay, nobody's gonna be judging you tonight. You're singing one song, and you're doing it for Scott," Will reassured her.

"You, my friend, are delusional. Any time there's a stage involved, there's also judging involved. But it's a good song. Not the song specifically requested by her highness Mother Violet, but good enough."

"So don't worry about it. Come on out, let's play. You know you want to."

"Will, your methods of persuasion haven't matured beyond your current dating age range," Bay said, rolling her eyes.

"And you are the same tiny stubborn person you were at twelve," Will jabbed back.

"Then you already know you won't win this day. I'll see you tonight?"

"Yeah, I guess you will. If I don't see you before, break a leg or whatever," Will said.

"There's an option," Bay answered before she hung up.

Breathe in. Breathe out.

When Mayor Lowman introduced Bay as the final performer later that night, she closed her eyes and steadied herself, then took the stage, pushing everything in her mind aside except for Scott. The audience may have been clapping or they may have been booing, but the only sound she heard was the soft click of her boots against the old wooden floor. The faces in the crowd may have been friendly, expectant, or hostile, but all she saw was the twinkling of the lights above them, the lonesome stool in the middle of the stage, the ancient microphone. By the time she'd settled herself on the stool and slung her guitar across her body, all that was left in the world for her were the strings beneath her fingers, the thrumming of her heart, the song she'd sing this once, for him. She immersed herself in what she'd felt for Scott one last time, and sang her heart out.

I can't forget the day you left
Your uniform, my old blue dress
I kissed your lips, you dried my eyes
We knew the drill, one more goodbye

We held the past inside our hearts
It kept us close 'til we fell apart
You left our future far behind
Dreamed your new dreams while I chased mine

But no one knows me quite like you
And I'm not sure how I'll get through
The storms that rage, the bitter blues
If there's nothing left of me and you

So I hope we'll still be friends
And there's nothing to forgive
If you'll come home again

It's hard to see life moving on
When all I knew before is gone
I tell myself I'll be alright
Just one more day, then one more night

They look at me like I should go
When there are things that they don't know
And I can't tell the simple truth
I can't take back what you chose to do

But no one knows me quite like you
And I'm not sure I'll make it through
The storms that rage, these bitter blues
If there's nothing left between me and you

So I hope we can be friends
And we'll forget and forgive
When you come home again

Bay didn't wait on stage to see who or what broke the stunned silence of her audience when the song was over. She didn't hear the applause building behind her as she took the steps from the back of the stage and walked across the open field with her memories of Scott to accompany her. Bay wasn't sure what had happened on that stage, but somewhere beyond her, she'd reached for Scott and found a certainty that he was okay, and that she could go on.

As she lay in the grass under the starlit southern sky whispering her song for Scott one last time, she didn't know that, thousands of miles away, in the mountains of Afghanistan, he was opening his eyes to the dawn of his last day as a prisoner of war. She didn't know that he smiled as he woke, thinking he'd heard the sound of her voice telling him everything was alright. She didn't know that somewhere in the place where the dark night sky above her met the early light of that December morning, Scott was making his way home.

EXTRACTION

Hondo kept his mind focused on his job as the Black Hawk made its way through the moonless night sky toward Khyber Pass in the mountains between Pakistan and Afghanistan. It wasn't the first time he and his team had been delivered to a remote and danger-laden area, but the energy was different than the kick they experienced with most missions. There were all kinds of political implications to consider with this one, given that they'd be crossing the Pakistan border, but that wasn't really his business. Men in suits would deal with that. Tonight, his team would extract and deliver Sergeant First Class Scott Jackson Murphy to an American airfield and escort him back to American soil. Nobody on the bird really cared where they had to snatch him from, they were just grateful they got to do it. Any one of them would be happy to grab him from the hands of the devil himself, if that's what it took. The air was swimming with adrenaline. You could almost taste it.

The boys of 160th SOAR flew expertly through the high-altitude terrain and slipped undetected into Enemy Central to deliver the team.

"Ten minutes," came the call through Hondo's noise-canceling headset. He surveyed the faces around him as they came to attention. The men began their silent preparations, checking gear, making final mental run-throughs, steeling themselves for whatever happened next.

The one minute signal was given. Hondo adjusted his night-vision goggles. The team would fast-rope into the compound where Murphy was being held in a mud structure with little ventilation, presumably guarded by less than four insurgents at this hour. The Black Hawks were loaded with the full force of their operational detachment, as well as several additional medics and gunners. Unmanned drones had been monitoring the facility in the previous two weeks, and given the intelligence gathered and the training exercises executed leading up to tonight's mission, they should be in and out within half an hour. Cakewalk.

The insurgents, for their part, had not anticipated a raid in Pakistan. It was a densely dark and quiet night, with little noise outside of the occasional braying or scurrying of an animal. The guards positioned outside of the makeshift holding cell slept more than dozed at their stations, so routine the post had become. They were slow to react to the sudden chaos when the night sky was shattered by the low whir of the Black Hawks overhead. Before they were fully aware of their dire circumstances, the forward extraction unit had leveled their weapons and fired. Hondo stood by impatiently as the explosives team set a C-4 charge to blast through the locked metal gate blocking the entrance to Murphy's personal prison. He was the first of the team to scramble into the pitch black of the room, where he dropped down in front of an alert, confused Murphy. He was on his knees, squinting into the darkness, stammering, "Sergeant First Class Scott Jackson Murphy, US Special Forces ODA-5126! I'm here! I'm here!"

Hondo forced night vision goggles over Murphy's face and gave him time for his eyes to adjust, time to register the moment. He grinned as he patted Murphy down, checking for explosives, grabbed his shoulders, and pulled him up when one of their teammates had cut him free of his chains. "Hey man, my name's Hondo. Try to relax and let us get straight here. I have a very important question for you, though."

"What's that?"

"Tell me about that sweet ride you got back home?" Hondo asked.

Scott made a sound as close to a laugh as he could muster. "Dodge D-100 Series, '67. If Bay didn't take it and wreck it yet."

"Let's hope it's still intact. What color did you say it was?"

"I didn't," Scott answered. "It's powder blue."

Hondo smiled. "Alright, then. Please work with me so we can get out of here together," he said. "We're taking you home, sir."

Twenty-eight long minutes had passed since the birds unloaded inside the compound. When the twelve men and their dog, Mika, trotted out, with Murphy among them, they quickly set for takeoff. Murphy was loaded in, seeming at once dazed and elated. Hondo stayed close by him with the team's medic, SFC Mike Sloan, who gave him an energy gel pack and a bottle of water while he checked him over.

"Take it slow with this, now," Sloan warned. "It's a little sweeter than that naan and jelly you've been eating. Your system will need some time to readjust to regular meals, although this isn't exactly a steak dinner."

"You okay, sir? Any injuries need immediate attention, anything else we can do to make you comfortable?" Hondo asked, noting Murphy's bruised face, his hand pressed against his rib cage.

Scott managed a smile and a shake of his head.

"Try to relax, man. You've been through a hell of a lot," Hondo said, in an effort to reassure him.

They sat still and silent as the Black Hawks climbed into the deep black of the sky and hurtled toward the air field. The helicopters would make one stop for refueling, in a dry riverbed where two Chinooks waited. Their crews cheered as the Black Hawks refueled, each man stopping with personal words of welcome and gratitude for Murphy. Then, as they neared the base forty minutes later, Hondo outfitted Murphy with a headset so he could hear the chatter as they approached. As the US airfield came into view below the helicopters, the chatter grew to a roar of cheers from the headset. Hondo turned to Murphy again and grinned.

"How does it feel, brother?" Hondo asked.

Murphy gave him a blank stare, then smiled like a man knowing what he was expected to say.

"Like nothing else," Scott said. "It feels like nothing at all."

CHAPTER 9

Bay half flew and half stumbled down the stairs late the next morning when Mel bellowed up to her from the den.

"Daddy, what's wrong?" she yelled, sliding at the landing in her socks, taking the corner too fast. She sprinted into the room and quickly assessed that he and her mother were both upright and breathing. Violet had the phone to her ear, and Mel was standing in front of the TV pushing buttons on the remote. A minute later, they all stood brushing arms, stunned into silence, as the CNN reporter narrated over the footage from Afghanistan. Mel moved to stand behind Bay, resting his hands on her shoulders.

"The Joint Special Operations Command Press Secretary confirms that a United States Army Special Forces Team carried out an extraction mission in the early hours of the morning. The mission took place along the Khyber Pass, a perilous no-man's land situated between the border of Afghanistan and Pakistan. No official word yet on whether the mission crossed the border into Pakistan. Sergeant First Class Scott Jackson Murphy, who is from New Hope, South Carolina, and a member of the Special Forces Fifth Brigade based at Fort Bragg, North Carolina, had been missing in action and presumed a prisoner of war or killed in action for nearly three months, after members of his team were ambushed in a night-time attack. Sergeant First Class Murphy has been recovered alive and in fair health. He is already en route to

Landstuhl Regional Medical Center in Germany, where he will undergo a medical evaluation before returning stateside…"

The news anchor continued his report, but Bay couldn't hear it above the blood rushing through her veins too fast, the pounding of her heart like shotgun blasts, the quickening pace of her breath. She didn't notice the tears streaming down her face until Mel's thumbs were wiping at them, and then he pulled her into his arms and helped her to the sofa when her knees buckled beneath her sobs.

When she'd calmed down enough, Bay fumbled around the coffee table and found the remote to rewind the news report so she could watch it again. She drank in the sight of Scott's face on the screen, still so handsome beneath the ragged beard, the bruises, the haggard expression. She wiped at her face with the back of her hands and laughed out loud when he flashed his brilliant smile toward the camera and gave two thumbs up. He seemed to be staring right at her, ready to crack one of his stupid jokes. She hit rewind again and paused the report at the instant he smiled so she could study him. She felt Mel's eyes on her and glanced over.

"He seems good, Bay. He looks alright," he said reassuringly, turning to the screen.

"Yeah, he does, doesn't he?" she replied, nodding her head. "Checking him over for cracks, as Mama would say." She got up and walked to the TV, laid a gentle hand on the screen.

"You'll have plenty of time to check him over, honey," Mel said. He paused, shook his head. "I can admit to you now, I didn't think we would ever see that boy again."

She felt the grin on her face falter at Mel's words.

"Sorry, sweetheart, I didn't mean—"

"No," she said, "Scott's coming home. That's all that matters."

"Yes, it is," Mel said, his voice thick with emotion. The exhaustion and worry lingering in his expression confounded Bay.

"What is it, Daddy?"

He shook his head. "Just thinking…"

"How is he, really?"

Mel sighed. "He's alive. Let's go from there."

"What are you two doing?" Violet said, stepping in from the kitchen.

"What are you doing, calling the whole town?" Mel asked. Bay didn't turn away from the screen.

"I'm leaving that for Leigh. I just called her and Ethan. Bay, we should get over to Scott's and start getting it ready. Lord, it's in a state over there. We didn't want to touch anything, but I sure wish we'd at least seen to cleaning." Violet was out of sight for a second before she came back, her hands raised in frustration. "Now, Bay, now!"

Violet clapped her hands together to get her attention, and for once Bay responded to her mother's command without bristling and rushed from the room behind her. In the foyer, Bay grabbed Violet's hand and pulled her to a stop. She turned, her face a study of focused energy. Her eyes softened as Bay's welled with tears again.

"Mama," she whispered, "is this real?"

Violet wrapped her arms around Bay and smoothed her wild hair, gently swayed her back and forth a moment.

"It's real, baby. He made it. He's alive, and he's okay. He's coming home." She pulled away and took Bay's face in her hands, throwing a glance up at the portrait of Willa Pearl hanging in the foyer. "You might get the chance to make things right after all, and I might get to put that pearl of yours around your neck before I'm too old to work a clasp."

Violet scampered up the stairs, leaving Bay in the wake of her words and what this could mean. She hurried up the stairs and stumbled into her bedroom, sat on the edge of the bed with her head in her hands and listened to her parents banging around. Her mind was racing so fast that the room was spinning. "Scott is alive. Scott is alive." She repeated it several times, out loud, as if the act of vocalizing it would fill it full of truth. As she attempted to wrap her mind around Scott's rescue as fact, the present reality of the way they'd wrecked things was almost too much to contend with.

When she could breathe again, Bay went to her dresser, pulled open the second drawer, reached in and grabbed an old gray Army tee shirt, one of the ones Scott had passed on to her that she'd slept in over the years whenever she was home. Somehow she could still tease out the scent of him from the worn cotton. She held it to her face and let her tears soak in.

"Scott is alive, Lillie," Bay said, keeping her voice low. "He's coming home."

Bay could feel her there, even if she couldn't see her in that moment. The energy and connection between them pulsed in the space of the room.

"I'm sorry, Lillie. I'm so sorry I lost you, that I let you go. I promise I'll make good on this chance with Scott. I won't lose him, too."

Bay shook herself, fighting to get a grip on her emotions, and hurried back to the guest room. She riffled through the clothes in her bag, discarding everything she had before she laughed out loud at herself, realizing Scott wouldn't actually be at his house that day. She threw on jeans and went back for the Army tee shirt, slipped herself into it, pulled her hair back in messy pigtails, and brushed her teeth before running down the stairs to pace as Violet got herself together.

Mel was standing at the kitchen counter pouring a steaming cup of coffee. Bay watched him stir the cup and take a long sip, his brow furrowed.

"What's going on with you, Daddy?" she asked, crossing her arms to hide her shaking hands.

Mel took another long sip. For the first time, Bay noticed the lines on his face, the way his age had suddenly settled on him, like the burdens that came with it were too much for him to hold up against. It should have been a happy moment, but something in the slump of her father's shoulders spoke of defeat. "Well, Bay, one of our own has practically risen from the grave, and your mama is all stirred up…"

"What about Mama?" Bay asked, stepping closer.

He closed his eyes and shrugged. "Be careful where you tread with her right now. That's all I'm going to say."

"Daddy, did she talk to you about that picture I found at Owl's Roost? That guy Marco, he looks so much like Scott, but Mama bristled at the idea of me even trying—"

"Bay," Mel cut her off, agitation edging his voice. "Leave it. Violet and I are in agreement on that—now's not the time to go poking around in the past. Focus on what's important today. Scott's on his way home, where his family is waiting for him. We're his family. Drop all the other mess, hear me?"

"Okay, fine," she said, "but we're gonna talk, Daddy. You're right, though, Scott's coming home, and we need to get ready for that. I realize he might not even want to see me. That...well, I'll deal with it tomorrow. I need to run out for a bit."

"Where do you need to go right now?"

"I need to pick something up." She plucked Scott's keys from the hook by the door. "I'll meet y'all at Scott's house."

Bay drove through New Hope to the far end of Main Street, with its one little restaurant, the car dealership, and the local hardware store. She thought she'd remembered seeing a few lonely Christmas trees left out on the sidewalk at the festival, and they were still there, leaning haphazardly against the brick storefront, unsecured. It was Sunday morning, and the store was closed, but she backed the truck up as close as she could to the trees anyway and left it running. If anyone was out on the street, she didn't notice. She searched through Scott's glove compartment until she came up with a napkin and a pen, and she wrote an IOU out to Mr. Collins, hoping he'd understand. It was for Scott, after all…most everybody loved Scott, and Scott had always loved Christmas.

When she'd selected the fullest, least lopsided tree, she hefted it by the trunk and made quick, noisy work of getting it up and into the bed of the truck. She secured it as best she could with the nylon cords she found behind the seat and lamented not using the gloves she also found there. Her hands were raw and dirty from the tree bark and needles, but she shook the discomfort off and drove away with her loot.

It wasn't much in the way of a peace offering, but driving to Scott's with the tree bouncing in the truck bed behind her, she felt a long-absent hope swelling in her chest, the hope that came with knowing they'd finally be able to put the burden of that last goodbye, and all the things they'd left unsaid, behind them. Scott was coming home, and she had a chance to make it right, or at least less wrong.

Using her elbow, she rang the doorbell twice at Scott's and waited, the tree propped against her. The yard was full of cars, mostly those of ladies from the church who came to help Violet get things ready, and she wasn't sure if anyone inside the crowded house could hear the bell over the chatter. She fought to stay upright as she was slowly overtaken by the unruly limbs of the Christmas tree.

As she waited on the porch, Bay heard a low hum from the tree. She pushed it away from her body, letting it fall with a thud against the door. The hum intensified into a buzz then, one she recognized immediately. Bay hurdled the steps and sprinted to the other side of the truck just in time to turn and watch the tree full of bees fall in on Violet.

"Bay?" Violet yelled as she stumbled back.

"Sorry Mama! There are bees!" Bay called back.

"Bees?" Mel hurried out and dragged the tree off of Violet and onto the porch. "Well, I'll be damned, and here it is December," he said, swatting around his head. "Let me go find something…" he trailed off and headed inside.

"Were you stung?" Violet asked, rushing past the tree and down the steps to Bay. "Do you have your pen?"

"No, Mama, I'm fine, I think," Bay said, checking herself over. She put a hand to her throat and took a deep breath, reassuring herself that she hadn't been stung, that she could still breathe.

But something else was there, hitching her breath as it rose in the back of her mind, surfacing with the appearance of a swarm of bees in winter. Worry itched its way up from her belly into her throat.

"Are you sure? You look flushed. Bay?"

Bay shook her head and looked at Violet. "It's not me, Mama. I'm fine."

Violet let out a breath. "Good. That's good. Let's let your daddy take care of that and make sure the house is clear before you go in."

Bay nodded, turning to watch Mel on the porch.

"Honey, it'll be fine. It was a sweet gesture," Violet said, squeezing Bay's shoulders.

"I know, Mama. It'll be fine. I'm fine," she whispered. "Let's go around back and get inside."

"Sure you're alright?" Violet asked, concern etching her features.

Bay nodded, struck dumb with a fear deeper than the sight of those bees could have stirred.

It was Christmas, and she'd made her way home, and now Scott was on his way back to them. But in this season of joy, a sense of dread was growing, thundering in her chest like a storm, buzzing in her ears like those bees, a warning that, even if they were all together again, they would never be the same.

HOMECOMING

I'm watching through the window of the tiny plane carrying me and the extraction team into Fort Bragg. It's a cold day for North Carolina, and misty with rain. Even with the dreary weather, I can see hundreds of people out there, waiting to welcome me home.

I guess the crowd shouldn't be a surprise. Fort Bragg is a large military base, a close-knit community, and New Hope's only two hours away. Even if the nation as a whole has all but forgotten this war, the ones here can't forget it. So, I get to be on display.

I hate this whole hero's welcome thing. Not to say I didn't imagine this kind of celebration more than once when I was in that shithole. I've been focused on survival so long, nursing dreams, that I forgot reality might not shape up to match them.

And now here I am, all my dreams about coming home realized.

All I feel is empty.

They told me in Afghanistan that Kedrick died instantly when we here hit. Simpson is making a slow recovery. Lost his right leg at the knee. So even though I've been to hell and back, I'm the lucky bastard. I'm alive. And aside from some cracked ribs, a messy face, and the fact that I still think I can smell my own hair burning from the electric shocks, I'm alarmingly healthy. I'm whole.

How can I be healthy and whole when one of my best friends

is gone? When one of my brothers left a limb in the desert that night? I can't process it.

Except I'm not. Not really. I'm a hull, burned out. At first glance, I bet I seem pretty sound, solid. If anyone looks closer, though, I'm scared they'll see it behind my eyes. I'm charred out, dead on the inside. Anybody feeling around for something left in there's gonna draw back from the heat of my rage with ashes in their hands.

I can't really make sense of it, though, how empty I feel. Angry. And alone, even though I've barely been left alone to take a piss since they found me. All I wanted over there was to get home. All that kept me going was what little escape I could find, at home in my mind. Now I'm here and it's real and I don't know how to do this.

Damn these nerves. I hate not knowing what's next. Hondo told me some of the details of what we'd do today, but I can't remember shit. My mind is everywhere and nowhere at the same time. I remember there's a celebration and ceremony to get through, more debriefings, evaluations, and interviews. Once that's over, they said I'll take leave. I'd rather go back to the field, though, to my brothers. They're the only real family I've got, anyway.

I close my eyes, clench my hands into fists, and take a deep breath, another. All those people will be cheering, waving flags and signs, wearing yellow ribbons to welcome me home. Had they been here to welcome Simpson? No, of course not. Simpson went directly to a military hospital and then to somewhere in Florida for rehab. And Kedrick has yet to be buried at Arlington. What a cold, cruel reality it must be for his wife and kids, his whole family, having their lives shattered to bits in some remote, faraway place, for reasons they'll likely never understand, and to have to wait so long to see him in his final resting place. Someone mentioned that I would be able to go for his funeral.

There's no way in hell I can do that.

"Ready for the party, soldier?" Hondo grins at me. He seems different today without all the gear. His smile is easy. He's confident, relaxed. The epitome of a Special Forces soldier.

I used to be like that.

"Negative," I answer, honing in on the smaller crowd of people hunkered beneath the breezeway between the small terminals. "There must be a quieter way to do this."

Hondo laughs and gathers his gear with the rest of the team. "What's the fun in that?"

"You know what would be fun, Hondo? A cold beer in a dark bar with my team. I should have gone back."

Hondo steps aside to let the others pass. "They're coming home in February. There wasn't enough time for that." He looks out of the window, then at me. "Listen, you'll get back in the game, Murphy. Give yourself some time to process. We're all here for you, man."

"Thanks." I turn to him from the window. "I don't mean to sound ungrateful. I know how lucky I am to be home. It doesn't feel right."

"It will. Give it time." He pauses and leans closer. "Listen, be careful, okay, with what you say? Call me if you need to talk. Just me. We'll keep it between us. After all this, I don't want to see you benched if you don't wanna be. Get me?"

I nod. I get it. I'm not sure that I care that much anymore, but I get it. "I want you to know," I start, but can't finish when my words get tangled in my throat. "Thank you, brother."

"It was my honor," Hondo says. He gives a quick salute and turns away from me fast.

As he deboards, I wait with the doctor and officer who will escort me off the plane, where I get to shake hands with the base generals and whoever they'd sent from Washington before joining whoever showed up in a private room. Nerves sit curled like a heavy fist in my gut. I don't know how to act my way through this. The last few months have been a steady practice in the art of emotional shutdown, objective strategy, and physical endurance. Now I'm home, and it feels like foreign soil, like being dropped behind enemy lines. I have to start all over again, assessing, engaging, strategizing, responding. But I don't want to deal with people. Any of them.

"Sergeant Murphy, come on down," someone calls from outside the plane. I nod to the medic and salute the officer before I make my way to the door. I try to ignore the pop of flashes as I concentrate on descending the slick steps to the ground. I salute, shake hands, and accept heartfelt gratitude from men who don't know anything about me.

I near the end of the line of Army brass who showed up for the opportunity to make it onto CNN, and I take a quick inventory of the faces watching from the breezeway. Mel and Violet are there. Will's there, too, on the other side of Violet. Jake, Leigh. A few other folks from town.

Soon as I think she didn't bother to come, there's movement in the doorway of the building to the right. That's when I see her, framed in the window of the gray metal door, her bright hair tumbling around her shoulders, wild from the rain.

Bay.

I'm led through the same door as the extraction team. Someone takes my bag, and they hand me paperwork and forms to start on—things I can't find the focus for.

"Hey," Hondo approaches and takes the clipboard from my hand. "Let's get Sergeant Murphy to his family, yeah?"

I nod my thanks to Hondo when I'm ushered to the inner door. Down the hall to the right, another turn, then another, until I stand before the final door separating me from the people who are as close to family as I have. And there's not one Murphy in the bunch.

"Can I have a minute?" I ask.

"Oh, yeah," Hondo answers. I watch him hurry down the hall, and then I lean against the wall. I consider the small group of people waiting on the other side of the door, and what they might expect, what they would want. I find my center and slip into myself—the Scott they know, the one they want back—and I open the door hoping I'll figure out how to get him home from here.

CHAPTER 10

The memory of her last trip to Fort Bragg weighed on Bay's mind as she waited for Scott's homecoming. She hadn't really been thinking about the war in Afghanistan as she stood on the blistering pavement that day in August. She hadn't been worried about Scott where the war was concerned. He had been to war before, after all, and he understood how to operate within its domain. Her thoughts had been dominated by the treacherous terrain of heartbreak stretching between them. She'd been smug, thinking that none of the skills of warfare he'd mastered in the last fourteen years could help him do battle with her there. She flinched at the memory of her resentment, the anger she'd carried like a clinched fist to swing at him that last time she'd seen him.

Why had she been so unwilling to understand, to forgive and forget something that happened when they were apart? She'd been so cavalier, and so naïve about what he might face. You never expect the worst to happen, and then it does, and you realize what you should have done…but it's too late.

Bay told Mel she was too cold standing outside in the rain, even under the shelter of the breezeway, and she'd come inside to wait alone. But her teeth still chattered, even in the warm room, and her heart flung itself around in her chest like a wild animal abruptly caged. Will caught her gaze through the window once and started toward her, but she warned him off with the flash of heat in her eyes. She needed to be alone, to watch Scott moving, to watch him breathing, to see him smile. And she thought putting the door between them while he made his way through the obligatory welcome committee might keep her from hurling herself into his arms like she hadn't spent one day out of them.

The extraction team members made their way off the plane and quickly to the other building through the rain. There was a moment when it appeared the plane was empty, and the Army brass, standing in the thirty-eight degree mist, shifted and squirmed in miserable solidarity until Scott appeared in the doorway.

Breathe in. Breathe out.

Everything else fell away as Bay watched him carefully come down the steps, one foot, the other, the next step, until he was on the ground, nothing but solid ground and a wall of people between them. She watched as he saluted and embraced people she knew he didn't even know. She closed her eyes against the tears that threatened to spill down her cheeks like icy snowmelt, and when she opened them again, Scott's eyes were locked on hers, through the window, through the crowd, through the pain and the bruises and the missing each other. He stopped where he was and waited. A smile broke like dawn across Bay's face, and she pressed her hand to the glass.

"Hi," she mouthed.

Scott stared at her a long moment, his face stoic, then turned away. Bay pulled her hand from the window fast, as if it had suddenly shocked her. Fresh tears stung her eyes as she watched him walking away.

What happened after that was a blur. Scott was ushered through the same door the extraction team had taken across the breezeway and his friends were sent through the one where Bay stood. Nervous energy bounced through the air in pops of laughter and static-like chatter about how good he looked, how healthy, how much like Scott. Anxiety knotted her stomach, stretched its fingers up around her lungs. They were right; Scott seemed fine, healthier than she'd expected, in most ways the same beneath the bruises. But something had struck her with that one look in his eyes, a sharp note of discord ringing now in her ears.

Violet came to stand beside her, slipped her hand into Bay's.

"What did you think?" she asked, doubt weighing her voice.

"I think he looks good," Bay answered. "He's so strong. He's going to be back to normal before you know it," she reassured herself as much as her mother.

The inner door on the far wall burst open. Scott walked through it and the room stilled. Mel stepped forward first, his eyes full of tears, and pulled Scott into a hug. Violet joined the hug, too, then Ethan and Leigh, and Will, until Scott was completely surrounded by the people who loved him.

Except for Bay.

She didn't know how long she sat there in a folding chair, her tears forming rivers down her cheeks, watching while everyone else celebrated a shared joy so deep it seemed to have stopped her heart. It was a noisy, exuberant dog pile of affection, and Bay found herself laughing and crying, near hysterical, by the time it broke up. When Scott finally came to her, she wanted to stand, at least meet him halfway, but her legs wouldn't cooperate. Then he was on his knees, his face buried in her hair as she sobbed against his shoulder.

"I'm sorry for putting you through this, Bay," she heard him say.

"You're sorry? Scott, you—oh my God. You're home. You came home!" All the emotions she'd been holding in for months overwhelmed her. Scott was here, in front of her, holding her. She didn't have to miss him, feel his absence in her bones, worry that he wouldn't come home, and regret every unresolved feeling, every word left unspoken for the rest of her life.

And yet, even in this happy moment, she felt the thread of uncertainty between them vibrate and hum. She pulled away instinctively, as if her body remembered before her mind and heart that his arms were not her home anymore. She opened her eyes and gazed into Scott's, confusion further shorting out the connection between them. Looking into those eyes set off a small blast in her chest. Her heart lurched, straining to shift into the old, familiar rhythm of loving him. It had been singing its quiet, certain song for him for so long, it never forgot the tune.

"You're skinny," she said. He laughed, and Bay felt the tension start to relax around them.

"I've been on a somewhat restricted diet."

"Well, it's good you're back in time for Christmas, then," Leigh Anne broke in. "Mama, we've got some cooking to do."

"Oh, don't you worry about a thing," Violet said, putting an arm around Leigh. "I've got a head start, and some of Scott's favorites already waiting in the car."

"Can y'all give us a minute?" Scott asked without turning from Bay.

"Sure, of course," Mel answered, nodding. "Violet and I are gonna go get us all checked in at that hotel they set us up in, off of Skibo?"

"Sounds good," Scott answered, still watching Bay. "I'll have to follow later on, so y'all should wait for Bay. We'll only be a minute." The lack of warmth in his eyes sent Bay's heart sinking. She remained in her seat, trying to gather herself together while everyone else made their way from the room. Scott was here, and whole, not lost. She'd touched him with her own hands. But something was off-key, like the wrong note struck to her finely-tuned ear, a subtle warning. The door closed, and for a moment they watched each other, the wariness building between them.

"Hi," Bay finally said, glancing away from him as she did.

"Hi? That's the best you got?"

"How are you?" She asked. Her words came out clipped, like she was biting off the ends. The sudden shift in the mood of the room knocked her off balance, and Scott hesitated a beat. His eyes were hard, his face a blank slate.

"Listen, Bay, you don't have to hang around. Neither do your folks. It's good to see them, obviously, and I understand that they worry about me not having family to speak of, but I don't have the patience to pretend we weren't off the rails when I left. It's clear you don't particularly want to be here. You don't have to be."

Bay sat up straighter in her seat. "No, how can you think that? I wanted to see you, Scott. Of course, I want to see you. None of us would be anywhere else today, you have to know—it's just—" She didn't know how to finish. She shook her head and forced herself to focus.

"It's that my sudden resurrection from the grave leaves you with an obligation you'd rather not have to deal with."

"That's not true at all," Bay said, her voice hitching. "How could you even say that to me?"

"You made yourself pretty clear on that before I deployed, Bay. And anyways, you're not the only one who's confused..." Scott bowed his head, flexed his hands into fists. "It would've been better all the way around if you'd stayed the hell in Nashville. I got plenty to figure out without this mess."

"Well, thanks for letting me know how you feel," she said, getting to her feet and putting a chair between them. "I'll go back to Nashville, then, soon as I can pack my shit and get the hell away from New Hope. No need to torture myself on your account, I guess."

"Torture yourself? The hell do you even mean, Bay?"

"I thought I'd lost you, too, Scott." Bay fought to keep her voice down, but it rose along with the temperature of her blood as it neared a boil. "And at first, I couldn't even show my face in New Hope when you went missing. Nobody knew what happened between us, except that we broke up, and then you were gone. Everyone could see it, the regret, the wishing I could take it all back and knowing I might not ever get the chance. I couldn't face the fact that I'd pushed you away like I did, when I had no right...Truth is, it wasn't just losing you that hurt so much. It was losing you and knowing how we'd left things because I was too proud, or too hurt, or just maybe too damn scared."

Scott stuffed his hands in his pockets and studied the laces of his boots. He sat down and leaned forward, his elbows on his knees, and ran a hand over his hair.

"You have to know I didn't mean..." She trailed off as she sat down beside him and gnawed at a fingernail.

"What?" Scott prodded.

"Nothing," she muttered, shaking her head.

Scott threw up his hands and let them drop heavy against his thighs. "Seriously? Can we not even manage one honest, open conversation, even on a day like this?"

"Hey, I'm trying. You're the one making it clear you don't even want me here," she fired back. "And you do realize you're being a complete asshole, don't you?"

He didn't answer, and she still didn't look at him, but she felt him watching her as she kept her eyes on the old "Army of One" poster hanging across the room. She tried to make her face a blank canvas. It felt like all the emotion had been drained from her body, like she'd already spent all she had reserved for this day.

"It's not fair of you to still be mad at me. I've been there for you no matter what, even at the worst times, even when I damn well didn't want to. I showed up. I realize you've been through a lot, and you're still going through a lot, but take it easy with the gut punches. I don't have to be here. It would have been easier not to be. But I showed up."

"Maybe I am being an ass." Scott blew out a heavy breath. "That doesn't mean you get a free pass for how you treated me before, though. The way you walked away, Bay, when we finally…you walked away. Maybe I shouldn't have told you about Emerson, but I thought we got past it, that we were getting past it. We weren't—I mean, I never, ever cheated on you. I met her when we weren't together. But then you broke things off again anyway, even though I didn't do anything wrong. You might be here now, but don't think I don't know that's at least in part for show."

The way he spat the words 'for show' at her made Bay think they must have tasted bitter in his mouth. She fought to keep her own temper in check, wary of this new brand of anger Scott was wearing like armor.

"Listen, you just got home from being held prisoner for months. I thought you were dead. We all thought you were dead. Do you really want to spend your first day home fighting with me?" Bay got up and walked to the door. "I can't imagine what you've been through. I'm not sure I want to know. But you're not the only one who's been suffering."

She stepped into the hall and closed the door behind her, then turned to watch him through the small window.

"God, please bring him back to me," she whispered as she studied his back through the tinted glass. "Please be okay." He sat up straight then, palms down on his knees, and she saw his shoulders rise with each deep breath he took.

When Scott turned, his gaze met hers through the glass, and he seemed to be looking through her, not really seeing her at all. The hum sharpened and rose up in her ears again. She wasn't sure what to search for in the deep well of his eyes, but whatever she hoped for she didn't find. She recognized the sensation then, that empty discord she'd felt all this time he was missing, the absence of him still resonating within her. He was here, right in front of her, but the Scott she'd loved all her life was still gone.

"LIBERATION": DAY 1

Bay walks away, and I drop my head to my hands. That's when I notice how bad they're shaking. Picking a fight with her is the last thing I want to do. We should be celebrating, clinking beer bottles and eating our way through a pile of junk food while she catches me up on the months of life I've lost.

I should feel liberated. That's the word they keep using on the news. But I don't. There's a slow boil starting in my gut, like acid, eating through me, scarring me from the inside out, scarring this day that should be perfect. I don't feel liberated at all. Part of me is still chained up on the other side of the world, dragged backward to the last place I want to be.

Should feel, should be, should have. If I could go back and do what I should have done…

I've been fighting for my life for so long, for this day, and now I don't even know if I have a life left.

Get hold of yourself, Murphy.

It's probably a mistake, but I pull the new cell phone from my pocket and dial my mother's number. It's the third time today I've tried. The tinny rings—one, another, a third—they hollow me out a little more. By the time the machine picks up, I'm out of hope. I listen to the brief message, *Hi, this is Janice. I'm not here. Leave a message…* Those words, *I'm not here*, get heavier every time I hear them. She must have gotten at least one of my messages.

I don't want Janice in my life—and I doubt she really wants back in mine. I don't know why I'm doing this to myself. Or why I'd do it to her.

Hell, maybe it's best to let her think I'm dead and gone. Most of me is, anyway.

☆ ☽ ☆

Bay's managed to avoid me the rest of the day, straight into the evening. I walk down the hall of the hotel to her room, determined to smooth things out.

But the woman makes me a little crazy.

"Headache my ass," I mutter at her door. I'm worn out with this day. The last few hours alone with Mel and Violet were exhausting. Bay's the last hope I have to feel normal for a while. I tap on the door with one knuckle of the hand I dangle a six-pack from.

"I don't want any," Bay calls through the door.

"Yes, you do. Don't lie," I say.

She cracks the door. "What kind of beer?"

"What do you think?"

"If it's peace offering beer, it better be a good wheat."

I hold up the six-pack of Bud Light to her eye level. She closes the door.

"Bay, come on." A beat later I hear the chain slide and she holds the door open to let me through. "I brought the leftover pizza, too. Figured you might be hungry, unless you got dinner elsewhere. Got another man stashed in here somewhere?"

"Seriously, why would I do that? You're picking a fight before I close the door? I'm not fighting with you anymore tonight." She crosses her arms and juts a hip out.

I put the pizza and beer down and sit on the edge of the bed. "I'm sorry. And I'm sorry about earlier. I don't know why I'm so irritable. Tired, I guess. I won't lie to you, I have no clue how to feel about anything, but you're my best friend. And I need my best friend. Can we put the rest on hold a minute?"

"Yeah, we do that a lot," Bay says, nearly smiling.

"And what does that tell you?" I ask.

"It tells me that you are a massive pain in my ass." She climbs onto the bed across from me and moves the pizza box between us. "Bet you didn't eat much."

"Some. My appetite's not quite right yet." I pull a slice from the box.

"Beer, please." Bay nods toward the table where I left it. "How did you get out of Mama's sight?"

"Told her I should bring the pizza down to you, see if you could eat."

"You know she's waiting up."

"Nah, I told them to go on to bed."

Bay swigs her beer. "I'm sorry about earlier," she says.

"I'm the one who should apologize. Things are a little mixed up, Bay. And I don't want to talk about it. I don't have my bearings yet."

I can't look her in the eye. She's staring at me, searching me…and I'm a blank damn slate.

"All that time, weeks and months you spent fighting for your life, I bet you didn't lose your cool once."

"Maybe for a minute here and there. I kept my mind busy, you know? Strategizing, planning, imagining this day."

"Hmmm. And I guess today isn't anything like what you thought it would be?"

I shrug. "I don't think anything could have lived up to the picture I'd painted in my head. Really, though, I wanted to get home is all. There are so many things that…I don't know. So many things to do."

"I'm sorry if it's not what you imagined."

"I know it sounds crazy, Bay, but I'd pretty much accepted my fate. I got used to the idea of being in captivity until they decided to execute me. And now…"

"What was it like, Scott?" Bay brushes the back of her hand against my arm. It's all I can do not to pull away from a touch like that, a gentle one. "Tell me what it was like."

I rub at my eyes, suddenly exhausted again. "I'd rather you tell me what it was like here, while I was gone. Please, not tonight with the heavy stuff."

"Agreed," she finally says after a minute. "Nothing heavy tonight. Enough already."

I feel some of the tension in my shoulders release. Sitting here with her, I can almost relax. Almost.

"Cheers," I say, clinking my bottle against hers.

"So, I should catch you up on New Hope events."

"Have you been in New Hope?"

"Well, for the holidays," Bay says with a shrug. "I avoided it as long as possible."

"I'm sorry—"

"No, don't. You know me. I've been rubbing Mama the wrong way since I learned to speak. I've got my own crap to sort out, I guess."

"Admirable level of self-awareness there, hon."

She rolls her eyes.

"So, what's the news?"

"Let's see… Will was apparently dating an adolescent."

"What?"

"A nineteen-year-old one, but still."

"Yeah, still."

"His mother found out. He's been on restriction since."

I laugh. "Why am I not surprised?"

"Because it's Will. And Will has no sense. And still lives with his parents."

"Fact," I say. "Emotional maturity of an adolescent himself."

"Who's talking?" Bay cocks an eyebrow at me.

"Hey now, I happen to have quite the sophisticated taste in ladies."

"That topic, also off limits," Bay says before draining her first beer. She gets up and grabs another, tries twisting the top off, winces.

"Gimme." I hold a hand out and take the bottle, open it.

"Also news, I punched Harry what's-his-name in the face, the Harry from the hunting club? Broke his nose. It was awesome."

"You're not serious?"

"Deadly serious," she answers. "Don't make me punch you."

"Please, have mercy," I say, holding my hands up in front of me. "I'm a POW. Spare me further abuse."

I regret the joke as soon as I see her eyes go dark. She closes the empty box and pushes it off the bed.

"Sure you don't want to talk about it?" she asks.

"Yeah, I'm sure. I want to forget it ever happened. Anyway, I mostly disconnected from what was happening when it was happening. Not much in the way of memories to go back to. And I thought a lot about home, you know?"

She almost smiles. "Home, eh?"

"Home, you…and wondering who I am, actually. Like, really, who am I?"

"You know, I've been sitting here thinking there's something else besides being suddenly thrust back out of an early grave bothering you. I mean, I'm bothering you, but…I don't know. You seem distracted."

"You are the perceptive one, aren't you?" I say, trying to smile and failing. "It's my mom, Bay. She'd heard about my capture on the news and wanted word when and if I was ever found."

Bay can't keep the shock from her face. "Janice? She's looking for you? Where is she?"

"Yep, Janice. She was trying to find me. I have a number to an apartment where she was staying in San Francisco when she'd called, but she left. They gave me another number where I might be able to reach her, but I haven't yet."

"Do you want to? I mean, you want to talk to her?"

I shrug. "Any other time, I wouldn't even blink. I'd throw this damn number in the trash and not think twice about it. But now…"

"You almost didn't have the choice, whether you ever saw her again or not."

"So I guess yeah, I want to talk to her. I'd like to know why she left the way she did, why she didn't try. And maybe she'd be willing to tell me who my father is. That's what I'd really like from her. To really know who I am."

Bay closes her eyes. "Let's try her again, then."

"Now?"

"Yes, now," she answers. "Why wait?"

I take the cell phone from my pocket and dial Janice's number. I put the phone on speaker. It goes straight to voice mail, and we listen to the message together. *No one is available…*

Bay lets out a breath. "I'm sure there's an explanation. I'm sorry, though, that she wasn't here for you, for today. If you wanted her to be."

I touch a finger to her chin. "Not like she ever has been, Bay. You can't miss what you never had, right? I'm glad you're here."

"Yeah, me too."

"Anyway, I've been thinking, I haven't tried to find out who my dad is. It occurred to me over there that I might not get the chance."

"Are you saying you want to find him?" Bay gives me an intense look, one that throws me off a little. There's something almost too earnest in her eyes.

"I don't know." I shake my head. "Maybe after some time. I need to let things settle a bit. I gotta get my head straight. I wasn't exactly thinking clearly. Let's drop it for now, okay? I don't know why I even brought it up."

Bay's brow creases with concern, and she runs a hand through her hair. "Okay, if that's what you want. But you're okay, right?"

I bring a hand to her cheek. I don't want to see that worry in her eyes. "I'm fine, hon. All the training really does pay off. I managed pretty well. I want to put it behind me now."

"Understood."

She reaches up to scratch a red spot at her neck, and it's then I notice why.

"You're wearing my promise ring," I say, fighting a smile off.

Bay smiles back. "I haven't taken it off since the day you went missing. It itches the daylights out of me."

I reach out to touch it. "I missed having it when I was…but then I was glad I didn't have it. They would have taken it."

She reaches for my hand then, and I shake off the thought. I wonder, if I kiss her…

"Want another beer?" she asks.

"I think I'm going to try to get some sleep." I get up and stretch. "I may sleep straight through the holiday."

Bay stands up too and walks with me to the door. "Do what you need to do. Take care of yourself."

"Yeah," I say, pulling her into a hug. Careful not to hold on too long. The impulse is tempting, but the fear is overwhelming. I can't hurt her again. I can't lose her.

We say goodnight and I check my phone on the way to my room.

"Pssst…" I turn to see Bay sticking her head out of her door. "It's better than good, you know, seeing your face."

I smile at her. "Roger that."

☆☽☆

When the door to my room closes behind me, I rush to turn on all the lights. The shadows are shifty. Dark spaces for the monsters to hide, the ones I carried back with me. I sit on the edge of the bed and know before I try to lay down in it that I'll never sleep there. I pull the blanket and a pillow to the farthest wall, where I can see everything, and fold it into a makeshift sleeping bag.

I close my eyes, but my mind keeps dragging me back to that night—the night I was captured. Our mission was one of the simplest we'd had in Afghanistan. It was information gathering. I was on point as my operational detachment's intelligence officer, with two other team members along. Kedrick and Simpson.

In our tactical review for the mission, we poured over the same data we'd been covering for days. We got lucky with the intel. A local spy on the payroll had lost a daughter during a mortar attack launched by the Taliban leader. When he heard the chatter about where the cell had encamped, he saw his opportunity to get revenge. When the information was passed to central command, there was a clear urgency to extract him sooner than later. The Taliban in the area had been slowly regrouping, reorganizing. They were preparing to take back control of the area.

The team broke with the mission planning confirmed complete. We packed up at a rapid pace, and in near silence.

We rode out into the darkness at 0200 on four-wheelers to set up surveillance. I was supposed to set up monitoring equipment while Simpson and Kedrick patrolled the area.

Once we reached our location, I got straight to work. I was focused on the task at hand. I knew my guys had me.

As I completed the last of my tests before we would return to the outpost, there was a blast to my left. Swear to God, it was out of nowhere. Knocked my ass sideways. I scrambled to recover my position in the rocks while my ears were still ringing and tried to get a spot on Kedrick and Simpson. Then the hot popping of bullets around me began, and I made a quick decision: destroy the equipment, unload what I could, and hunt for cover.

We hadn't expected a heavily armed cell, and we weren't prepared for a firefight. The area had been swept for roadside bombs recently, but in war, things change fast. I worked to get in position to return fire, but I still wasn't sure where my teammates were.

Left with no radio, I hunkered down in a rocky gulch and held my own for as long as my ammunition lasted. By the time morning broke, I was certain I was watching my last sunrise. I'd managed to avoid anything more than surface wounds, but as I heard the maddening chatter of the Taliban soldiers approaching, I closed my eyes, hoping my death would be swift and less than torturous, that they would fill me full of holes and leave me there in the gulch to die.

But for whatever reason, they decided to keep me alive. As I was dragged from the gulch, wrists and ankles tied, head bagged, I half wished I'd held one last round in my pistol to end it. I wasn't proud of that thought, but it occurred to me.

Where did she come from? They beheaded her. I watched. The girl with the eyes like Emerson's, the one who tried to help me.

How did she get in here? Bees swarm around her face, cover her arms…does Bay have her EpiPen here? Why this girl, and not Lillie?

Swarms of bees.

Voices outside the door.

I hear them coming and push myself closer to the wall. They're not whispering tonight. Laughing. The assholes are laughing.

If I ever get out of these chains I'll beat their shady faces in. I'll find a way out—

Why are they speaking English? Talking about a football game?

No chains. There are no chains. No girl. No bees. Bay is safe, down the hall. I haven't lost her. Not entirely.

I sit up and feel the blanket around me, wipe the fresh sweat from my face. I'm not chained. I'm not in that room. I'm not in Afghanistan anymore.

But I'm not here, either. Not exactly.

Because I'm not the same. I won't ever be the same.

```
Scott Jackson Murphy.
Sergeant First Class, United States Army.
Serial Number 224278972.
```

I brought this home with me. I brought this all home, straight from hell.

CHAPTER 11

New Hope's second Christmas Parade in the span of a week spiraled into a scene of pure downhome madness. The weather had turned warm again—the midday sun raised the temperature into the sixties—and encouraged a crowd of people to descend on the little town in bare-legged, rowdy droves. There were the floats that remained assembled from the first parade, marching bands, Shriners in silly little cars, and motorcycle rally clubs stretched out for miles, it seemed. And then, of course, was the hometown hero, Sergeant First Class Murphy, and half the United States Army along with him. It would take the entire day for the caravan to pass through town.

Bay settled into a camp chair between Mel and Violet to watch until Scott passed by. She hoped he was near the beginning rather than the end of the steady stream of chaos. He'd asked her to ride on the back of the car with him. He outright refused the idea of an actual float, and while Bay wasn't sure, she thought the Army might have had to order him to participate at all. The idea of riding with him sent her stomach churning. They'd had an awkward exchange the night before about giving the wrong impression, not giving the gossip mill more fuel for the fire of speculation that was already lapping at their heels.

Scott's rescue and return after the festival set their little hometown ablaze with rumors, there was no denying it. Bay conceded the timing was a wild coincidence, but the mystical, written-in-the-stars significance some folks placed on the timing of her performance at the festival and Scott's return was over the top. Her tongue was sore from all the biting down on it she'd done in the last two days.

"I don't understand why you didn't want to go ahead and ride with Scott for this thing, since he asked," Violet said. "It would have been a nice gesture."

Bay cut her eyes at Violet. "May I remind you, Scott and I are not a couple. I'm overjoyed he is alive, and home, and safe, like everybody else. But that doesn't mean the reasons we weren't together before aren't still valid reasons for us to not be together now. We can't pick up where we left off." She paused to watch a group of Army veterans riding through on Harleys. "In fact, if we picked up where we left off, we wouldn't even be speaking."

"Well, I realize all that, Bay, but if you could try to—"

"Violet," Mel interrupted, leaning forward around Bay and raising his voice to compete with the noise, "can you please give our child a moment's peace? It's not our worry."

"You say that now," Violet huffed. But she turned her attention to the parade, and for that Bay grinned her thanks at Mel.

"She'll make you crazy if you let her," he grumbled, low enough that only Bay could hear him. She laughed, patted his arm.

"It's a two-way street, I guess. I think she's gotten her fair share of hell from me over the years."

"I can't argue that point. You two are more alike than either one of you will ever admit," he said.

Bay laughed at Mel. "Okay, now you're going too far."

"It's the truth," he answered. "Stubborn as mules, always right, and can't give up on an argument 'til long after you've lost it. Good thing you're both beauties, else no one would tolerate you, including me." He cut his eyes at her, the twinkle in them giving away his teasing. "Big hearts, though."

She leaned into his shoulder. "You're a saint for putting up with us."

"Hardly, but I know what's worth the effort and what isn't. That's something I hope you can figure out for yourself soon."

The noise at the far end of the street picked up from a loud hum to a roar. Bay peered past Violet and saw people getting to their feet in a wave, American flags up and fluttering in the air.

"Looks like the man of the hour is approaching," she shouted, but her voice got lost in the clambering noise. Bay stood up and took in the moment as the high school's marching band led the way, their red and black Marauders uniforms providing a crisp backdrop for their instruments glinting in the bright sun. The classic red Mercedes convertible followed slowly behind the drum majors. Scott sat perched on back, posed like a small-town beauty queen and smiling through the discomfort that Bay could sense coming off of him in waves. His knees bounced as he scanned the crowd with a pained expression on his face. A pang of guilt heaved in her chest: she should have ridden with him. She would have hated every minute of it, but at least he wouldn't seem so alone up there.

When he was close enough to spot her, Bay stepped to the edge of the sidewalk and held up the bright yellow bandana he'd given her to make it easy for him to find her in the crowd. He knew she'd be right at the road by Blossom Hill, so it didn't turn out to be too difficult. Their eyes locked, and she saw that his were full of something close to desperation.

"Please come up here," he mouthed to her, bringing his hands together as he pleaded. "Help me."

She shook her head and mouthed "no" even as she moved closer to the car, and the driver pulled to a stop beside her. There was an actual guard unit flanking the car, and they made her wait in the street until Scott gave them clearance to let her approach. Two guys launched her over the side and up beside Scott, and the noise from the crowd ticked up a notch. He put an arm around her and moved closer so she could hear him.

"This day makes me question why anyone ever wants to be famous. Is this how it is being on stage?"

Bay laughed. "I can't say I've ever drawn quite this much of a crowd, and even small crowds give me palpitations. Not the same thing as this, though. Have you noticed all the women? You've got groupies."

She watched all the people closing in around them, all the breathless anticipation she'd noticed earlier in the younger female faces around her hosed down with a mixture of resentment and utter disappointment. Bay thought if it weren't for Scott right beside her, some of them would be hurling stones.

"I'm sorry to drag you up here, but I desperately needed a buffer."

"Don't worry about it," she said, resting a hand on his knee. "You need a human shield, I'm your girl. I gotta say, though, you may have to shield me from some of your admirers."

"Yeah," he said, taking her hand. "Sorry about that."

She should have been paying more attention to the cameras flashing around them, the reporters jockeying for the shot of the hero and his childhood sweetheart reunited, but she gave it up beneath the urge to protect him from the scrutiny he struggled to bear. This was something she could do for him, after feeling helpless for so long. And it felt good, being by his side.

They rode holding hands through the end of the parade, Scott waving from time to time while Bay reminded herself to smile at the people who occasionally called her name. But the glares she got told the story—the wrong impression she didn't want to give had been exactly the message the throngs of people received when she joined Scott in the car. She turned to Scott as they pulled to a stop at the park marking the end of the parade route. He bent to kiss her forehead. The warmth of the gesture cemented her firmly in her confusion. It was hard to care what anyone else thought, now that he was here beside her.

"Thanks for climbing aboard," Scott said before he slid over the side of the car. He reached up to help her down. "It was less terrible with company for that last bit."

"Yeah, when I saw you up there alone…" she didn't finish.

"You have a knack for knowing what I need." He dropped a hand on her shoulder and steered her past the gathered reporters toward Will. A few of the more aggressive guys called out questions, but Scott didn't make any move to answer. There had been a press conference in Fayetteville, and one that morning at the local library. Bay hadn't attended either one for fear of making a spectacle of herself, and judging from some of the questions being tossed toward them, it was the right call.

Scott fell into conversation with Will, covering their hunting schedule ahead of the new year and the private party planned that night. Bay half-listened as the parade participants began crowding into the park, many of them making their way toward Scott.

"Hey, why don't we head on inside?" Bay nudged Scott with

her hip, indicating the growing crowd with a nod.

"Yeah, definitely," he said. They hustled down the road and up the hill to the house and through the front door.

"Bay, I can help get things set up for you tonight so you can play at the party," Will said when they settled in at the kitchen bar.

"Oh, I'm not singing tonight," Bay answered, clipping the words out too fast. She got cups down for them and pulled a full pitcher of sweet tea from the fridge. "Is anyone hungry?"

"Not so fast, little lady," Scott came up behind her and grabbed the pitcher from her hand. "I've been hearing about this song that is the stuff of legends since I got to town. Don't I get to hear it, since it happens to be about *moi*?"

"Sure, you can hear it, but not tonight." She grinned and batted her eyes in a way that let him know arguing the point was futile.

"No fair. I'm a returning war hero. You're supposed to humor me, woman."

"Unfair would be playing a song in front of an audience tonight that I've played in public exactly once, and haven't played since. I don't want to spend the rest of the day practicing, or panicking. I'll do it for you later."

"Oh, I get a private show," Scott teased.

Bay rolled her eyes. "Did I say that, Sergeant Murphy? I don't believe I said that."

Will leaned back on his stool and squinted up into the lights over the island. "Can y'all please get this worked out? All this tension is gonna give me indigestion for Christmas."

"Fine. Why don't you tell me how to sort it out?" Bay asked, bracing herself against the island. "Trust me, I'd welcome the help."

"Tell Scott you love him, get married, and live happily ever after?"

Scott held in a laugh when Bay glared at Will.

"I will punch you in your face."

Will raised his eyebrows and pushed Scott between them. "Restrain her, man. After seeing what she did to poor ol' Harry, I need a head start."

"That won't be necessary," Scott said, laughing. "I surrender."

Will looked from Scott to Bay, but no one spoke for a moment. Finally, Bay shook her head and went to the refrigerator and stuck her head in to end the conversation. "We can make sandwiches, like I said," she called over her shoulder, "or I can heat up some lasagna."

"Or we can go on down to the festival," Will said. "They'll have those food trucks again, maybe even more than last week. I love those funnel cakes."

Bay waited for Scott to answer. He shrugged. "Suits me. I guess I'm supposed to be down there anyway."

"Okay, then," Bay said.

"But we're not done about this song. I do want to hear it."

"I told you, later," Bay said, stepping around him toward the mudroom. "Y'all coming?"

Bay stumbled through the door of her parents' house hours later, having braved the festival crowd with Scott for the better part of the day before driving him home so he could clean up for his party later. She pulled her boots off by the door and limped into the kitchen. The smell of fresh apple cider and cinnamon led her to the kettle on the stove.

"How was the festival?" Violet asked, watching Bay over her mug.

"It was fine," she answered, stirring her cider before taking a seat by Mel. "But it was exhausting for Scott. I don't think he wants to be famous."

Violet furrowed her brow. "The attention will die down after the holiday, I bet. It's turned into the feel-good story of the season."

Bay nodded. "It seems like it. I mean, I expected there to be interest in the story and some media around, but it's a madhouse."

"Plenty of women circling, too, I noticed," Mel added. He shot Bay a glance and she smiled at him.

"Yeah, he was feeling a bit intimidated, I think. That's why he dragged me everywhere today."

There was a pause as Violet considered her across the table. "Bay, what happened?"

It was Bay's turn to furrow her brow. "What do you mean?"

"Between you and Scott. The last couple of years, with the on-again off-again."

"Well, I believe that's my cue to go." Mel bent to kiss the top of Bay's head on his way out.

"I don't really want to talk about this, Mama," Bay said, watching the steam rise from her mug of cider as she gripped it between her hands absorbing its warmth.

"You have made that abundantly clear, but people are talking around town."

"Ask me if I care what people in this town have to say," Bay barked. "Because no, I do not give two flyin—"

"Language," Violet broke in before Bay could finish.

"Flips."

"Well, I'm going to tell you anyway. If nothing else, you can help me understand. People are saying you broke up with Scott, that you broke his heart before he left for Afghanistan, and now that he's come home a hero and getting all this media attention, you're trying to win him back, get some of that limelight."

Bay shook her head and held a tight-lipped smirk in check. "Scott and I had broken up well before he left. He wanted to work it out, and we gave it a shot. It wasn't like I didn't try. I did. So much had happened..."

"But it was your choice, in the end, this last breakup, because he transferred and deployed again so quickly. You wanted him out of the army."

Bay crossed her arms over her chest. "That wasn't the reason. I supported Scott's service, from the start until the bitter end, whenever that turns out to be. But I didn't want him transferring to go back over there, not after I found out that he'd met someone else when we'd broken up before, when he was deployed to Afghanistan. She's an aide worker from England. Her name is Emerson."

Violet stared at Bay, slack-jawed. "You think he transferred and returned to that hell—to that war—for another woman? How would that even happen?" she finally asked.

"No, it's a longer story than that. The transfer wasn't something he had a lot of control over, I know, although there were other options that would have kept him home longer. After everything that happened, I felt like I had to draw a line in the sand. We were on shaky ground already. I needed time to feel solid again, but he couldn't give me that."

"Bay, why have you let us all think that you broke up with him because of the transfer?" Violet's voice strained an octave higher.

"Because I didn't want to talk about it, and it wasn't anybody else's business," she replied. "I mean, come on, Mama, it's not like we're one of those mother-daughter pairs that has to talk on the phone every day and share intimate details. It's never been like that with us."

Violet winced. "It hasn't, Bay, you're right. Maybe it should be, though."

A surge of fresh tears pricked at Bay's eyes, catching her off guard. She took a sip of cider, gathered herself. "Maybe. Anyway, then we didn't know if Scott would ever come home to us. And it isn't like he cheated. I mean, we were apart when he met her. That's probably why it happened. I didn't see the need in spreading it around. Why would I do that to him, his memory, if things had turned out differently?"

Violet reached a hand across the table but stopped short of taking Bay's. "It was a very selfless thing to do, keeping that to yourself. Even if you were apart, I can't imagine Scott with anyone else."

"Ha! Let's not make this about me being selfless. Truth be told, it's partly because I was embarrassed. And the way he talked about her… she's not just some girl, some fling. I was afraid if he went over there, and somehow saw her again, he'd change his mind about wanting me, wanting us again. I was pissed off, and scared, and I didn't want to face it. So it was an easy decision. Then he was captured, and I—I just couldn't make that part of the story, of our story, if it was ending like that. But, for the record, it wasn't some irrational ultimatum on my part. Just because we've been together forever, and our relationship seems so natural and simple from the outside, people assume it's never complicated. The last few years got really complicated."

"I understand that, better than you know," Violet said, a wistful sadness haunting her voice.

Bay met Violet's gaze in the silence that fell between them, hovering for once over common ground. She realized for the first time that she'd always judged her parents' relationship the same way. Her stomach clenched at the thought that she had likely been wrong.

"Well, now you know." Bay leaned closer to her mother, deciding to shift gears. "Did you know Janice has been in touch with him? Or I should say with the army. Before they found him."

"Janice Murphy? His mother?" Violet asked, eyes wide.

"Yes, his mother. Apparently when she heard about his capture she wanted to know what was happening, and wanted to be contacted with news. But now he can't reach her at the number she left. I hate to say it, and I wouldn't dare say it to him, but with her history all I could come up with was that she was hoping for some kind of death benefit from the army."

"And now that they've found him alive, she doesn't care to hear from him," Violet said.

"That's how it appears to me," Bay replied.

"It's a wonder she didn't try to contact us. I guess if she'd wanted to be informed, to know whether or not he was dead or alive..."

"Exactly. I doubt she had some renewed interest in his welfare. And she knew if she called somebody in New Hope, they'd tell her to drag her sorry ass back and be here for him. That's not what she was after."

"I wonder why he hasn't said anything to me or Mel about this."

Bay sighed. "I think with all the fussing over him, everybody making such a big deal over his return, he didn't want to seem ungrateful. He doesn't want you guys to feel like the family you've worked so hard to give him isn't enough."

Violet stared up at the ceiling, blinking tears from her eyes. "Oh Lord, that poor precious boy. He deserves so much more. I wish I could—if I could—"

"Give him a chance to have some connection with his biological family, with one of his parents? You know, we could try."

"No," Violet said, shaking her head, clipping the word. "No, Janice is probably in no position to be a positive influence on him."

"But if we can find her, we can give him the chance to decide that for himself. And maybe she could give us some idea about finding his father. He brought it up to me the night after he got home, finding out who his father is. He said he couldn't miss something he never had, but that didn't ring so true. I think he's missing a whole lot. And it's nagging at me, Mama. I know y'all told me to drop it, but that Marco guy? My gut says there must be a connection."

Violet got to her feet and crossed the kitchen, kept her back to Bay. "Now's not the time for this. What Scott needs is stability, to be surrounded by the people who love him—who have always loved him. I need more time."

"You need more time, Mama? For what?" Bay asked, her voice barely rising above a whisper. "Why are you so dead set against Scott looking for his father? I mean, every time I bring it up, you shut me down before I can even form the thought. But now that Scott's back…don't you think he deserves to know, if there's any possibility we could find something out?"

Violet hesitated. "Bay," Violet started, not turning to look at her, "maybe it's best we just forget about Janice, okay? Just let it go. She'll be in touch again if she really wants to be."

"I wish I could forget a lot of things, Mama," Bay said, then remembered one of Violet's favorite old expressions. "But you know what they say…you can't unsmell a skunk."

"LIBERATION": NIGHT 3

I'm so sick of this day. I should have said no to this party, but that would have been an admission of…something, and I don't feel like letting on to all these people that I'm any different than I was before. Eighty-eight days of my life in a black hole. A party wasn't what I was dreaming about when I was over there, wondering if I would ever come home again.

I was dreaming about her. I watch Bay through the window as I drain my fourth, maybe fifth beer, I don't know anymore. She looks as uncomfortable as I was feeling, which makes me feel like shit for leaving her in there, but I needed some air. Not that the Lowman Lodge didn't provide plenty of room, lots of open space, vaulted ceilings with exposed beams, three iron chandeliers, six bulbs each, two dining tables with twelve seats each, pine floors, two fireplaces—probably why it was too warm in there right now—and three visible exits. All that and a crowd of forty-seven of my closest New Hope pals gathered in loose knots, either at the buffet or the tables, or the grouping of sofas near the window.

That's where Bay sat, shifting every now and then to get a look around the room, scouting for me.

"Speak of the devil and he walks in the door," Will says, grinning from where he sits beside Bay on the sofa. I put on my best smile for the audience, like it's any other day and the last few months never happened. Even so, I feel Bay tense as I settle in on the other side of her. I sling my arm around her, but don't quite let it rest on her shoulders.

"You okay?" she asks, tipping her chin so that her gaze meets mine.

I fight the urge to look away. "Yeah, I'm good. Just getting some air. It's a little warm in here."

"Mmhmm."

She doesn't buy it. Of course, she doesn't. I can hide from everyone else in this room, but not Bay.

"I see you didn't bring your guitar," Will says. "I guess we didn't convince you to play tonight?"

"Nah," Bay answers, shaking her head. "Maybe next time, but not tonight."

"Not even for Scott, at his homecoming party?" Will asks, his eyes narrowed.

"Scott doesn't need me serenading him tonight," Bay answered, her tone making it clear the conversation is closed.

"Better watch yourself with her, Will," Tommy Patterson, Bay's cousin, breaks in. "She'll bloody your nose, I hear."

"Yeah, from what I hear, she's got my back in a bar room brawl." I nudge Bay and give her a wink, but the teasing doesn't seem to settle her. She's on to me.

"Poor ol' Harry, felled by a ninety-pound ball of rage," Will says, getting a laugh from the group.

"She told me all about that," I say, turning to Ethan. He seems more willing to accept my act than his sister. "We taught her well."

"Taliban would've never got a hand on you if she'd been with you over there," Tommy says, laughing.

The entire room seems to go quiet, and I feel every pair of eyes near us turn to look at me. I don't react. I finish my beer and let them all squirm in the uncomfortable silence.

"Sweet Jesus, Tommy, and your mama worries over my manners," Reva mutters under her breath, glaring at her husband.

Another beat of silence stretches out to two. I can feel Bay's jaw clenching, the tension pulsing through the rest of her body.

"I should have a word with my aunt about that, Reva. Tommy definitely married up with respect to manners. Hell, with respect to everything. He just married up, period."

Bay stands, holding her empty bottle underhand. Tommy's smart enough to back away. I'm tempted to tell her not to fight my battles, but the expression on his face is too precious.

"Looks like I need a beer," Bay says.

"Grab me one, will ya?" I ask, sliding my fifth—sixth?—empty onto the table in front of me.

"I could use one, too," Leigh Anne says, locking arms with Bay and hauling her toward the kitchen.

"Hey man, I didn't mean nothing by that. Just a joke," Tommy says. I feel his fear, coming in waves as he watches me carefully. I don't respond, don't even move. I won't give him the satisfaction of assuaging that fear, of reacting at all.

Reva kneels beside the sofa where I sit, keeping her voice low so that only I hear. "Scott, I don't really know what to say after this ordeal you've been through, but I hope you know that many prayers were answered when you made it back. We're likely making a mess of welcoming you, throwing parties and parades and all before you've had a chance to catch your breath. Just know we're all here for you. One hundred percent. Even if that means leaving you the hell alone for a minute. Just say the word, okay? And my apologies for my ass of a husband."

I can't help but crack a smile. "Thanks, Reva. So you know, regardless of whether you wear one around your neck, you are a true pearl. Tommy's lucky to have you."

"You got that right," Bay says, scooting back in beside me and leaning in to our huddle. "I'll have a word with Aunt Olivia about this pearl situation. If Leigh—"

Reva holds up a hand. "I appreciate the sentiment, but I'd rather not rock that particular boat at the moment. We seem to be patching things up okay."

"Bay wouldn't show up to a barn party without her instrument. It would break tradition," Will is saying, getting our attention as Reva slides away from our group.

"Well, some cycles need breaking, Willis," Bay answers, narrowing her eyes.

"That ain't one of 'em," Will says, standing on his shaky ground.

"When's this barn party?" she asks.

"New Year's Eve, if everybody's in for it. The first one in a long while, to honor the return of two legends."

"Bay, it's a small crowd tonight. You sure I can't hear this history-making song you wrote for me?" I drop my hand from the back of the sofa to her shoulder and squeeze, wrap a curl around my finger. I'm pressing her for Will's benefit, but I know she won't budge. And I don't want her to, not tonight. Not when I'm eight-beers-in relaxed and feeling things I don't want to deal with.

Okay, if I'm honest, nine. At least.

"Not a chance," she says. "I'm woefully unprepared and apparently a couple of drinks behind." She takes a few gulps of the beer in her hand.

Will leans forward and grins at Bay in a way that speaks trouble. "There is a chance we can hear Bay play tonight, if you really want to."

"Really?" I join in the game, lean in, move my hand to Bay's knee. I try not to squeeze too hard as my stomach churns.

"See that flat screen up there over the fireplace?"

Bay turns her head to see what Will means. "You didn't."

"Oh, but I did," Will says. "I posted it online and brought my little streaming device. It's already hooked up and ready to go, baby."

"Nice work, my man." I hold up my beer in salute. Guess this is better than a live performance. Easier to disengage. Except for all this beer. "Let's roll it."

"No!" Bay shakes her head. "Can't we wait 'til later?" She takes in all the people scattered around the room, then turns to me. "After dinner, okay? Maybe the crowd will thin out. They all already heard it, anyway."

I pull her against me and kiss the top of her head. I suddenly have the urge to kiss her mouth, to take her upstairs, where I know there are several bedrooms. But all these people. When will they leave? "Sure, babe, whatever you want."

"Hmm…" Bay leans in long enough to let me know she feels the same way. "You mean it?"

"I mean it," I whisper close to her ear.

And then I wonder if I have anything left to give her. The mood leaves me just as fast as it came on.

The party drags on for an hour or two longer, I think. People cycle in and out of the space around me. Some of them I'm not even sure I know. Right on through dinner, no one asks questions about Afghanistan. Not even Tommy brings it up again. They're all content to drink, live it up like nothing ever happened. Tonight could be any other night Bay and I spent together in New Hope. As long as I can sit here, looking in command of myself, work the room, they're all content to pretend, to ignore the bruises like shadows that linger across my face, to act like I'm not mourning one brother, and hurting for another. All these people, they laugh and chat around me, like I'm not still at war.

Except Bay. Her eyes are on me, no matter where she is. She sticks close, and she watches me even closer. Nobody else knows I'm putting on a show, but after all the years of art school, theatre people, the constant dramas of Nashville, and a lifetime of loving me...Bay knows.

When dinner is done and the dishes are cleared, Will stands on the stone hearth and taps a fork against his beer bottle, but when the chatter doesn't subside, gives a loud whistle. "Hey, everybody, gather around over here," he calls.

Bay takes my hand and we stand together in the center of the room, surrounded. I don't like the feeling. She turns to me, concern drawing her mouth in a tight line. I'm squeezing too hard, but she doesn't pull away. Instead she edges closer and wraps her other hand around my arm.

"So, a lot of you were present for Bay's performance at Christmas Festival Part One," Will starts. There is clapping and whistling. "Alas, our friend Sergeant First Class Murphy here was not, and since he was the inspiration for that stirring, fantabulous performance, I thought he should have the pleasure of the experience." He pauses for more clapping and cheering. "Lucky for us, someone had the foresight to record the occasion. So, without further ado, I present to you Bay Laurel LaFleur with her live—and quite heartfelt—performance of 'When You Come Home Again'."

Will starts the video, and Bay covers her face when she appears on the flat screen. The room goes quiet as she starts to play, and her head drops to my shoulder.

I listen, lost as ever in the sound of her voice, the lyrics and what they mean, all that's happened between us. Somewhere in the middle I can't hold on to myself anymore, so I hold on to her.

My face is in her hair, and I think there are tears—hers? Mine? I don't know anything except I won't ever let her go again.

☆ Bay ☆

With the last guests pulling out of the driveway, Ethan hands me the lodge keys. "Mayor Lowman said for you two to stay as late as you want," he says, hugging me and then Scott before he turns to leave. His eyes are still red from his own tears. Scott's reaction to the song had the whole room crying by the end of it. Even the two reporters in the room left sniffling.

"Thanks, Ethan," I answer, whispering as if the sound of my voice might send Scott back into some black pit of despair. "Some quiet time will be nice."

"The bedrooms are all made up," he adds. "The bathrooms, too, fresh towels and the works. Drop the keys by his office next week, okay?"

"Will do." He waves from the porch, and I shut the door behind him. I stand against it and study Scott. He's stretched out on the sofa, hugging a pillow to his chest.

"Hi," he says, his voice still thick with emotion.

"Hi. Are you okay?"

His face crumples as if in answer to my question. He sits up and puts his head in his hands, his shoulders shaking. I cross the room, wrap myself around him and hold on.

"You don't have to do this alone," I tell him. "I'm right here. You don't have to do it alone."

"Bay, do you understand what I've done? I can't stop thinking about it…I keep reliving that night, over and over. They came out of nowhere. And I let them down. I let my brothers down."

"What night, Scott?"

"What night do you think? The one those reporters keep wanting me to tell them about…Kedrick was a good man, a father. His kids aren't even in school yet. And Simpson…his life will never be the same. And here I am, fine, getting the hero's welcome they deserve. Do you think anybody threw a parade for Simpson, that reporters circled around his hometown? He lost his leg. I lost a few months. How is this right? None of this is right."

"Scott, you were ambushed. None of this is your fault. You did what you could."

"It wasn't enough. It was my job to know what we were headed into. The information was wrong. It was all wrong. And I couldn't find them, I couldn't do anything."

"No one blames you—"

"I blame me!" The words burst from him like a shotgun blast. He pushes away from me and off the sofa, like he wants to find something to punch, but he comes up empty. "I thought I was gonna die, Bay. It was over. Every day, every night, I thought it was the day I would die. And then all of a sudden I was out, alive, getting my life back. I should be happy, right? I did what I was trained to do. I survived."

I stand in front of him and put my hands on top of his clinched fists, trying to find the right words to comfort him, knowing there aren't any. "Yes, you did, Scott, you survived. Thank God in heaven, you survived. You made it home to us, and that's all that matters."

"It doesn't matter to Kedrick's family, or to Simpson," he says, pain straining his voice. "How is it I get captured instead of blown up, everybody assumes the worst for months, that I've already been beheaded, or worse. But suddenly I'm home, and I'm healthy and whole, and everybody treats me like a damn hero. I'm not a hero, Bay. There's nothing heroic about managing to stay alive."

"It is to me," I say quietly.

Scott raises his hands as if in surrender, then lets them drop. "And then this thing with my mother…God, Bay, why did she even bother? I kept thinking over there, you know, that I don't even know…that I would die and not even know who I am. I thought maybe if I could talk to her…"

"Have you heard from her at all?"

When he doesn't answer, I blow out a breath, hold my temper, and search for the right words to say. "We don't know how she's been living all these years, Scott. It might be drugs, or she's wandered somewhere else, or—"

"Or that I was worth something to her dead, but not alive."

I wrap my arms around Scott's waist, press my face to his neck. All I want is to comfort him, to somehow ease his pain. I'm a little drunk, and he's a lot drunk, and all of a sudden I'm feeling things I haven't allowed myself to even think about in ninety-one days.

But right now, in this moment, it's the most natural thing in the world, tilting my face up, rising up on my tiptoes to press my mouth against his. I run my hands over his body, pulling at his clothes.

The alarms sounding in my head, telling me to slow down, drown under the waves of want I feel when Scott kisses me back, his mouth hard on mine, his hands sliding beneath my shirt. All at once, he is tasting me, touching me, claiming me in all the ways I desperately want him to. We stumble up the stairs together, unwilling to separate for a second, for fear of losing the moment.

Scott leads me into the first bedroom at the end of the stairs, his hands working on the buttons of my shirt, sliding it from my shoulders, his mouth trailing over the exposed skin of my breasts. Then he is on top of me, inside me, his body both familiar and different, sparking a mixture of memory, desire, and regret.

Later, beyond the heat of the moment, we lay facing each other. I'm drifting off, but I feel him studying my face in the moonlight.

"Merry Christmas," he whispers, resting a hand on my hip.

"Merry Christmas, Scott," I say, reaching out to touch his stubbled cheek. "Thank you."

He laughs. "Thank me for what?"

I move to press my lips against his chest. "For coming home. For being my home."

☆ Scott ☆

I should be sleeping next to Bay, but I can't.

I have to watch the door. I have to watch the door. I have to watch...

I watched as they dragged the girl away from me, the night she helped me try to escape. I don't know how she'd even managed to slip over to where they had me stashed then, to get her hands on the keys. But she did. That young girl with the wide, sad brown eyes did it.

And when they came for us, she didn't even struggle. She turned her head to watch when they knocked me to the ground. An apologetic expression on her face, in her eyes nothing but sorrow. Maybe she didn't think she had much of a life ahead of her, anyway. Whatever that life might have been, I took it the moment

I manipulated her into a bond with me.

I think she didn't regret trying to help me, even if it was the end of her. They took her head, not mine. Her own father did it. I did that to her. I couldn't save her.

Just like I couldn't save Lillie.

But here she is again, the girl with the dark eyes. I don't understand how she's here. And when she holds up her hands, swarms of bees pour from them, big clouds of them. Like a hurricane blowing in from the coast, they're advancing on us, blacking out the sky.

How did this girl's soul follow me home? It's like that place, those people, sent her for me, to take everything I wanted to come home for away from me. I brought this war home, and it's raging in my head, a danger to us, to Bay…I was wrong. She has more than one weakness.

It's not the bees. It's me, the me she remembers. The one she still loves…the one that's gone.

Bay has come back to me. This is what I wanted. All I wanted. But it's not fair, asking her to do this. I'm not the same. It's never gonna be the same.

I can't lose her, but I can't put her through this. Can I?

I close my eyes again, and when I open them, the girl is gone. She left one bee, one lone bee making its way up Bay's leg.

I have to save Bay. I have to save her from me.

CHAPTER 12

"Well, look what the cat dragged in." Violet scolded Scott and Bay with a glare as they came through the door Christmas morning. She was perched on a barstool reading the paper, her glasses already so far down her nose they were close to falling off.

"Calm down, Mama," Bay said as she gave Mel a quick kiss on the cheek. "We both overindulged a bit last night. Didn't want to get on the road like that."

"Merry Christmas, Ma," Scott said. His voice carried through the room as he hugged Violet.

"Merry Christmas, son," she replied, her voice suddenly thick with emotion as she held on to Scott. "I can't tell you how good it is to be spending it with you."

Scott obliged Violet and watched Bay over her shoulder, a half-smug, half-guilty smile on his face. Bay rolled her eyes at him.

Violet folded the paper and moved to the stove where Bay stood opening pot lids and peering into the oven. "I'm starved," Bay muttered.

"I bet. You could have called us to come and get you," Violet said to Bay, keeping her voice low.

"Please leave it be," Bay whispered. "He needed me. I couldn't leave him alone, and I couldn't bring him home like that."

Violet studied her for a long minute and shook her head. "Yes, you could have. You could have brought him here to us if he needed comforting. You could have given us the chance to be there for him, too."

"Mama, you really have no idea what you're talking about, but I refuse to have this argument with you right now," Bay hissed under her breath.

"Right, Bay, your ignorant old mother has no idea what on earth you and Scott might have gotten up to when you got drunk and spent the night together on Christmas Eve." She put a hand on Bay's arm and faked a smile to fool the rest of the room. "Please, won't you enlighten me?"

"No, Mother, I will not. You are unenlightenable," Bay said, then kissed Violet on the cheek. Then, louder, she said, "Merry Christmas, Mama. I love you, too."

Violet turned away from her and opened the oven. Bay fell in beside her to help set breakfast out, and the four of them fixed their plates and gathered around the table, an uncomfortable silence settling in with them.

"One thing's for sure, Miss Violet," Scott said when he finished his plate a few short minutes after they sat down, "if I was in Afghanistan, my Christmas breakfast wouldn't come close to this. Thank you for having me."

"You're welcome, Scott," Violet said, letting her gaze land hard on Bay.

"You're quiet this morning." Bay nodded at Mel. "Did y'all open presents already?"

"No, your mama wanted to wait for you, even though we planned to give you cash."

Bay nodded while she chewed a bite of breakfast casserole. The conversation didn't pick up much, and she gathered that Violet must have told Mel about Janice reaching out to Scott. Her daddy wouldn't be happy, but he wouldn't say anything, at least not to Scott, given the circumstances and it being Christmas. But she knew to prepare for an earful herself when he got her alone.

Scott and Bay did the dishes while her parents had more coffee in the den. They worked in companionable silence, Scott washing plates and silverware quickly while she dried and stacked them. He smiled every time their eyes met, the way Bay thought he might at a woman he had to impress, one who actually required some effort to win. He must have sensed her uncertainty, the way he was trying to put her at ease. And she couldn't help herself…it was working.

"You want to come on over to the house with me while I get showered?" he asked her while she was putting the dishes away.

Bay gave him a wink. "Of course."

"Hey kids, come on in the den. We got a little something for Scott," Violet interrupted, waving them into the family room.

"I haven't exactly had any time for shopping," Scott said, aiming a sheepish grin at Violet. She laughed.

"Me, either," Bay said. "I waited 'til last minute, and Scott managed to completely blow my schedule this year. Punk." She cut her eyes at him and bumped his shoulder with hers. He wrapped his arm around her and pressed his lips to her temple.

"I'll do better next year, promise," he said into her hair.

Bay felt her cheeks blush red at the intimate gesture.

"Amen," Violet said, handing Scott a small box impeccably wrapped in brown paper with an army green bow, just as she always wrapped his gifts. "It's not much, but we thought you might enjoy it, after the last few months."

He carefully broke away the bow and paper and pulled open the slender box. Inside was a leather-bound journal and an expensive-looking pen. Running a hand over the journal's cover, he smiled. "It's perfect," he finally said, looking from Violet to Mel. "I'd been talking with—" he hesitated. "Before, I'd been thinking about writing a book, but I wanted to do it old school, you know, pen and paper. Maybe I can get started now."

"A book? That's incredible, Scott," Bay said, surprise sparkling in her eyes. "We knew that you'd dabbled with some poetry from what was sent home to us, but I hadn't imagined a whole book."

Scott's face flamed, and he avoided Bay's gaze, even though she was teasing. "Well, I haven't written it yet."

"Yeah, but the fact that you've been thinking about it is awesome. You have an amazing story to tell."

"I didn't really want to write about me," he said. "I've seen so many things in Afghanistan, it's a whole different way of life, and it's dying. It's a bittersweet thing to experience, really. If you haven't seen it with your own eyes, it's hard to understand. We all know we're trying to give people an opportunity for a better life, but not everyone sees it that way." He paused, fanning the blank pages of the journal with his thumb. "Imagine it: you've lived your life the way you've been taught is right, only to have outsiders come in with a different faith, a different culture, telling you that their way is better. Now, that's not how we see it, and it's not what we try to do. But it's how it seems to them.

"I don't know, though. After the last few months…maybe not. I'm not sure I want to revisit that place again, even in my mind."

There was a long pause before Mel spoke. "You do the best you can, son. I understand that all too well. The questions you're asking yourself, Scott, they're a sign that you operate within the boundaries of honor. If you didn't have those questions, then we'd worry."

"No worrying today," Scott said, breaking the sudden somber mood with a flash of his grin. "It's Christmas, I'm home, and there's a lot more food to eat. Let's get to celebrating."

"There is one thing for you, Bay…" Violet trailed off.

"I was wondering about that," Mel said, smiling at his wife.

"I wonder if it's too much?" Violet asked, eyeing Bay.

"Well, now you've mentioned it, and there's no time like the present, anyway," Mel said, smiling. "I think we should have all learned our lesson about that."

"Fact," Scott nodded at Violet. "What's this one thing?"

Violet didn't answer. Instead, she got up and headed into the foyer, where she dug around in the coat closet.

"What is she doing?" Bay wondered out loud.

"It's not wrapped. I wasn't sure about giving it to you this year," she was saying as she came into the room. Bay sat her coffee mug down to take the large box as Violet handed it down to her and Scott, where they sat on the floor. "Now that Scott's come home to us, I hope it's something you'll both get a kick out of."

"This is for both of us?" Bay asked.

"Well, it might as well be. I've worked on it for quite some time. I didn't know when or if the right time would come to give it to you, but—well, Mel is right. No time like the present."

They pulled the top off of the box together, and Bay carefully unfolded the heavy tissue paper. She pulled the corner of a heavy quilt out, then stood with it, stretching her arms as far as she could and letting it fall in front of her. She recognized the squares, numbers from Scott's high school jerseys, her favorite band tee shirts from the same time period, a sweatshirt from Belmont College, tee shirts from Bay's summer gigs performing at random theatres through college, their senior cruise shirts, and a slew of Army logos.

"Wow," Scott said, looking up at Bay. "It's... wow."

Bay studied the quilt, a sort of cumulative history, a literal representation of over half their lives spent together. She turned to Violet, overwhelmed by the meaning of her gift. "I don't know what to say. Thank you."

Bay stood and wrapped herself in the quilt, smiling down at Scott as he stared up at her, his eyes soft, near brimming.

"So you like it?" Violet asked, running a finger along the hem near Bay's arm.

"I don't have words to say how much. It's like...our past, bringing it forward. All this history that almost ended, and now..."

The doorbell rang and broke the spell of the moment. "Oh, Will said he might come by for coffee. I'll get it." Bay shuffled to the door with the quilt still wrapped around her, along with all her newfound hope for the future.

When she swung open the door, she found herself face to face with a woman she recognized vaguely, a tall brunette with her hair in a messy ponytail and round brown eyes, eyes that appeared as stunned to see Bay standing there with her quilt as Bay felt seeing her. Bay didn't know how long they gaped at each other before Scott was behind her, before she heard his voice crack over the name that had broken her heart.

Emerson.

This must be the emotional equivalent of falling on a grenade, Bay thought. All her senses numbed at once and the world shrank to a pinhole. With every beat of her heart she felt shattered from the inside out. This was her reward for letting her guard down, for setting the fact of the other woman in Scott's life aside.

"I apologize, I've obviously interrupted a family gathering," Emerson was saying, her lilting British accent lending charm to her husky voice. She stood there, managing to be elegant in yoga pants and a long-sleeved tee shirt. Bay couldn't look away, as much as she wanted to.

"Emerson," Scott said again, pausing to squeeze Bay's arm before he moved past her and her parents to the porch. "I—I'm surprised to see you here. I was going to call you, but..." He had his arms wrapped around her already, and she buried her face in the curve of his neck. Emerson clung to him like he was a life raft, like she would never let go of him again. Her sobs shook them both.

After several minutes that felt like years to Bay, Emerson took a step back and composed herself enough to speak. "I was out in the field, and it took a couple of days to get the news. As soon as I heard I headed home to London. I had the address from the letters you sent when you were stateside. But when I got to the road," she tilted her head down the lane, "I couldn't tell which box went with which house. So I came to the one with all the cars. I hope you don't mind, but—well, I came straight here."

Scott laughed, shaking his head at her. "I should have known," he said. "I should have known you'd jump on a plane."

Emerson studied his face, ran her hands over it reverently, and Bay's stomach flipped. "It's surreal," she said, took a few shallow breaths. "I never thought I'd see you again. When I watched the videos, I nearly fainted."

"You, faint? That's unlikely," Scott teased. He wiped her eyes with his thumbs.

Bay tasted bile rising in the back of her throat. She wanted to speak, to break whatever spell Emerson had cast over Scott with the sound of her own voice, calling him home to her side, their reality, their fresh start. But when she opened her mouth, nothing came out.

"I know perhaps I shouldn't have presumed, Scott, but I had to come," she said.

"Scott?" Mel finally stepped up and broke through the bubble of their happy reunion, and Scott jumped at the sound of Bay's daddy's voice booming from the doorway. It was as if he'd forgotten that he and Emerson weren't alone.

"Oh," he said, a nervous laugh breaking loose when he glanced at Bay. "I lost track of where I was for a minute. I think I'm in shock. Em, this is Bay, and her folks, Mel and Violet."

Emerson beamed at all three of them and extended a hand to

Mel. "It's a pleasure, really. I've heard so much about all of you. I apologize for the abrupt arrival, and for my disheveled state." She touched her free hand to her hair. "I'm in desperate need of a bath."

The group's stunned silence stretched a beat too long. "You must be exhausted," Scott said, jumping into action. "Where did you fly in? Are your bags in the car?" He peppered her with questions as he jogged down the steps toward the nondescript Toyota she must have rented. Emerson watched him, shifting from one foot to the other, her discomfort obvious.

"No need to worry," she called after him. "Really, I don't want to intrude on your gathering. If you'll direct me—"

"I'm going to take Em on over to my house," Scott said, turning to Bay, pleading for her understanding with his eyes. "She's come a long way, so let's let her clean up and rest? I'll come by a little later, okay?"

"Sure, of course," Bay answered, letting the quilt drop around her feet as she crossed her arms over her chest.

"Don't forget your gift," Violet said, turning to go get it.

"Here, take this too." Bay reached down for the quilt and tossed it out toward him. It landed on the porch steps.

"Bay, you should keep it here for now," Scott said, gathering it up. "Miss Violet—"

"No, take it. You probably need some extra over there, if you're having company." She nodded in Emerson's direction, but kept her eyes on Scott.

Violet came outside and handed Scott the small box with his journal. "Bay's right—there wasn't much over there when we cleaned, and I guess this is something for both of you. You'll have to share custody."

Scott spoke softly to them with Emerson out of earshot. "Okay, then, if you're sure. Bay, I'll be over in a bit, okay? I should set things right with her. I wouldn't have dreamed she'd come all the way here. Don't worry. I just—I can't just send her back, you know?"

Bay nodded. She couldn't think of anything appropriate to say, so she bit down on her tongue. She resolved to handle this better than she had before, for Scott's sake.

They tossed around goodbyes as Scott walked Emerson to the

car and took the driver's seat himself. With the door closed behind them, Violet and Bay stood in the foyer in stunned silence as Mel poured himself a drink.

"Well, that was truly uncomfortable." Violet put her hands on her hips and shook her head at Bay. "I can't believe how quick Scott ran off with that woman. He sure seemed happy to see her."

"Violet, please," Mel said, taking a sip of his drink. "No use stating the obvious, unless you enjoy kicking the girl when she's down."

"Never mind it, Daddy," Bay said, starting up the stairs. "It was plain to see, wasn't it? Anyway, I'm the one who opened the door for her, in more ways than one."

☆ ☽ ☆

Bay got some clothes from her suitcase and headed straight for the bathroom, near desperate for a shower and a quiet moment alone. She started the water and held her hand beneath the stream until the temperature was right, then undressed in a hurry. Before she turned to step into the tub, she caught her reflection in the mirror. Moments from the previous night with Scott flashed through her mind, then Scott driving off with Emerson. She closed her eyes, unable to face the shame she saw in them.

"What the hell am I doing?" she asked out loud as the steam from the shower began to fog the mirror.

"That's a really good question."

When Bay opened her eyes, Lillie was there behind her in the mirror. She studied her sister's face, her anger flaring at the amusement she saw there.

"It's not funny, Lillie. Do you have any idea what a huge mistake I made last night?"

"Well, I know you weren't here, so I'm guessing maybe you and Scott…"

"Dammit Lillie, aren't ghosts supposed to be omniscient or something? Yes, me and Scott."

"You know, even when I know, I do like to give you the chance to tell me things from your perspective instead of giving you mine right off."

"I'll take yours, please. I got nothing here except a bucket full of confusion. Especially now that I've managed to get my hopes up, only to watch him walk off with Emerson. Ugh…what did I do?" Bay sat on the edge of the tub and held her hand under the shower.

"Scott knows Emerson isn't what he wants. Maybe he was happy to see her, but that doesn't mean they'll ride off into the sunset. He needs you, Bay. He already chose you. And maybe he needs to explain that to her, for her to accept it. He's always needed you, but…well, he's going to need you in a bigger way now. You're his safe harbor. But he's never had to come back from something like this. And so much more is coming. Don't add to the confusion if you can help it, okay?"

Bay's head snapped up at Lillie's foreboding words. "What do you mean? What's coming, Lillie?"

Lillie smiled. "When you find what you're looking for, you'll know. You need to be there for him."

"I'm trying, but there's something missing, something not right. Being here, and being with Scott, it feels like coming home to something familiar to find it all abandoned, all empty rooms and empty spaces, and realizing that all your memories aren't enough to fill up the voids. We can't settle in because it's familiar. That would be too easy and way too damn difficult all at once. Scott needs to rebuild from the inside out."

"And what do you need?"

Bay knew the answer, at that moment. "I need to help him."

Lillie nodded, and the butterflies resting in her hair fluttered their wings. "Because you love him." She whispered, "It's okay to love him, you know."

"I do love him. Of course, I do. But—"

"But what, Bay? You're afraid? Tell me something, all this time he was missing, how did you feel?"

Bay took a while to think before answering. "Lost. Like I was lost, wandering across this desert of hurt, choking on the sand, hoping something else might fill me up. It was nothing but pain…"

"And when you saw his face, that first moment you saw his face?"

"Like I'd stumbled across an ocean full of fresh water, an ocean made up of love, and it swallowed me up."

Lillie sighed.

"Jesus, I'm sorry. Poor choice of metaphor." Bay reached toward her sister, who smiled in return.

"Well, good for you that you can't literally drown yourself in love and fear, because you would. Here's the thing, Bay. You have to let go of this fear that it's gonna hurt. Because it is. You can't worry about that all the time. Let go of the fear, and let Scott see the love in you. Let him see how you felt in that moment, when you saw his face again, because in that moment, you knew, and he needs to know, too."

Bay covered her face with her hands. "But, Lillie, it's not that simple. I don't know if I can…"

"You have to. See it through, Bay. He's still so lost. This time around, you have to carry him home."

CHAPTER 13

Bay walked outside and sat in Scott's truck, rolled down the window and lit a cigarette. She held the picture from The Owl's Roost, her phone, and Janice Murphy's number in her lap. She had some questions for the woman, and she needed an opportunity to ask them out of everyone's earshot. She drove down the dirt road past the barns and parked by the small pond where she and Scott and Lillie fished as children. An old bicycle boat was still tied to the little pier. She smiled, recalling the one like it they sank, Lillie screaming bloody murder about the dirty water and the mudfish she was so afraid of lurking around their feet as the three of them scrambled for the pier. "Good times," she said to herself, blowing smoke out of the window.

She dialed the number Scott had for Janice, hoping there was a good chance she'd be in on Christmas morning. By the third ring she was discouraged, but in the middle of the fourth, someone picked up.

"Hello?" The voice on the other end was female, but rough, lived-in and worked over.

"Hey, Janice," she said, hoping the quick use of her name would keep her on the line. "Merry Christmas."

"Who's this?"

"This is Janice Murphy, right? Scott's mother? I'm Bay, Bay Laurel LaFleur. I have news on Scott." The line was silent for a long stretch. "Janice, are you there? Please don't hang up."

"I already saw on the news."

"Oh, well, I thought you might want to hear from somebody who knows him, you know. Personally."

Another pause. Bay bit back her frustration and waited it out.

"He okay?"

"Yes ma'am, he's doing well. I think it'll take some time, you know. But physically he's well, and he's tough. He'll get through."

"Thanks for letting me know."

"Janice," Bay started quickly, afraid the woman would hang up, "I need to ask you something. Something personal. I know you don't know me, but Scott is my best friend. He has been since we were kids. And you should know, he's a good man. He's a really good man, with a good heart. But all this has been hard on him, and he confided in me the very day he came home about your call. We've done our best to give Scott a family. We consider him family. But he'd like to know his own, you know?"

Bay hesitated, afraid the tumble of words might cause Janice to retreat. She stared out at the tree line beyond the pond and willed herself to continue.

"Janice, are you there?"

"I'm sorry, Bay. I can't come back there, not now. I'm glad to know he's okay. When I saw on the news that a soldier had gone missing, a Special Forces soldier…" She seemed hesitant to continue, so Bay waited patiently for her to gather her thoughts. "It probably sounds ridiculous to anyone else, knowing how I up and left, but I knew before they said his name. Believe it or not, I've kept up as much as I could over the years."

Bay considered it, recalling the night Lillie died and the heightened sense of distress she'd felt within her own body when her sister was drowning. She knew it was possible to be that in tune with another human being, to be that aware of the very breath, the heartbeat, of someone else. But how could Janice claim such a bond with Scott when she barely knew him? She said it herself—she chose to leave him behind. But Bay couldn't claim to understand a mother's bond with her child. Surely there was some innate connection, some tether, that time or distance couldn't break.

"…the hell are my cigarettes?" Janice mumbled. "Anyway, when I saw the news that he'd been rescued, I was so relieved, but

I don't want to mess up his life. And I don't have the cash to get to New Hope, anyway."

"Maybe you could answer his calls, though?"

Bay heard Janice fumbling with a lighter, then taking a long drag. "I wouldn't know what to say," she exhaled. "What do you say to the kid you left to convince them you actually do care?"

Bay heard Janice's voice crack, and for the first time she understood the shame the woman might feel when confronted with the son she abandoned, who someone else raised into a wonderful man, something she didn't believe she could have done herself.

"I get that you might feel that way, but try to understand why he's reaching out now. He almost died, and knowing it was possible at any moment when he was captured, he knew he'd be dying with no real relationship with either of his parents. He has us, the LaFleurs, and lots of friends, but he has no family, flesh and blood. He's feeling a little lost in the world. So maybe if you could talk to him?"

Janice sucked in a breath. "I'll think about it."

"Good," Bay said. "And the question I wanted to ask you, the personal one?"

"Might as well," Janice said with a quick laugh.

"Scott's father…he'd like to know. If you could tell me who his father is, I think it would be good for him to have the opportunity to reach out, if he wanted to."

Janice blew out a breath, coughed. "I wouldn't even know how he'd go about finding the guy. He wasn't from around there or anything. He was army, just passing through visiting friends."

Bay closed her eyes. "Do you remember where he was from? Or his name? Anything at all about him?"

There was a long pause, then Janice coughed again.

"Could that man possibly have been Marco Ramirez?" Bay blurted, losing her patience.

The question was met with a sharp inhale on the other end of the line. "What do you know about him?"

"Not much, really. I saw some old videos and pictures, and…well, they've got this same dimple, the same grin. And there's something about his eyes. I don't know, my heart lurched when I saw him. It just feels like there's a connection, you know?"

"Marco was the guy. I couldn't have told you his last name,

though. Your mama ought to know, though, that's for sure."

Bay's brow furrowed, and she held the phone tighter to her ear. "Why would you say that?"

Janice laughed. "Oh, so you don't know that story? Everybody always knew my dirty laundry. The same rules didn't apply on the other side of the road, I reckon."

"What are you talking about?" Bay asked, her voice pitching.

"You better ask your mama about that. I probably shouldn't have said anything," Janice said, the humor quickly leaving her voice as she caught on to Bay's surprise. "That doesn't have anything to do with Scott, anyway. Forget about it. Anyway, I answered your question, so will you do one thing for me?"

"What's that?" Bay asked, trying to catch her breath and hoping Janice wasn't about to ask her to do anything illegal, like ship her drugs. Or for money, because she sure didn't have any of that.

"Call every now and again, let me know how he is? It was good to hear that he's okay. And it's nice to hear a friendly voice."

"I can do that. Take care of yourself, okay? Merry Christmas."

"Merry Christmas."

Bay sat her phone in the seat beside her along with the notes she scribbled while she talked with Janice, got out of the truck, and walked down to the end of the pier. She sat down over the murky water, studying the reflection of the sky in its still surface.

In all likelihood, Scott's father was Marco Ramirez. But who was he—and who had he been to Violet? Why had her parents been so against Bay finding out more about him? Scott deserved to know who his father was, but Bay couldn't put all the pieces of the puzzle together yet. She had a face and a name, the fact that he was an army man himself, a hint of something to do with her own mother…but where was he now? And what skeletons might she find in this particular closet she was opening?

Bay got up and headed to the truck, determined to find out, for Scott's sake. First things first, though, she had to smooth things over with him. If they were ever going to move forward with their lives, the whole lot of them would have to come clean. And if she had to, Bay told herself, she'd go first. She could do that, for Scott. After all, she loved him. "I love him. I love Scott," she said to herself, out loud. They were the simplest, truest words she'd ever spoken.

☆☽☆

Breathe in. Breathe out.

It was all Bay could manage to do as she walked up the front porch steps of Scott's house. How many times had she bounded up them and rushed right in the front door, made herself comfortable on her stool at the bar, the one closest to Grandma Aggie's at the end? When all of them—Bay and Scott, along with Lillie and Will—weren't in and out as kids, you might find her here, listening to Aggie's stories, taking advice and wisdom from the kindest, humblest woman she'd ever known. She'd always felt welcome here before. But this day, it felt like the space had been invaded.

But she refused to knock. This was still Grandma Aggie's place, and Scott's, an extension of Bay's own home. Scott might expect her to overreact, to come in guns blazing, but she was determined to keep her cool. She turned the knob and walked inside, noting the lit Christmas tree in the corner, the luggage left in a pile at the end of the sofa.

"Scott's in the shower."

Bay stared at the back of Emerson's head. She was in the kitchen, making herself at home here while Bay stood in the awkward area between rooms, her hands shaking. Emerson wasn't even stretching to reach the top shelf of the pantry, her limbs long and elegant.

Bay threw her jacket down on the sofa and sat down in her seat at the counter. Her seat. "I need to talk to him."

"Of course," Emerson said, turning to Bay, holding out a box. "I'm making hot cocoa. Would you like a cup?"

Bay shrugged. "Sure. Okay."

"I'll have to make it with water," Emerson said as she moved around the kitchen. "No milk. I believe a trip to the grocery is in order first thing tomorrow."

Scott prefers almond milk. Bay didn't say it out loud, though she was tempted to take the opportunity to point out something she knew about him that Emerson didn't.

Emerson handed a mug over the counter to Bay and took a sip

from her own before she sat herself right down on Aggie's stool. Bay squeezed her mug, fighting the urge to shove Emerson to the floor. She sipped at her cocoa and forced her knees to stop jumping. She hated that she was nervous. She wanted to be composed, sure of herself. But she didn't even know what to say.

"I'm glad to have a few moments alone with you, Bay," Emerson started. "I know it must seem…well, it must be maddening, me showing up on your doorstep today. Merry Christmas!" Emerson extended her arms and laughed, the warm, rich sound of it almost startling. It was the kind of laugh that could draw you in, seize your attention. Bay studied the other woman, her dark hair and eyes paired with dark, flawless skin. She was attractive, sure, but when she laughed, she was stunning. Scott would fall in love with a laugh like that. Bay's heart stuttered at the thought.

She took another sip of cocoa. Somehow Emerson had made the perfect cup, with water and powdered cocoa from a packet. "This is good. Thanks," she said, fumbling for words. Emerson's open smile left her disarmed, and flustered.

"I love cocoa. Sadly, I'm not much of a tea drinker. Although, I must admit, now that I've been introduced to the wonders of sweet iced tea, that may change."

"Welcome to the South."

They sat in awkward silence for a moment, Emerson staring into her mug while Bay willed her knees to be still beneath the counter. It was actually a relief when Emerson finally spoke.

"I'm sorry we haven't had a chance to talk until now, until this…happy little miracle?" Emerson's eyes slid from Bay's face to the window. "I mentioned to Scott more than once that I'd like a chance to talk with you. I believe he was concerned we wouldn't behave like civilized adults."

"You mean he was afraid I wouldn't behave like a civilized adult."

Emerson shrugged. "I have my moments like anyone else. But if anyone had a right to outrage this past year, it was certainly you."

"I was outraged last year, but I won't go so far as to say I had a right to be." Bay sat back, wrapped her hands around her mug, but didn't pick it up.

"Still," Emerson said, "I understand, I think, how you must feel, me showing up like this. You set everything aside that happened before, and you've been here for Scott since he was rescued. And then I swoop in from nowhere, on Christmas no less…"

Bay tapped her fingers on the counter and stared out of the window, too. She would rather have stuffed Emerson into her suitcase and shipped her back to England than sit at the counter making small talk, but she wanted to show Scott that she could handle it, and that they could move on from Emerson. So, she would talk. She'd even open up a little, woman to woman.

"Really, this whole thing caught me off guard. Scott and I weren't together when he left. I didn't know where we were. And then he was missing. One day I thought he was gone forever, the next…" Bay trailed off.

"The next, there he was, large as life on the telly, grinning that grin of his. I do understand that."

"Exactly." Bay tried to smile, but failed. "I've spent a lot of time reflecting on the past these last few months. I see it more clearly than I could before. He changed a lot in the last few years. The war changed him, even before he was captured. He said I didn't understand what it was like. I didn't want to admit that he was right, but he was. I'm trying now, though. I want to understand it, and what he's been through. I want to be here for him."

"He certainly saw things—and did things—for his job, that change a person." Emerson clasped her hands in front of her. "I've been to Iraq and Afghanistan, and both experiences, both wars, altered the course of my life. You can't go into a situation like that, see the widespread suffering, experience that level of fear, and not be changed."

Bay bit the side of her cheek, hesitant to ask questions of the other woman in Scott's life, to ask anything of her. But Emerson knew things she didn't, and she was sitting here, in Aggie's kitchen. "Tell me what it's like, really. The things he doesn't tell me."

Emerson rested her chin in her hand. "My first experience as an aide worker in a war zone was in Iraq. I'd been there almost two months the first time I saw, up close, an IED explode. We were on our way to deliver supplies to a school, and we had to pass through the Red Zone. An Iraqi ran up to the Humvee, screaming about terrorists the next street over, lying in wait to attack. Three of the troops in our convoy got out to sweep the street ahead of us." She paused, took a deep breath, exhaled through her mouth. "The bomb was hidden in the carcass of a dog. One of the soldiers tripped it with the muzzle of his rifle and set it off. To this day, it is the most horrific thing I have ever seen."

"Did he survive?"

"He died on the way to the base hospital." Emerson sat back and rubbed her arms with her hands, as if she'd felt a sudden chill in the air. "His name was Jason J. Conroy. He was nineteen years old, from Indiana. Can you imagine, he was engaged to be married? No one should be engaged to be married at nineteen. Ha! I'm sorry—I don't know why I said that."

"Scott wanted to get married as soon as he came home from basic training."

Emerson put a hand to her throat again, her round eyes going even wider. "He did?"

Bay nodded. "It's the army way, you know. I wasn't ready for that, being in school and all, and I really wanted to pursue music. I couldn't do that and be where he was all the time."

"No, that's a good thing. It's dangerous, surrendering your dreams to the tide of other people's expectations."

"Anyway," Bay said, "I understand the impulse, wanting to have someone there to come home to. I imagine that's the main reason why a lot of kids in the military get married young."

"Do you wish you'd made a different decision, when Scott asked the first time?"

Bay tipped her head, thinking. "Nah, it would have been a disaster then. I'm a little selfish, but I'm working on that. I would have resented the hell outta him for dragging me out of Nashville. Now, though…everything is different now."

"I wonder, how different does he seem to you now than before?"

Bay's forehead creased as she thought about it. "Well, you said yourself, war changes people. And being held a prisoner...I don't think even he knows how this has changed him yet. Not really. He's been grappling with it. I can see him struggling, but I haven't figured a way through it yet."

"Scott's going to need support, and time to heal, but he's strong. He will get through it. I'm going to see to it that he gets through it and back on his feet, doing what he loves."

Bay pushed her stool out and put her feet on the floor. "What do you mean?"

"I'll be staying on, of course, to help Scott get over this hump. He'll need me now more than ever, Bay. Surely you can see that he needs someone here who understands—"

"Oh, I see. I see exactly what you think he needs." Bay sprung to her feet.

"I know what he needs." Emerson said the words with quiet confidence, her shoulders squared, as if it had all been decided.

Scott emerged from the bathroom then, still damp from the shower in his tee shirt and sweats. Stung by Emerson's words, Bay grabbed her jacket and the box with the quilt her mother made from the sofa and headed for the door.

"Bay, wait. Can I talk to you?" Scott's hand went to his hair when she stopped to look at him.

"Now isn't the time, Scott," she answered.

"You and I need to—"

"Not now," she said through gritted teeth. "Unless you want to have a knockdown drag-out in front of her, let me go home."

"What the hell is wrong with you?" he yelled at her, the veins in his neck popping.

"What the hell is wrong with you?" she shouted back at him, unable to keep the control she'd be hanging on to by tattered threads. "What do you expect from me, Scott, congratulations? I know you're confused but…you know what? I'm not doing this. I refuse to lower myself to this silly middle school game of grappling over a boy with you two. So yes, congratulations. And go to hell."

Bay stormed past Emerson and out the door. She held the box with the quilt to her chest and flew down the front steps with Scott trailing behind her. She dropped the box in the passenger's seat of his truck, slammed the door, and walked to the driver's side. Scott was leaning against the door, his hands in his pockets, anger etching his face.

"Get off." Bay put her hands on her hips and lifted her chin a notch.

"This isn't at all what you think," he said, turning his eyes up to the deepening blue sky.

"Then what is it, exactly?"

He closed his eyes. "Bay," he whispered, his voice so soft she stepped forward to hear the rest, "I have no idea what to do here, about anything. Part of me is happy to see Em—I mean, I didn't think I'd ever see her again, either. And she came all this way, so I couldn't leave her standing in your driveway. Please give me a chance to explain to her. Please."

"No, Scott." She jerked her hand away when he reached for it. "Get out of my way, and from now on, stay out of my way."

"Can we talk tomorrow?" he asked her, finally relenting and stepping away from the door.

"No," she said, her voice rising. "I shouldn't have come here, and I shouldn't have written that stupid song, and I damn sure shouldn't have sung it, and I shouldn't have been here for you. So, no, you can't talk to me tomorrow. Talk to Emerson, since she's the one staying."

Bay got in the truck and slammed it into reverse, backed up over the grass to turn around and kicked up gravel going down the driveway. When she saw Scott standing with his hands on his head in the rearview mirror, she almost stopped. There was a time she would have stayed, she would have yelled, screamed, fought for him. She would have snatched Emerson up from her barstool and shown her the door herself. But that was all in the past, along with her hopes for a future with him that wouldn't require her to live in Emerson's shadow.

CHAPTER 14

"Mama?"

Bay trudged through the back door at Blossom Hill, dragging the quilt Violet had made for her and Scott behind her. Part of her wanted to burn it in the back yard, but there was another part of her—the one that was absolutely falling apart—that couldn't let it go. She lifted the corner she held and wiped the tears from her face.

"Mama?' she called out louder as she stood in the kitchen, looking around her as if she expected Violet to materialize from thin air. It had been a couple of hours since she'd left Scott's house. She'd driven around town for a while, then down to the pond, where she'd sat on the little dock, trying to sort things out. No such luck.

She leaned against the island and surrendered to a fresh wave of tears. After her disastrous run-in with Emerson and her fight with Scott, all she wanted, ironically enough, was her mama.

There was light coming from the front rooms of the house. Bay moved toward it, sure she would find Violet curled up in the corner of the sofa with a Christmas romance and a cup of cocoa. But when she rounded the corner, she found the sofa empty. She found Mel instead, sitting in a straight-backed wingchair, his long legs stretched out in front of him, a drink in his hand, and a defeated expression on his face.

"Daddy," Bay started, tears welling as she dropped onto the sofa, letting the quilt fall in a heap at her feet, "I'm so glad you're up. I can't believe this is happening."

Mel sat forward. He glared at Bay. "Exactly what part of it can't you believe, Bay? You're the one who set this whole mess in motion."

Bay leaned away from Mel, crinkling her nose. "What do you mean, Daddy?"

"I don't care to get into it with you, not right now," Mel said, his tone one of disgust. "You'll have to go talk to your Mama, and may the Good Lord help you with that."

"What—where is she?" Bay asked, glancing toward the staircase.

Mel sipped his drink. "She's gone down to Edisto. You should get on upstairs and pack an overnight bag. Sooner you get on the road the better. If you leave in the next ten minutes, you'll make it by midnight."

Bay's instinct was to get up off the sofa, to argue with her daddy, to fight. But the weight of the day's events seemed to press her further into the cushions, and into herself. All at once, she felt far too tired to wade through any more confusion. "Can you please just tell me what the hell is going on? I can't possibly have had time to do something to send Mama into a fit since this morning."

"What's going on, Bay, is that we got a call from Scott's long-lost mother, Janice. She wanted to discuss pieces of our collective history we'd left long buried, pieces it seems you've busied yourself digging up."

Bay straightened in her seat and forced herself to meet Mel's eyes. There was a hardness in them she'd never seen before, an undercurrent in his tone that made her stomach twist new knots.

"Scott's been wondering about his mom since he got home. I was just trying to help him along getting in touch with her. Why is that such a big deal?"

"If that's all you were trying to do, Bay…hell, it would still be a big deal. But the real problem here is Marco Ramirez," Mel said, spitting the name out like it was all sharp edges in his mouth.

Bay recoiled as if he'd tossed hot coals in her face. "Daddy, I don't understand…why is he such a big problem? I mean, you knew the guy. Don't you remember him, what he looked like? You have to admit that there's a resemblance to Scott. And if there's some connection between the two, how come you and Mama are so opposed to me trying to find out? Does it have something to do with Mama?"

Mel heaved a sigh and shook his head at her. "We both asked you to drop it, Bay. It would have been better all the way around if you could have just done that."

"Except for Scott, Daddy. Y'all seem to be forgetting that dropping it might not be better for Scott. Anyway, all I did was make one phone call."

"You have no idea the old wounds you've opened with that one phone call." Mel closed his eyes and dropped his head like he might fall asleep where he sat, except for the way he tilted his glass this way and that in his hand.

"You know, I didn't go looking for that picture of Marco. I found it kind of by accident, and I didn't know that by trying to help Scott I'd be causing anyone else pain."

"That's between you and Violet now. To be honest, I don't care to hear it. All the time I've spent over the years trying to forget that whole thing, and then trying to figure out the best thing, and then wrestling with the regret of what I did and didn't do…for you to bulldoze over it, Bay, without considering the consequences or respecting our wishes…well, I don't want any part of it. You and Violet can figure it out."

Bay held her hands up in front of her. "What 'whole thing'? Daddy, I'm not sure I understand what—"

"Enough!" Mel's voice shook the house like thunder, rattling the windows. He hurled his empty tumbler across the room. It exploded against the mirror hanging above the fireplace, sending shards of glass and crystal raining down over the hardwood floor.

Mel and Bay both froze in place and stared over at the damage. Neither of them spoke for a long moment, until Mel finally turned to face his daughter. She hesitated to meet his gaze, she was so horrified to have pushed him to this point.

And then he laughed. A roaring, deep, long laugh, with knee-slapping and tears. Bay got caught up in it, too. They laughed until they were both out of breath.

"Whew, that felt good," Mel said, scratching his head. "I've never thrown something in anger in my life. I didn't realize what

I was missing out on."

"Holy hell, Daddy," Bay said, giggling again. "I better warn everyone to duck for cover when they come over now."

"Lord, Bay," Mel said, settling into the chair and wiping his forehead. "This is a fine mess."

Bay got up and walked over to Mel, then bent down to kiss his head. "Don't worry," she whispered. "We'll sort it out, all of us, together. But I guess I need to sort some things out with Mama, too."

"Yes, you do, Bay. Whatever else happens, whatever else is true, the two of you are gonna need each other."

"I know. I love you."

"And I love you. I'm sorry."

"No need to be. Did you good to get that out." She smiled at him before turning to go upstairs to pack. "Now you have to clean up your mess while I go clean up mine."

Breathe in. Breathe out.

Bay stood watching her mother through the kitchen window at Pearl's Place, listening to the water rolling onto shore just beyond the cottage, a low tide languishing beneath the full moon. Even though she'd not yet made the ranks of the Pearl Girls, Bay knew this was where the women in her family congregated to share their lives, tell stories, heal wounds, restore their souls. Of course, this was where she and Violet would come to share their truths. She just wondered if either one of them was ready for it.

Violet spun the old-fashioned glass on the table in front of her, lifted it to her lips and drank, gently placed it on the table, spun it again. She didn't break her rhythm when Bay walked in and stood across the table from her.

"What are you doing, Mama?" Bay asked.

Violet let out a sound somewhere between a laugh and a sob. "Waiting for you, my darling daughter."

Bay picked up the bottle between them and sat down. "And you needed a visit with good ol' Captain Morgan for that?"

"No, honey, but telling you about the green-eyed island boy your Mama almost ran away with? Well, it requires a healthy dose of rum and tears. And since you insist on unearthing the whole sordid story..."

The look in Violet's eyes scared Bay more than any she'd leveled on her before. She didn't know what the hell had happened to her parents over the course of the last few hours, or what Violet was talking about, but whatever it was had them both unwound in a way Bay hadn't imagined possible. She popped the cork from the bottle and poured her own healthy dose in the glass Violet had set out for her.

"I'm not entirely sure I know what this is about, Mama. You gonna fill me in?"

Violet raised her glass as if to toast, then drank. "Once upon a time, your Mama was young, and beautiful, and a little bit wild...a whole lot like you."

Bay lifted her glass to her lips and sipped, her hands trembling with nervous energy. "And what does that have to do with this Marco Ramirez? And Scott?"

Violet tented her fingers over her glass. "Everything, Bay Laurel. Everything."

"Mama, for the record, I didn't go snooping into this thinking it had anything at all to do with you. I saw Marco in that video, and then I found the picture…he just reminded me so much of Scott. I thought it might be important for him, if I could find out something about his family. I wasn't trying to up-end ours in the process."

"It doesn't really matter now, does it?" Violet said with a wave of her hand. "To be honest, I'm glad to get this out in the open. I've never told anyone. Not the whole story, anyway. Your father knows the parts he had to know, and what he figured out." She paused long enough to give Bay a wicked smile. "But you get the distinct pleasure of being my one and only confidante."

Bay propped her chin in her hands. "Okay, Mama. I'm all ears."

Violet laughed, a little too loud. "And where shall I start?"

"Try the beginning," Bay answered, looking her mother straight in the eyes, trying to seem braver than she really was. Seeing this kind of turmoil bubbling up in her strong, solid mother made Bay wonder if maybe there were some things she didn't want to know. But she nodded her head and encouraged Violet forward. "Your secrets are safe with me."

"Maybe, maybe not. We'll see how you feel about that when you've heard them," Violet said, one eyebrow cocked, her glass swaying in her hand.

"Okay," Bay said. "So, the beginning…"

Violet let out a sigh, then started into her story. "I suppose we should start with Marco Ramirez. I met Marco the summer before my junior year of high school, when my daddy hired his parents to do some work here. A couple of weeks turned into all summer after Daddy found out that Carlos, Marco's father, had experience sailing. That's when he got the grand idea to buy that boat."

"The Witch Hazel?"

"Yes, that one. So, he bought himself a sailboat, and the Ramirezes stayed through the summer while he learned the ropes. I didn't pay Marco much attention. I didn't pay any of them much attention, really. I was running around the beach with my summer girlfriends, you know. And growing up on the farm, workers came and went with the seasons. I figured it would be the same with the Ramirezes. There was no reason to think they'd be around very long. But then Daddy decided Carlos was indispensable to him, and next thing we know they're living on the farm."

"So that's how Marco ended up in New Hope, Grandpa brought him there?"

Violet nodded and got up from the table. She wandered into the den and stared out past the dunes. Bay poured a splash more of the rum into her glass and followed, hanging back, watching her mother. Violet was lost in her memories, in her buzz, and her defenses were down. Bay fought the urge to charge her with questions, or accusations, and waited for her to continue with her story.

"Carlos could fix anything with moving parts, I remember Daddy saying. And they'd become good friends in a short time. Even so, junior year, I was friendly with Marco, but I pretty much kept my distance. Everybody around town did."

"That's what Amelia said," Bay broke in, "that the Ramirezes kept to themselves."

"You could say," Violet said, wrapping her arms over her chest. "I don't know if it was more that they kept to themselves, or that us locals kept them out. New Hope was a small town, still is. Most families have been there for generations. Newcomers aren't necessarily unwelcome, and weren't then, either, but it's hard working your way into a tight community. Well, I imagine it is. Not like I ever had to try."

"Yeah, I imagine it is hard, Mama, trying to gain acceptance with people who are constantly judging you," Bay interjected, her words dripping sarcasm.

Violet turned and squinted at her. "Are we telling your story tonight, or mine?"

Bay couldn't help smiling at her mama's quick retort. They could do battle all night and not get anywhere. "Sorry. Carry on."

"Anyway, Marco made a place for himself in school. He was quite the athlete, but he wasn't cocky about it. He earned some respect on the football field, and that spilled over to school, but he still pretty much kept to himself. When the rest of us were hanging out, he was usually working with his dad. He was quiet—quieter than most of the rowdy boys from around here, and thoughtful.

"My relationship with Marco started to shift when, a few days before the end of our junior year, your daddy did the unthinkable."

Bay stood shoulder to shoulder with Violet and turned to study her profile. "The unthinkable? What did he do?"

"He broke up with me. Dumped me cold for Ella Kay."

"What?" Bay's voice pitched up, her eyes going wide. "Ella Kay Foster?" Bay thought of the woman who ran the hair salon in New Hope, with her over-teased, over-dyed red hair and bedazzled sweatshirts. She couldn't reconcile the thought of her straight-laced father getting caught up with an Ella Kay.

"Hudson then," Violet answered, rolling her eyes. "Seeing as my family was the only one that left town all summer, and Mel wasn't invited along, he decided he didn't want to spend the last summer before he graduated at home with no girl. He was going through a lot, mind you. His father died not long before that, and he was taking on so much already. I couldn't be there with him, so he dumped me. And I was heartbroken. I begged Mama and Daddy to stay home that summer, to let me stay home that summer, but I suppose you can guess how that went."

Bay chuckled, bumping her shoulder against Violet's. "I'm sure Gramma Olivia insisted you would not lower yourself to hang up around New Hope all summer moping because some boy had the audacity to dump you."

"You got that right. They packed me up and dragged me right on down here to Pearl's Place. And, since Daddy still wasn't altogether comfortable on The Witch Hazel himself—and never was—we had the Ramirez clan in tow again. Well, Marco and his Daddy, at least. Mama decided it would be good for me to take care of the house myself, have a bit of a job and earn some money. Then, as luck would have it, Granny Sarah got sick a few weeks into the summer. I was packed and ready to high tail it home in five minutes flat, but Mama wasn't having any of that. Daddy felt safe enough leaving me with Mr. Ramirez and Marco to watch out for me, and Mama told me to rest assured that she'd see to it that Mel knew I was having the time of my life without him."

"Wow, Grandma was devious!"

Violet laughed and cut her eyes at Bay. "We've always known where you get it from, and she got it straight from Willa Pearl."

Bay shrugged her shoulders. "So, they left you here, and then what happened?"

"Well, I did what all teenaged girls do best. I sulked. I didn't even step foot out of my bedroom until the second day. That evening, I decided to walk down to the beach before the sun set. I was out of sorts, still upset over the breakup, and being left alone for the first time in my life to fend for myself. I took a blanket with me and sat near the dunes. I noticed this guy a little ways down the beach, doing sprints, then running into the waves and diving in, swimming out, then back, starting it over. Like some sort of drill. I remember thinking that he was beautiful. I don't even know how long it took me to really look at his face, to recognize that it was Marco. But once I did, I couldn't drag my eyes off of him.

"He finished up after a while and jogged a little closer to me where he'd left his towel. I was debating whether or not to wave, or maybe even call him over, when he caught me staring. That was the first time I think we ever really looked each other in the eye." Violet paused, her face flushed from the mix of the rum and her memories.

"It must have been a powerful moment, if you remember it that well," Bay said. She walked to the table and poured more rum in each of their glasses, brought them over and handed Violet hers, then sat on the sofa. Violet eased down at the other end and they faced each other.

Violet sniffed at her glass, then took a long sip. "That was a moment I'll never forget, Bay. I know it must sound terrible, but it was the first time I really saw him. And when he smiled at me, I couldn't help smiling back. I couldn't imagine in that moment how I'd managed to overlook that smile for the better part of a year. It took my breath. We sat on the beach and talked for hours that night."

"What did you talk about?" Bay tucked her feet beneath her and rested her head on her hand. Her mother's eyes sparkled as she shared her secrets, radiating a warmth Bay had rarely seen in her. She wondered whether it was the rum, or the relief of finally telling someone this story, or a combination of both that had her glowing. Either way, Bay found herself fascinated by this side of her mother she hadn't known existed, this love story she'd kept buried for so long.

Violet grinned and tilted her chin, gazing somewhere past Bay. "Everything. Nothing. He asked about Gran, and how I was holding up, if I needed anything…he finally sat down beside me and asked why I wasn't ever out at the docks. I hadn't even seen The Witch Hazel then—I didn't spend a lot of time with Daddy, and it was his thing. And that was enough to give Marco ideas."

"Ideas?"

"Daddy had called Mr. Ramirez to bring some things to New Hope the next day. Marco thought we should make an adventure of the day while we were unsupervised, take The Witch Hazel out for a spin. He said he'd teach me the ropes, and I could surprise Daddy when he came to Edisto. I hesitated at first, but then he linked his fingers through mine and promised me I was in good hands with him. Something about the way he said it, the way he looked straight into my eyes, the gentle way he touched me…I couldn't say no. No wasn't even a word I remembered at that moment."

Violet closed her eyes and fell into the sofa. "When he walked me to the house and said goodnight, my hands were shaking. I couldn't settle down. It must have taken a good hour for the shaking to stop, and I barely got any sleep. I was excited, and at the same time scared. Mel was the only boy I'd ever dated. I'd rarely even paid attention to any other boy. And to see Marco, after not really seeing him…" Violet said. "Refreshing isn't the word. In those few hours with him, the world suddenly seemed expansive to me. It was like all of a sudden I realized the New Hope boundaries, the social rules we lived by, they weren't real. Here was this gorgeous young man, who was smart and funny and interesting. And I realized I'd been overlooking him because he was different. I also realized that my little moment of insight wouldn't have been a shared one by all of my friends back in New Hope. So, I decided to enjoy it while I had the chance."

Bay put a hand on her Mama's. She was lost in the story, almost so lost that she forgot it was true, and what it might mean. She was all at once afraid and desperate to know the rest. "So, did you go?"

Violet nodded. "We met at the marina the next morning. He'd told me the night before that his grandfather on his father's side was a passionate sailor who took him out on the water as much as he could when he was growing up, along with his dad. It was in their blood, really. And no matter where they seemed to go after their family left Puerto Rico, his dad was drawn to the water. It was meant to be, he said, when he stumbled across the old boat so much like the one he remembered from those treasured childhood trips with his grandfather. The Witch Hazel felt like home to him.

"I found our boat slip at the marina without much trouble. Marco was on deck, his back to me, bent over something I couldn't even identify. *"Hey there, sailor,"* I called from the dock, striking a pose in my white sundress and strappy sandals. I didn't exactly dress for the occasion. He looked over his shoulder at me and whistled. *"Hey, mi querida,"* he said. That was the first time he called me that. He held out a hand to help me up, and when I put mine in his, it was like the most natural and magical thing in the world, all at the same time. Marco could tell I was nervous, and he chatted while he worked. It put me at ease."

"You're not very comfortable in the water," Bay pointed out.

Violet shrugged. "No, and it was the first time I had ever been on a sailboat. You know I'm not much of a swimmer, and I explained to Marco that while I'd spent many a summer day sprawled on a towel in the sand, I avoided watersports as much as possible. He shrugged it off, said that sailing was a different experience, a different kind of moving through the water.

"People say things like 'sailing through' or 'smooth sailing' like it's an easy thing to do," he said as he checked the ropes, made adjustments. *"Sailing is a study in planning, in learning the details and paying attention to them, but understanding that everything around you is in a constant state of flux. Doesn't matter what you'd planned for, at the end of the day. Sailing is what taught me how to make the right adjustments rather than go with the flow, or try to motor through without adapting. Sailing teaches you how important it is to make graceful changes. To keep your head about you."*

"Sounds like a pretty wise teenaged boy," Bay said. "Actually, like a player. He sounds like a player."

Violet laughed. "I don't think it was ever that. Marco was an old soul, even then. And God, was he smart. It scared me, how smart, how eloquent. And in his second language, even. He told me then that learning to change, to grow, was the only way to be really free. And that it's hard work.

"Anyway, we went out on the water that day, and Marco covered the basics with me as he moved around the boat. I was pretty useless though. When we dropped anchor to have lunch, I told him I wished I'd brought my guitar, so I could at least play something for him."

"What?" Bay asked, eyes wide. "You played guitar?"

Violet chuckled. "And where did you think you got that from, dear, your Daddy? He can't carry a tune in a bucket."

Bay laughed along with her mother. "It's almost too much to take in. I mean, a hot summer romance with a sexy Puerto Rican is one thing, but you and a guitar? I gotta see this with my own eyes."

"Maybe I'll show you a thing or two when we get home."

"But…I don't understand, Mama. You haven't really supported me pursuing music, playing guitar. I'd have loved so much to share that with you, for you to have taught me. Why didn't you ever play with me? Why did you fight me on it so hard?"

Violet studied her glass. "Maybe I'm a little jealous of your talent, Bay Laurel. Or maybe I don't want to see you disappointed if you don't make it. I feel like a different person than that girl. I put my guitar away after that summer. I never touched it again."

"Okay, we can get back to that. Now keep going. What happened next?"

Violet closed her eyes again. "We dropped anchor to have lunch—he was prepared for that as well—and we were sitting side by side, arms and legs brushing. Every now and then he pushed at the wide brim of my hat, which I kept hoping would keep my face from burning to beet red. I mentioned the guitar again, searching for something to do with my hands.

"You know, you don't have to provide entertainment everywhere you go," he said to me. *"You could enjoy the freedom you have in this moment to just be here, in your beautiful skin, with someone who absolutely adores you."*

"He caught my eyes with his, and Lord, it was like staring into these deep green pools flecked with gold that glinted like the sun on the sea, and I realized in that moment how easy it would be to fall for him, if I let myself. I was in trouble, real trouble, when he kissed me. It was like something lit beyond a spark, past fire, like after the longest night of my life, the sun might rise again."

"Wow, Mama. That's so romantic." Bay said, drawing out the words.

Violet smirked. "It was. And, then again, maybe I've over-romanticized the memories in my head. That happens, you know, when you look back on a love affair. Rose-colored glasses and whatnot.

"Anyway, the next few weeks were intense. After our parents came back, we snuck in time where we could. Lord, could that boy ever kiss. He tasted like mango and honey and something else exotic I don't even know the name of."

Bay giggled, feeling herself blush at her mama's admission. "And after summer, then what?

"Well, when school started in the fall, it was almost like it had been a dream. We didn't know how our parents might react if we tried to date openly. And then Mel saw the error of his ways, and we made up."

"Did he know about Marco?"

"He suspected, but I denied it, and he didn't press the point. After all, he'd broken things off with me, which your Gramma Olivia reminded him of daily. Anyway, at Christmas our senior year, your daddy and I got engaged. I started planning our wedding for the day after graduation. But every time I saw Marco, I couldn't help but wonder…"

Violet got up from the sofa and wandered to the windows. She took a deep breath and let it out.

"What if…" Bay said, picking up her train of thought.

"Yes, what if," Violet whispered. "Marco had plans. He was leaving New Hope, joining the army so he could see the world, get an education. And he asked me every time he could get me alone, every time, to come with him. And, of course, I said no, every time. But there was a part of me, Bay, a very big part of me, that was dying to say yes. I wanted the world, too, to see it and touch it. To experience it. God, I wanted that, too. But that's where you and I are different. I was so scared. Too scared. And you never have been.

"Then there was this one night, a few weeks before the wedding, Mel and I had a big fight. We were both terrified. I don't think either one of us really knew for sure what we wanted. I was walking around the farm, up and down the lane, really, and Marco spotted me. We met in the middle, and he wiped my tears. He didn't say a word. He took my hand in his and took me with him. We laid a blanket out under one of the willows, behind Daddy's old barn. The way he kissed me that night…nobody had ever kissed me like that. I'd never felt wanted like that. That one night, that one time, we made love. Without one word spoken, before or after, we made love."

Bay sat on the sofa, staring at her mother, who had once been a girl, a girl at war with herself over conflicting dreams. For once, Bay could see herself in Violet. Maybe they had more common ground between them than she'd thought.

But then her thoughts drifted to another question…her brother. Bay recalled what she'd seen on her parents' wedding video—Violet's illness, her emotional upheaval…and Marco's anguished expression as he watched the happy couple setting off for their honeymoon. Was it possible that Ethan had been conceived the night Violet spent with Marco, that he was Marco's son?

Bay studied her mother, working up the courage to ask the question and only finding enough to whisper one word. "Ethan?"

Violet shook her head. "No, no. Ethan was born thirteen months after our wedding, Bay, and I assure you, since the one time with Marco, there hasn't been anyone but Mel. You're right, though, there was a baby conceived that night." Tears spilled down Violet's cheeks and she swiped at them. Bay got up and grabbed a box of tissues. She held it out to Violet and waited for her to continue, her own eyes threatening to spill over.

"I realized on my honeymoon that I was already pregnant, and with Marco's baby, and that's why I'd been so sick. I thought it was nerves about the wedding, about the choice I was making. And then—I didn't know what to do. God, Bay, I didn't know what to do." Her sobs shook her, and Bay wrapped her arms around her Mama's shoulders.

"It's okay, Mama. Whatever happened, it's okay."

Violet pulled away and looked at her. "No, Bay, it's not. It's not okay. What I did…I didn't know what else to do. I was married to your father, and Marco was gone. I couldn't pretend that baby was your father's child, and I couldn't tell him it wasn't. But I should have. I wasn't willing to take the chance, to give him a chance to accept it, or to forgive me. And I wasn't ready to face the consequences if he left me. Can you imagine, Violet Hampton LaFleur, newly minted Pearl Girl, so thoroughly shamed? I thought my parents would disown me. So, I did what I thought I had to do." Violet turned away from Bay.

"What did you do, Mama?" Bay whispered, resting her hands on Violet's shoulders.

Violet took some time to steady herself. "Isn't it obvious?"

"I think you need to say it. Out loud. If you've never told a soul before tonight, and if you never tell a soul after, say it now, Mama. It won't make it any more or less true." Bay turned Violet to face her, letting her own tears spill over her mother's unspoken pain. She took Violet's hands in hers and held them tight. "Tell me, Mama."

"I found a clinic, Bay, and I went early one morning and I had an abortion. Hired a driver in from Charleston and had him drop me off at a restaurant close to the clinic, and pick me up there after." Violet choked back a sob as Bay wrapped her in another hug. "I changed my mind a thousand times, but in the end, I did it. I'd told your father I was coming here for the day, that I wanted to lay on the beach a while. When it was over I called to tell him I'd come down with an awful bug and was staying overnight. He almost caught me in it then—he wanted to come get me, to come take care of me. But I told him I didn't want to get him sick, too, and he finally agreed."

"It must have been so hard to go through that alone. And to carry that burden all these years." Bay pulled Violet to the sofa and sat her down, then went to the kitchen to put on a pot of coffee.

Violet laughed, the sound as sad as any wail of grief Bay had ever heard. "Mel asked me during that phone call if I might be pregnant."

Bay stopped the stream of water running and turned to Violet.

"I made up another lie, that I'd also started my period that day, and that I'd been hoping to be pregnant. He said the most comforting thing he could think of, I know, that we'd be pregnant in no time."

Bay wiped tears from her eyes. "That sounds like Daddy, looking for the bright side in any situation. If he'd have had any idea how much that thought might hurt you in that moment…"

Violet curled up at the end of the sofa. "But I didn't tell him the truth, or give him the chance. And when it was said and done, I went along with it like it was my plan all along to start a family immediately."

"But that's not what you really wanted?" Bay asked. She leaned against the counter and watched the coffee begin to drip into the carafe.

"I don't think I ever found out what I really wanted. I went home, and I healed, and I prayed to God that if he would forgive me, I would live the rest of my life making up for it, being a model wife and mother. And I thought that was exactly what I was doing, right up until the night we lost Lillie. That night the lies caught up with me, and we all paid such a price," Violet said, bringing her hands to her face.

"Mama, what happened to Lillie couldn't have had anything to do with any of this," Bay said as she took down two mugs.

But she hesitated with her hand on the handle of the coffeepot. Lillie's drowning couldn't have had anything to do with this…but of course it did. Bay squeezed her eyes shut as the memories she'd locked away began to surface, the sudden awareness bearing down on her, making her queasy.

"See, that's where you're wrong. You were just a kid, being a kid. The three of you, you did what kids do. How many times had Ethan and your cousins done the same thing?" Violet paused and took her mug from Bay when she brought it over. "Countless times. But we knew. We always watched, even when we let them think they weren't getting caught. Same with the three of you. Except for that night, because of my stupid mistake. We weren't paying attention."

Bay poured the coffee with shaking hands, added cream and sugar, then sat down close to Violet. "I don't understand. What happened that night? Why weren't you paying attention?"

"There were letters, Bay, ones I kept hidden here. Until your daddy found them that night."

"Marco wrote you letters."

Violet nodded her head. "He did. I never wrote him back, though. Not until then. That week, shut up in my little reading nook, I wrote a letter to him. All those years, after he sent letters, I did the right thing. At least that's what I told myself. I'd made this promise to God, you know? Perfect wife, perfect mother. And perfect wives don't return letters to their old lovers. I can't tell you how guilty I felt, when Marco asked outright about Ethan. If he'd known about the baby I aborted, he'd have been over the moon. It was his child, too. I didn't give him a choice.

"Anyway, you and Lillie and Scott, you were getting older. Scott seemed to become a young man overnight, and one day that summer it hit me. Scott was jogging down the beach toward the house, and I was standing on the boardwalk, not thinking of anything in particular. Then I saw him, and the first thought I had was *Marco*. As he got closer, he waved up to me, and I realized it was Scott. I also realized that Scott looked a hell of a lot like Marco when I'd first met him, but a little younger. I came in here and went straight to those letters. The last one he wrote me was in September of 1983, when I was pregnant with you and Lillie. He had come back to New Hope, just…I don't know, I guess just to revisit those memories. To check in on me. We ran into him at the football game that Friday night he was in town. Lord, I was shaking all over when I saw the date."

"Scott's not even a half a year younger than me and Lillie, so you would have been showing."

Violet nodded. "That was the last time Marco was in New

Hope, and I realized that's when Janice could have conceived Scott. That it was, in fact, possible that Scott was Marco's son."

"So, you wrote him a letter."

"I did. I didn't come out and say in the letter that I thought he may have a son, mind you, but I felt like I had to ask if he'd had any involvement with Janice when he was in town. It was a chance, you see? If Scott was his…well, then he'd have a chance to know one of his children. I thought maybe I could give him that chance.

"The letter was laying on my desk that night when your dad came in wanting to talk. I'd left it, trying to decide if I could even send it, and walked down to the beach. When I came inside, he was furious. He mistook my questions as jealousy over Marco, as an invitation into my life."

"Daddy didn't think Scott looked like Marco, too?" Bay asked.

Violet shrugged. "It hadn't occurred to him, and I was dodging it. I spent hours that night dodging it. We'd gone upstairs, and he demanded answers…how long we'd been communicating, if I'd sent other letters, where the letters were that I'd gotten from Marco…it was a disaster. I finally asked him to think back, to really try to recall Marco, what he looked like, how he carried himself, and to tell me if he didn't see him all over Scott."

"Did he?"

"At first, he brushed it off, said I was reaching." Violet laughed. "So, I reminded him how we'd run into Marco that night, when I was pregnant with you and Lillie. The timeline fit, and Janice insisted before she left that Scott's father wasn't a local, that he was an army guy passing through.

"Once he worked out the timeline himself, and I pulled out some pictures, Mel didn't have much of a choice but to see the possible connection. Then we fought over whether or not to send the damn letter, even after Mel tore it to shreds. I went downstairs and I got a bottle of wine. He brought up a bottle of bourbon. And we never came to a decision, whether or not to pursue it. We drank and fought and cried until we both passed out, exhausted. That's why we didn't hear…"

"But I heard you," Bay whispered, pressing a hand to her chest. "I shouldn't have been listening, but I heard you when I was walking by the door."

Violet covered her mouth with her hand and shook her head.

"I was scared, and so mad at you. I remember now. That's why I ran. I thought you and Daddy must be getting divorced," Bay said, looking at Violet with fresh pain in her eyes. "I wanted to scream. I wanted to run as far away as I could, and Lillie and Scott, they followed me, and so I went for the water..."

Violet let out a low moan that rose up into a sob. "Oh, Bay, I'm so sorry. I'm so sorry. I didn't know...if I'd been more careful. God, if I'd just left it alone."

"Oh, Mama..." Bay took Violet's hand and put her head on her shoulder. "That doesn't make it your fault that Lillie died that night. There was no way you could have known. And if I hadn't run off, if I hadn't gone in—"

Violet turned to Bay and took her face in her hands. "No," she said, her voice firm and low. "You listen to me, Bay Laurel, it wasn't your fault. Not for one second did I ever think it was your fault."

"But I did, Mama," Bay said through tears. "It seemed like you did, too, like everyone did. I wouldn't stop, and I told her to go away. I told her to get lost, and then—"

"I was the one who should have been looking out for her, Bay. Baby, it wasn't your job, it was mine. If not for that stupid letter, my wondering what could have been, we'd have been watching. We'd have been able to do something. Don't you see, Bay? I lost two children because of my own selfish need to save face, because of the lies I told to hold on to Mel, to this perfect life, so I could seem so perfect. And now you know. Your mama's not so perfect after all."

"I don't see it that way at all," Bay said, shaking her head. "What I see is someone who loves her family very much, and tried to do the right thing. You weren't being selfish—you were trying to do the right thing by Scott, weren't you? And Lillie's drowning...I guess we can both blame ourselves all we want, but we can't change it. It was a horrible accident. It was an accident, Mama."

Violet's sigh was a heavy, burdensome thing. "On some level, I believe that. But I think I'll always blame myself for being distracted." She reached out to touch the little butterfly Bay wore around her neck. "She meant so much to you, I know," she whispered.

"She still does," Bay said.

Violet closed her eyes. "And Scott…after Lillie's death, it didn't seem like the right time to say anything about Marco, about the possibility that he was Scott's father. I don't think Mel and I could have navigated that. I don't even know how long it was before it came up again, but we didn't have another real conversation about it until Scott went missing. Your daddy took it so hard. Scott's been like one of our own—well, you know that. We all love him so much, and everyone took it hard, I guess. But Mel took it especially hard. I noticed his drinking picking up a few weeks after we got the news, and I forced him to sit down and talk to me. He was grieving Scott, and also feeling such guilt for not setting aside his pride and helping Scott find his father. It was killing him, thinking Scott had gone to his grave not really knowing who he was, not having a connection to either of his biological parents. Mel lost his father at such an early age, and the idea that he may have denied Scott time with his own father, feeling like we were responsible for keeping that from him…I think it's been too much."

Bay sat forward, her elbows on her knees. "So now Scott is home, and we have a chance to make this right."

Violet nodded. "Yes, we do. Mel and I are in agreement on that, but not on exactly when or how to tell him."

"I see," Bay said.

"Bay, now that you know everything, I have to ask you to please give your daddy and me some time to sort through this and handle it together. I hate to ask you to keep things from Scott, but we need to be sure of this."

Bay stood up and walked to the windows. The sky was shifting to a lighter shade of blue, the sun promising to rise over the ocean soon. She pressed her hands against the cold glass. "How do we do that, Mama? When I called Janice, she confirmed Marco could be Scott's father, and given the resemblance, you have to believe it's a high probability."

"Well, I'd like to try to find Marco. Mel isn't sure that's the right thing to do. He thinks Scott should have that choice. But I don't know how we confirm, beyond a shadow of a doubt, that he is or isn't Scott's father."

"I won't say anything," Bay said, turning to Violet. "But I'm glad you told me. I'm glad you told me everything."

Violet looked up at Bay from the sofa, sadness pulling down the edges of her face. "I hope, now that you know the worst of it—the worst of me, I guess—that you won't hate me, Bay. I'm sorry to have laid it all at your feet, but it does feel good, having told the whole story to someone."

Bay knelt in front of her mama and took her hands. "I don't hate you. I've never loved you more in my life than I do right now, now that I understand some things a little better."

"I love you, too, so much. Please don't ever doubt it," Violet said, sniffling.

"So, what now? What's next?"

"I think maybe we get a little sleep, then go home," Violet said. "We both have some fences to mend there."

Bay handed Violet a pillow and tucked a blanket around her. "I'm going to walk outside a bit, watch the sunrise. You get some rest."

Violet grabbed Bay's hand before she walked away and pressed her lips to it. "Thank you, Bay."

"For what, Mama?" she asked.

"For coming home to me."

Outside, Bay thought through all her mother had told her that night. As painful as it was for all of them, all the secrets, all the heartache her parents thought might tear them apart, was bringing them all back together. For the first time since Lillie's death, the moment that broke them apart, Bay felt close to her mother. She had her family again.

Except for Scott, she thought.

What she still didn't know, and what scared her the most, was that Scott might find his way to the family he desperately wanted, and everything he needed…and that he would do it without her.

“LIBERATION”: NIGHT 4

I can’t sleep with her here. And I know she’s not asleep in the guest room, either. I can tell by her breathing. Even that irritates me.

I want to be glad she came, but I’m not anymore. She brought that place with her. She reeks of it. Wants to talk about it. All of my memories of her are tied up in Afghanistan. I can’t stay tied up in Afghanistan, and as long as she’s around, part of me is there.

The first time I met her, we were offering a medical clinic to a small village, and the aide organization she worked with sent her and another member with us. They were delivering notebooks, pencils, basic supplies for the kids. When I told them they could send the supplies with us, that we would deliver them and they could stay out of harm’s way, she insisted on coming along.

“Really, it’s important that we make a connection with the people,” she said. Then she smiled at me, and I felt warm from the inside out. We talked the whole way there and the whole way back. That was the start of it.

For months, she was the person I talked to the most. We became the best of friends. War zone friends. She’d seen almost as much as I had, and understood the culture, the people, the needs they had. She understood me.

She still thinks she understands me, what’s happening now. Because she’s seen it all and she has all the answers.

I don't want her here, with those eyes like the girl's. I don't want that war here.

"Scott?"

Dammit, I didn't hear her get up.

"Yeah."

"You can't sleep?"

"Bay hasn't come home yet." I'm staring out of the kitchen window, up at Blossom Hill. "I want to make sure she gets home okay."

Emerson sits on Grandma's stool. "You don't know if she is coming home, darling."

I glance at her. I can't look at her too long. Her face makes me angry.

"You should try to get some sleep."

I get up and walk to the window, lean against the lip of the old porcelain sink. How many times did Grandma watch for me out of this window? "I'll sleep when she's home, where she belongs."

She groans. She's aggravated.

"Go back to bed."

"Maybe we should talk instead. Would you like to talk about it?" she asks.

I don't turn to face her, but I see her reflection in the window. She crosses her arms over her chest.

"I don't need to talk."

"I think you do, Scott. Talk to me."

"Let me rephrase that. I don't want to talk about it. I know what you want to hear…yes, I'm having bad dreams, flashbacks, all the things you'd expect. I'm dealing with it. But I don't want your help dealing with it."

"Scott, please, let me help you—"

"I need you to stop. And I need you to leave. That would help me right now. I'm gonna deal with this in my own way, on my own time. I know enough to understand what I'm going through, and how to get through it."

"This is really about Bay, isn't it? You want to fix things with her, and I—"

"I don't mean to sound ungrateful, Em. God, I don't. But I'm not ready to go to that place, not in my mind, and not in my heart. All I've wanted, all these months, was to get home. Now that I'm here, I'm actually here…it's like it followed me here. And what we had, everything we were, it's a part of that time and place. Maybe one day I can get some perspective on it, but I can't yet. Home is what I need. To not think about it. And yeah, home is about Bay. Just like you're all tangled up with Afghanistan."

"You'll always come home to her, won't you?"

I don't answer.

"What is it about her, really?" Emerson whispers.

I stare out over the dormant fields, across the road to Blossom Hill, where Bay Laurel should be sleeping. "It's her heart, the way it beats in time with mine. It's the only comfort I had in that shithole, knowing I'm part of her heart. Every day, all I wanted was to get home, and I escaped somehow, in my mind…I relived some of the best moments of my life trying to get through the worst moments, and all of those memories I made with her. Bay Laurel, she's the best part of me. She has been my whole life, the one person left that I've loved every day since I can remember. And if I let her go now, I don't think I'll ever feel at home again."

Emerson drops her head to her hands. "I'm going to get a little rest. You should try to do the same. Things might be clearer in the light of day."

I hear her soft steps as she walks barefoot across the hardwood floors, down the hall to the guest room, where I told her she would have to sleep. Away from me.

"I'm sorry, Em."

It's all I have left for her. It's all I can say.

CHAPTER 15

Back in the quiet of her room at Blossom Hill, Bay stripped out of her clothes and climbed into bed. All she wanted was to close her eyes and drift off to sleep, but she couldn't stop turning over the night's events in her mind. And she couldn't stop her mind from drifting to Scott, and to Violet and Marco.

"Lord, Bay, you look a mess."

Bay cracked her eyes open. Lillie was sitting at the foot of the bed, grinning at her.

"Hey, Lillie," she said, yawning.

"Are you gonna update me?"

Bay swallowed, looked out the window. "I really don't know what to say. Me and Mama, I guess we just hashed things out pretty good. She's had to keep so many things hidden inside, Lillie…"

"So have you," Lillie whispered.

"I remember now," Bay whispered, tears welling in her eyes.

Lillie shook her head. Two butterflies fluttered up and landed in her outstretched palm. Twins. "And now you know it was never your fault, and she knows it was never hers, either."

"Lillie—"

"It's not important now, Bay," Lillie said. "What's important now is fixing things with Scott."

Bay groaned. "I don't know if I can. Everything got mixed up.

I guess I wrecked Christmas. The other woman is here, the one he met in Afghanistan. And she's staying."

Lillie closed her eyes and sat quietly for a few moments. "That's hard to believe. It's not right." She shook her head. "No, can't be."

"Well, tell that to Emerson," Bay said, her voice too sharp in her own ears. "She's the one next door with him."

"I don't see that happening. She's not meant to be here."

Bay got up and paced around the room, unable to be still with the emotional war raging in her heart. "I really don't know what to do about that. I don't know if I can win Scott over this time. But the rest, Lillie…the other part, about Scott being lost, not knowing who he is? I think now we know."

"Of course, you do," Lillie said, smiling. "But does he?"

Bay shook her head. "Not yet. And given the situation, I'm leaving that in the capable hands of our parents."

"Oh, Bay, you can't." Lillie flopped on the bed, sending up a cloud of butterflies. "It's been in their hands forever. If you don't get hold of this situation—"

"What? What am I supposed to do? Scott is with Emerson. Our parents are gonna come unwound if I put any more pressure on them. And I happen to have no idea what the hell to do about any of it myself."

"Here's the thing: I don't really care what Scott says he's doing with Emerson. You love each other. And you're going to keep circling back to each other 'til you get it right. So maybe the first thing you need to do is put up a little of that famous Bay Laurel LaFleur fight for your man. Don't run off with your tail between your legs because y'all ran it in the ditch. You're gonna have to work this out. For once in your life stop running. Stay. Try something new."

"Something new?"

"Yes, new, Bay. Not the same old. Something new."

The gears in her head rolled forward, shifted, and she pushed herself off the bed. "Something new with you…"

"You need to figure out what's right for you, really right. But it's for you to figure out, on your own. It doesn't matter what anyone thinks about it, Bay. It matters how you feel."

"Okay, yeah, I can do that," she said, her words rushing out and scrambling over each other. "I can figure it out on my own."

Lillie laughed, faded. "You need to write something…Merry Christmas, Bay."

"Merry Christmas, Lillie."

Bay grabbed a notebook and pen from her old desk, then snatched Sally from her case and sat cross-legged on the floor. So much had happened in the course of the last few days, this holiday could provide enough inspiration to last her years. She hummed the tune that was forming in her head, played a few chords, stopped, started, and did it all again.

She could certainly have written a song about Scott's being found, about the two of them coming together only to fall apart again. Emerson's stage-worthy appearance at the front door, the shattering apart of the pieces that were falling into place on Christmas day—that scene would work, too.

But her mind was somewhere else that night. The familiar pang of heartache was there, but it was dulled beneath the renewed hope she felt, the happiness peeking over the horizon, on the far shore of this ocean of uncertainty she'd been drifting over. All she had to do was find the courage to cross it, to steer them into something better, something that she and Scott could build together.

She wrote late into the night, not of heartbreak or loss, all the old traps laid out for her heart when she came to New Hope. This trip home had revealed so much to her, how stuck in place she'd been, living the same mistakes over and over again, because it was easier than doing something different. Finally, she saw it, at the end of this day that embodied all that was her past and what might be her future: it was time for something new.

Sleeping half wrapped around Sally wasn't what Bay would call comfortable, but it put a smile on her face to wake up with her old guitar in her arms all the same. She sat up and stretched her shoulders, wincing when a sharp pain shot up her neck. She took in the bed that was covered in notebook paper and colored pens, the product of an intense and productive night's work, and yawned as she got up to gather the loose sheets of music. She arranged them in a tidy stack on the desk and then settled Sally into her case.

It wasn't until she stepped out into the hall and found Scott pacing in the upstairs rec area that her mind rewound to the less gratifying details of their Christmas day together. She saw the turmoil in his face and winced again as a familiar note of discord thrummed in her chest. Turning quickly on her heel, she stomped to the bedroom, slamming the door behind her, in an attempt to avoid any further confusion between them. She wanted so much to run to him, to throw her arms around him, but she needed more time. If they were going to start over, it had to be with everything out in the open, and she still had work to do. Of course, she knew if Scott had bothered to show up here this morning, he wouldn't be deterred by a slammed door. She rolled her eyes at the firm rap of his knuckles on the other side of it, wondering how long he'd wait her out if she ignored him.

"Bay, come on," Scott said, his voice soft. He continued when she didn't answer. "Requesting permission to enter, Miss LaFleur."

"Request denied, soldier," she answered, staring at the white paneled barrier between them. She pressed her hand against it, wishing she could reach through and lay her palm over his heart, feel it beating in time with her own.

But she needed time.

"We need to talk, Bay," he started, hesitated. "This whole—"

She jerked the door open but didn't move to let him pass. "Who let you in?"

"Nobody," he said. "I walked over, snuck in the front door. Your dad's banging around in the kitchen. He didn't hear me."

Bay cursed under her breath. Her parents never locked that damn door. "Okay, we can talk. But I'd like to put some clothes on and brush my teeth, if you don't mind. Meet me in the tree house?"

He frowned. "That thing's still back there?"

She turned away from him to riffle through her clothes. "Yeah, far as I know, although it may be falling down. Anyway, you go first and see if it holds."

"Okay, if you say," he said, but didn't make a move to leave.

"What?" Bay asked, turning and cocking an eyebrow at him.

"I was thinking …we had some moments in here."

Bay felt her face flush and turned away in a hurry. "I'll meet you down there in a few minutes, okay?"

"Sure, yeah."

When he still didn't move, Bay shooed him with her hands. "Seriously, I need a minute without you staring at me like I'm, I don't know, your favorite old GI Joe doll and you accidentally pulled off all my limbs. Go. I gotta pee."

Scott snorted in reply. "You do have a way with words. See you out there."

Bay decided it was okay to make him wait—she needed time to put her thoughts in order for this conversation. She showered and took her time getting ready, bothering to style her hair and carefully apply her makeup. This would be the last time Scott would see her for a little while, since she'd already decided to head out as soon as she could pack up. This time, she wanted to leave him on a high note.

Her nerves hummed in her limbs as she made her way silently down the front stairs and out the door, following Scott's lead and taking a route that wouldn't put her daddy on alert. Scott's decision to sneak in was a wise one—Mel would have likely chased him out with a rifle if he'd found him out. Even though Scott and Emerson met when he and Bay were apart, Mel was none too happy about Emerson staying with Scott right there by Blossom Hill, rubbing Bay's nose in it.

As Bay made her way around the side of the house, she kept a close eye on the door and windows. When she was sure she'd made it past the thick stand of evergreens that separated the formal yard from the smaller play area, she stopped and let her eyes wander the space where she'd spent countless days wasting time in various ways with Lillie and Scott. The old swing set was gone, replaced by a newer model with monkey bars and a big slide. She watched as one of the last of the leaves fell away from a Japanese maple and fluttered on the wind. The line of azaleas and dogwoods that would be brilliant in the spring were now empty of color, their bare branches against the gray sky lending a desolate feel to the scene, as if to remind Bay to keep her expectations in check, that she still had to get through the rest of this season before her hopes could take root and blossom.

"Hey," Scott called to her from the window of the dilapidated playhouse. "You coming up?"

"Is it safe?" she asked as she approached the planks that served as steps, nailed into the old oak tree.

He nodded and held a hand out to help her in when she reached the last plank. They had to kneel to keep from banging their heads on the low roof of the structure, and Bay made a futile attempt to wipe some of the dust away, catching a splinter or two for her efforts, before she plopped down in the middle of the floor cross-legged. Scott followed suit, and they sat side by side in the stillness of the moment, each searching the empty space and cobwebs around them as if some shared memory might solidify and save them from the uncertainty of their future. Finally, Bay looked up at him.

"So," she said, "where to start?"

Scott stared out of the little window, watching a winter bird smoothing its wings on a branch beyond it. He took his time answering. "I got no clue here, Bay. Nothing's right and nothing's wrong all at the same time. How can everything already be so damn crazy?"

"Because we're making piss poor emotional decisions at the worst time possible?"

"I can't think straight, Bay. I'm sorry things got so messed up yesterday. When Emerson showed up, I—I don't know, it overwhelmed me. I'm overwhelmed."

"Last night took me back," she said. "Remember when you first told me about Emerson?"

Scott nodded. "I remember fumbling all over myself telling you about Emerson."

"Yeah, you did try to avoid it for the longest time, even though I knew something was off."

"Well, I wasn't sure I should ever even mention it. It seemed like the biggest mistake I ever made, until yesterday. Telling you, I mean."

"Yeah, yesterday would have been a hell of a lot uglier if I didn't have any forewarning." She nudged him with her shoulder.

"I thought I was doing the right thing at the time."

"I can understand that now," Bay said. "Damn, was it ever a fight that night, though."

Scott gave a weak laugh. "If my memory serves, you did most

of the fighting. I've never seen such hollering and breaking shit."

"And crying," she added. "You couldn't possibly forget all the crying. My eyes were nearly swollen shut the next day."

"I regret every time I've ever made you cry, even if technically I didn't do anything wrong."

Bay waved off his apology. "Truth? I should have seen it coming. We'd broken up. I guess I didn't expect you to move on, especially while you were deployed. I thought I had time to sort things out. And then you told me about Emerson...and it unstitched me."

Scott bowed his head. "I'm sorry. I didn't want to hide things from you."

"You talked about her like she was some kind of saint that night. I think, more than anything, I was mad at myself for not measuring up."

Scott took her hand in both of his and squeezed it. "I'm sorry if I made you feel that way. We were fighting. I'm pretty sure I said some things out of spite, but I didn't mean any of it."

Bay stretched her legs out in front of her and shrugged her shoulders. "Looking back on it now, I think the main thing I felt that night was scared."

"Scared? Of what?"

"Of what was next. Of trying to hold on to you, and of letting go. I'm afraid of what I've been afraid of forever, Scott. That I won't be enough. Especially now that my life is a complete mess. I don't know what's next for me, with my music. I don't know where I'll go. And I'm scared that I'll lose you, too. For real. Forever."

Bay felt Scott's eyes on her but didn't turn to meet them. She was terrified of what she might see there.

"Maybe you were right to worry before, when we were apart, but I promise you won't have to worry about that now," he said, his voice barely a whisper.

Bay turned then and searched his face, finally settling her eyes on his.

"What do you mean?"

He turned to the small window. The bird that had been perched there fluttered up from the branch and away. "Everything feels different now."

"Well, that's not surprising," she said, leaning against his shoulder. "Considering all that's happened—"

"I don't want to consider what happened," he broke in, his voice firmer. "I don't want to think about it or talk about it ever again."

"Okay, I get that," Bay started, "but maybe…I don't know. How do you even know what to feel now?"

"I can tell you what I know, Bay. I know that you get it, that you get me, and that we've been through just about everything together. This whole ordeal, maybe it was God's way of helping me see where I'm meant to be."

"And where do you think that is?"

Scott squinted, peering out over the yard, into the sun. "I can't go back there. That place, and those people—before, I felt compassion for them. Now…"

"You don't know what you feel right now. Don't try to rush your way through this, Scott. It'll take some time to get your head straight."

He made a weak attempt at a laugh. "Get my head straight? Yeah. My head's as straight as it'll ever be." He looked at her, reaching over to tuck a stray curl behind her ear. "But my heart…my heart wants to be home, and home is here. And here…I don't know how to separate here from you."

"Sure, you can," she said. "I don't live here anymore, remember? I don't much feel like I belong here, and I don't have to come around that often, not once I get myself together, get on my feet. And I can do that now, I think. You're safe, and I can breathe."

"You are a part of this place, and it's a part of you, whether you like it or not. And we're a part of each other. Maybe if you learn to accept who you are, you can figure out what to do with it."

Bay raised an eyebrow at him. He did know how to push her buttons, challenging her like that.

"Brad Singleton came by this morning," he said, before she had a chance to light into him.

Bay's forehead crinkled with confusion at the change of subject. "That was nice of him."

"Yeah, it was. He made me an offer."

"Offer?"

"Know how your folks deeded me the plot right by the pond a while back? He brought some house plans by, told me to choose whichever I wanted, that he'd build it at cost."

"Wow." Bay's eyes went wide. "That's pretty generous of him."

"Very generous," Scott said. "Bay, do you…" He looked past her, to the corners of the tree house, his breathing picking up pace.

"Do I what?"

"Do you hear that?"

Bay shook her head. "Hear what? What do you mean?"

Scott grabbed her arm and pulled her to him, then pushed her to the steps.

"Bees!"

"Bees?" Bay started down the steps from the tree house as fast as she could, still trying to see around him. "I don't hear any bees. It's the middle of—" Her foot slipped on the loose bottom slat, and she felt herself falling backward when the one she was holding onto came loose in her hands.

"Bay!" Scott called as she went down with a grunt. He leapt from the tree house and managed to land on his feet in front of her. "You okay?" He looked over his shoulder, his face twisted with fear.

Bay scowled up at him but accepted a hand up when he offered one. Giving him the weathered remains of the slat she'd pulled down with her, she brushed herself off and threw up her hands. "I'm so sick of ending up on my ass, literally and figuratively."

"Are you hurt?" he asked, walking around the tree, squinting up into the sun.

"Nah, my ass is fine, thank you very much. What are you looking for? A hive?" She thought back to the Christmas tree, the bees—the foreboding she felt then. It washed over her again in an instant.

"Listen, I didn't mean—"

"Scott, stop. Stop what you're doing," Bay said.

"What is it I'm doing?" He stopped and faced her.

"You're—I don't know, you're confused, and you don't know where to start or what to do about putting your life together."

Scott was peering up into the treehouse again, half listening to her.

"Don't try and rush us into a life you're not even sure you want anymore."

He finally turned to her. "Bay, haven't you thought about it, too?" Scott took a step toward her, his eyes on the plank he still held in his hands. He turned it for her to see. "I mean, look at this, Bay."

Bay reached out and ran her hand over their names. "That's what we were, Scott plus Bay," she whispered. "It's not what we are."

He dropped his eyes from her face and spun the wood in his hands. "Maybe it's what we still could be. What if we really made a go of it, Bay? Maybe all this is a sign that we could have a fresh start, right here in New Hope. Build the house, get married, start a family. We can even add a studio to the plans. Maybe this is how it's meant to be."

Bay crossed her arms in front of her. "Before you left this last time, how long had we been at odds, on again and off again, going in different directions, wanting different things?"

"Well, I've had a little time to reconsider my perspective. Haven't you?" Scott argued.

Bay dropped her gaze, unable to bear the desperation in his eyes. She wanted so much to say yes, yes to it all, to every bit of it. But first she had to finish what she'd started, and she needed to be sure that Scott was choosing her for the right reasons.

"You don't know what you want right now, I get that. And I get that it's all different, that you need to adjust. And what about Emerson? She told me she's staying. Whether or not that's the case, I think you need to get clear about your own feelings, and be clear with her. In the meantime, I need a little time to catch my breath."

"I know I need to straighten things out with Emerson, Bay. Nothing has happened between us since she showed up, I swear it. I came over today to make sure that you and me—that we're solid, if you want us to be."

Bay turned away, fighting the urge to fling her arms around him.

Scott held her by her shoulders and studied her face. "What aren't you telling me, Bay?"

"What?" Bay asked, still not able to bring her gaze up to meet his.

"I'm pretty sure that right up until yesterday, this is what you wanted, too. Something happened. You're hiding something from me. What is it?"

"Why would you even think that?"

Bay picked at a nail, then turned away from him. She wanted to tell him what Violet had told her, the possibility that he had family somewhere, family who would want to know him, that he'd want to know. That there was this huge secret that could change everything. But she couldn't tell him, not without knowing for sure, and somehow he sensed it. He knew her way too well.

"Good instincts, training. I can read between the lines. You're holding something back, something important. You seem highly agitated, and aggressively confused. There's some sort of disturbance, something hanging over your head."

"How can someone be aggressively confused?" she asked, internally cursing the irritation tweaking her voice.

Scott laughed, but there was no humor in his tone. "You're the master of it, hon. When you don't know how to make up your mind, or deal with a thing, rather than stepping away and assessing the situation calmly and forming a plan, you get mad at the world and go in full blast."

It infuriated her to hear him say that the one time she was actually being calm and making a plan. "I'm not mad at the world," she shouted.

"Then why are you yelling at me? I don't recall having done anything to incite your anger."

"You're taking that tone. Being a pro," she said, throwing air quotes at him. "And it gets under my skin. You're not allowed to interrogate me, remember?" She started toward the house.

"I'm glad to know I can still get under your skin. That's something."

"Scott, I—"

"Bay, stop," he broke in. "Don't talk anymore, please. Listen to me. I don't know what's been going on here, where you are in your head, but—"

"Do you think I know?" she asked.

"You can't just listen a minute, can you?"

She answered him with an extended silence. He stared past her again, put his hands to his head.

"Where are these bees coming from?"

Bay looked around again, listened hard. "Scott, there are no bees. I don't see or hear anything. Are you—Scott, are you okay?"

"No, I—Jesus. I don't know what's happening to me. Maybe you're right, Bay. I don't know. You're probably right. I'm no good for you now. Not like this. That must be it, the bees…what they're trying to tell me. I'm no good anymore."

Bay stepped forward and put a hand against his cheek. "I think you need some time. And I need some time. But listen, I'm worried about you. What's happening here, Scott?"

He bent down and kissed the top of her head and lingered a moment, his hands in her hair. Then he took her hand and pulled her back to the house, all the way to the front door, looking back behind them now and then.

"I gotta go. You're right—I need to sort some things out. Please remember I love you," he said.

"Scott, wait—"

He turned to her and flashed her favorite grin. "I'll be back, Bay. I promise. Don't worry, okay? Remember."

Bay closed her eyes and listened to his footfalls when he turned to go, listened as he picked up pace and jogged away from Blossom Hill.

"I'll never forget it again," she whispered.

CHAPTER 16

"Well, there you are," Mel said when Bay came into the den. He pulled off his reading glasses and tossed them down on the coffee table, then fell into the pile of throw pillows, rubbing the bridge of his nose. "I was about to come in there and check you for a pulse. Half the day's gone."

"Admit it, Daddy, you were really worried I might have thrown myself out of the window during the night." She plopped down beside him and picked up a cookie from his plate.

"Nope, we checked the front yard first thing this morning, just in case. Violet already checked all the bathroom floors last night."

Bay grinned at him. "Was Mama terribly disappointed when I wasn't all mangled in the bushes?"

"Now, Bay," Mel said, his eyes going sad. "Neither one of us could stand to see you any further mangled than you already appear to be. And anyway, from what she tells me y'all made some progress."

"Yeah, we did. Thanks for checking on me, but I'm alright, or at least I will be soon as I get myself together and get moving. It's time to get back to work, get some things settled."

He studied her face, his eyebrows drawn together with concern. "I hope you won't rush off too soon. This is your home, Bay. I want you to feel safe and welcome here."

"I know, and I'm sorry, but I'll feel better getting back to work.

I'm feeling inspired. I got a couple new tunes to get out of my head, and a few other ideas that could round out an album. Making it through that performance at the festival convinced me that I can still do it. No matter what."

"Well, we'll both feel better when I've given Scott a piece of my mind," said Mel.

"You just missed your chance, but you don't need to anyway," she said.

"What do you mean?"

"He snuck in here this morning. That's what took me so long—we've been outside talking for a while."

Mel's face went red. "That boy needs his ass cut, if you'll excuse the expression."

"Excused." Bay shrugged her shoulders. "Scott and Emerson, though…he didn't know she was coming, and he doesn't seem to want her to stay."

"Still, the fact that he even got involved with that woman…" Mel sat forward, his brow furrowed.

Bay considered telling Mel what happened at the tree house, but she didn't want to burden him with more worry. Not right now. "Yeah, well, we'd broken up, Daddy. We've both made some mistakes. His just happened to ring our doorbell on Christmas morning. Maybe you made one or two back in the day yourself." Bay cocked a brow and waited for Mel's reaction.

A deep blush crept up Mel's neck to his cheeks under Bay's scrutiny. "We're not talking about me and my past today, we're talking about you and Scott. Where do things stand with you two?"

Bay hesitated, propped her feet on the coffee table. "I've still got some things to figure out, Daddy. And you and Mama have to figure out how to handle some things, too."

"Bay, let me ask you something. Do you love Scott?"

"What do you think?" Bay answered, pulling her head up to roll her eyes at him.

"What do I think? Huh." Mel shook his head. "I think most people get it wrong, what love's about. Think it's all long kisses and gazing over candlelit dinners, holding hands, seein' nothing but the good in each other. People seem to think if it's not all sunshine and roses, it can't be the real deal. Truth is, that sunshine and roses kind of love is a lie. Love is getting slapped down, busted up and broken, it's hurt and disappointment served up by this person who doesn't quite match up to what you got built in your head about 'em. It's having your ass handed to you and getting back in there anyway, getting your hands dirty fixing it, because it's worth going an extra round. Love isn't real until it's really been tested. And you and Scott…well, you've been testing it your whole lives."

"I think we're failing this current test. Definitely failing."

Mel chuckled. "You say that right now because you're hurting, but you hurt because it's real, what you feel for Scott, it's a true thing, and that is one beautiful piece of pain, isn't it?"

"It is?" Bay asked, looking around her for an answer. "I reckon it is, if pain can be beautiful. But I don't know what I can do about it right now."

Mel rubbed at his forehead. "I need more coffee for this, I believe."

"I may need an IV drip today. It's been two long nights." Bay hauled herself up and led the way to the kitchen, where she started unpacking and washing the new Cuisinart coffeepot her mama had gotten for Christmas.

"Violet was intimidated by all the technology, I'm afraid," Mel said. "She wants to keep her old one-switch coffeepot."

"Huh. Well, I'll set the new one up and program it before she gets home. She'll be fine." With that, Bay unceremoniously dumped the old pot in the trash and set up the new one.

"Well, you might want to act a little more depressed when Violet gets home. Maybe she'll take it easy on you," Mel said, shaking his head at her.

"I'm helping her see the light, Daddy. She needs to embrace change. Besides, you can set the timer on this pot to have the coffee ready when you get up in the morning. She's got to love that."

"You better sell her on it hard," Mel said as she took a stool across the island from him.

"We'll see how long it takes her to get sick of our truce."

"You're not hoping it's gonna last?" Mel raised an eyebrow at her, sipped his coffee.

Bay took a deep breath and let it out. "Maybe. But you know, it's like you've said in the past, we butt heads because we're so much alike. I see the truth in that now. It's the stubborn streak that gets us in trouble. And the deep desire to be right about everything."

Mel shook his head. "I think I'll enjoy the peace while we have it." He visibly relaxed onto the stool.

"So, have you and Mama had a chance to talk?" Bay toyed with her coffee cup as she waited for Mel's answer.

Mel shifted forward again, flattened his hands on the marble slab between them. "We have, a bit."

"Did you come to any decision on—"

They both jumped when the door banged open. Will burst into the kitchen wearing his hunting gear and a panicked expression.

"Sorry, I should probably knock," he said, looking sheepishly in Mel's direction.

"Don't worry, everybody in town lets themselves right in," Bay said, rolling her eyes at Mel.

"Sit down before you bust a vessel, son. Everything alright?" Mel asked.

Will followed Mel's suggestion and took the stool beside Bay. He scratched away at a red welt on his arm. "Why's your phone off? I've been calling and calling."

"Because it died, and I don't have a charger in here, and I've been too lazy this morning to go plug it in. What's the problem?" she said, turning on her stool until her knee bumped his.

"You need to go charge it." He reached into the pocket of his jacket, pulled out a napkin, and held it out to her.

"What's on it?" Bay asked, taking it from him gingerly between her thumb and index finger.

"It was clean, and it was all I had in the truck to write on. Lucky you, your old roommate's still got my number. She's been trying to get hold of you. There's some music producer on your trail. Seems that little video I posted online got linked to a few news stories about Scott. Bet you can't guess how many people have viewed it?"

"Will, don't play with me."

"It's six figures, the views," Will added quickly.

Bay looked from Will to Mel, who was standing by the sink with his mouth gaping open. "Six figures? So, like, hundreds of thousands?"

"Over six hundred and thirty thousand, if you want to get real specific about it," he said. "One of those military guys they made a movie about? He saw it and posted it on his Facebook. Things took off from there. It seems you've stolen all of Sergeant Murphy's thunder, Bay Blue."

"And this producer who's been calling, who is it?"

"I don't know, some old white guy who maybe wrote books, Brent or Brandon or something," Will said. "Sounded like maybe y'all had a run-in at one of your shows before, but he's hoping to talk about this song with you anyhow," Will said.

"Brandt Thoreau?" Bay's voice hitched up a notch. After that night she got the call about Scott, when she walked off stage, she'd just assumed he'd never want to work with her. If she hadn't blown any chance she ever had to work with them that night, it was a wonder.

"Yeah! That's it, Brandt Thoreau."

"Brandt Thoreau wants to talk to me about my song?"

"Yeah. Now can you please call him before I itch to death? He's done ruined my hunt this morning." Will scratched at the fresh hives breaking out on his neck.

Bay turned to Mel, wide-eyed, and he slipped the cordless phone into her hand.

"Go get 'em girl," Mel said, nudging her off the stool.

"Thanks, Daddy," she said on her way to the den, then turned around and looked over the two of them as they followed her. "Better yet, I think I'll go up and grab my cell, make the call from the truck. Think y'all can wait inside?" She held the phone out to Mel and watched as their faces fell. "Good Lord, I'll be right back."

Bay jogged up the stairs and then down again, sparing a glance at her daddy and Will still standing around in the kitchen before she went out the door. She got in the truck and plugged in her phone, her knees bouncing while she waited to turn it on. When it finally powered up, she saw the missed texts and messages scrolling on the screen.

She laid the napkin with Brandt Thoreau's number on her lap and made the call. Two minutes on the phone with an assistant and she'd made an appointment with the man, but she put him off for a few days. There was somewhere else she had to go first.

In the house, Mel and Will followed her around as she threw things in her bags. She strong-armed Will into driving her up to the airport in Columbia.

She had to demand a moment alone, and when the two men finally relented, she sat down and wrote a note to Violet.

Dear Mama,

I'm sorry, I know it's not what you wanted, but this is something I have to do. I have to try, anyway. I hope you'll understand, but if you don't, I hope one day you'll forgive me.

Love,

Bay Laurel

"LIBERATION": NIGHT 5

Scott Jackson Murphy.
Sergeant First Class, United States Army.
Serial Number 224278972.

Bay's gone. She left. Everyone's been coming by the house all damn day long, checking to see if I'm alright.

It's for the best. God, if I was her I'd run off, too. Maybe it's because of Emerson. Or maybe it's because I'm out of my skull. It doesn't matter. At least I won't be able to hurt her anymore.

I sat Emerson down and I told her to pack up and go home, and to never look back. She wanted to fight me, but I made her understand. She won't get what she wants out of me. Nobody will.

Now I'm hiding in the tree house, counting the bees. They're forming black clouds in all the corners. The girl sits across from me. She stares at me, her dark eyes unblinking. She's the only one who sees me, sees what I really am. What I've done.

I have to sit very still, in the center, to keep count of them. If I can keep them all here, they can't follow Bay. She can escape from here. From me.

The only way Bay gets to have her life is if I keep her out of mine. Because this nightmare, it comes with me. And I can take it, but it would destroy her. I get it now.

Why can't somebody get me out of that room?

Water, fire, blood, or bone?

Fire was the worst. Makeshift devices for conduction of electricity are unpredictable forms of torture at best. Bee stings. A million bee stings.

I feel it now more than I felt it then.

But I can take the pain if she can escape from it. I'll let her get away to keep her safe.

```
Scott Jackson Murphy.
Sergeant First Class, United States Army.
Serial Number 224278972.
```

I know they wanted to save me. Truth is, nobody can.

CHAPTER 17

Bay stood on the sidewalk of New York Boulevard in Brooklyn, checking and rechecking the address she'd written on the outside of the folder she held in her hands. It was too cold for her—she was shivering even in the thickest coat she could find in her old closet at Blossom Hill. The air smelled of wood smoke and reminded her of sitting by the old Squire stove at Grandma Aggie's with cocoa and marshmallows on sticks. A part of her wanted to rush home, to the comfort of that memory. Instead, she braced herself against the wind and hustled across the street.

The red brick building in front of her was plain but tidy. A sign on the left spanned the height of its top four floors, listing numbers of bedrooms and square footage. A smaller, faded sign read CALL NOW FOR APPOINTMENT. Tucked around the corner was a small portico leading to the lobby of the building. Bay kept to the sidewalk, avoiding the spots that seemed slick with ice where the sun couldn't reach into the shade to melt it. She thought the bare flowerbeds might be pretty in spring, but now they were covered in slushy gray snow.

It was easy enough to find the call box and the number for C. Ramirez, but not quite as easy to find the courage to press the button. She crossed her arms over the folder and hugged it to her chest. She'd found a current address for Mr. Carlos M. Ramirez using a people finder site on the Internet. Bay assumed this had to be the address for Scott's grandparents, but now that she was here…

Maybe, she thought, it was a mistake to dig all of this up. She hadn't told her parents that she'd found Carlos Ramirez, and things were so fragile with both of them when she left. Plus, Scott was already dealing with so much—she couldn't be sure if this would help or hurt him.

Bay had no luck finding any information on Marco. This may not even be the same family. There'd been multiple listings for Carlos Ramirez around New York. But this was the only Carlos M. in Brooklyn, and somehow that M. made it feel right to her. This had to be them.

Breathe in. Breathe out.

She'd maxed out her emergency credit card Mel getting to New York. It didn't make sense to turn back now. Bay punched the button hard before giving herself time to change her mind.

"Yes?" A male voice answered after a moment.

"H—hi," Bay started. "My name is Bay Laurel LaFleur. I'm Mel and Violet LaFleur's daughter, from New Hope. I'm looking for a Carlos Ramirez?"

A few seconds passed, and Bay wondered if she'd lost the man until the intercom buzzed again and made her jump. "LaFleur? That's a name I haven't heard in ages."

"I'm sorry to drop in, but I'd really like to talk with you, if you have some time. It's about—well, I have some information I'd like to share with you. And I'm hoping you can share some with me, too."

Another pause. "Okay, come on up."

"Thanks," Bay said, not quite getting it out before the front door buzzed and she could open it. She hurried into the elevator and pressed the 4 button, then bounced on the balls of her feet as she ascended.

The elevator stopped and the door chimed as it opened onto a hallway with old hardwood floors and scuffed white walls. The dark gray trim stood out, especially in the places you could tell it was painted over previous paint colors. The fixtures were newer, though, she noticed, and the old hardwood floors gleamed. It was obviously well kept. She scanned the doors until she noticed one near the end of the hall was cracked. An elderly man stepped out and smiled when his eyes met hers. Bay found herself immediately at ease, sensing his genuine warmth as he waved to greet her. It seemed he was glad to have company.

"My, my, Miss LaFleur. You look so much like your grandmother, but I guess you know that," he said as Bay approached. He wrapped her in a gentle hug rather than taking her extended hand. Mr. Ramirez was a slight, graceful man. His hair was almost completely silver and receding a bit, but his thick mustache and eyebrows were an intense black. His dark skin was lined with age, but his eyes—the same forest green as Scott's, she noticed—danced like he was still a man in his prime.

Bay tidied her wild hair as best as she could and smiled at Mr. Ramirez. She liked him immediately. "I do get that a lot," she said. *And you might be surprised to find it, but you look a whole lot like someone I know*, she thought.

Carlos tilted his head to the side and studied her a moment before inviting her to come in and take a seat at a small table tucked beneath a window in the space between a tiny kitchen and living room. Bay was surprised how sleek the space was, with dark hardwood floors and bright white walls. The living room was tastefully decorated with a cozy red sofa and old wooden coffee table. There was a modern yellow chair near another window, and a bookcase stuffed with reading material within reach. The kitchen was also updated, with white cabinets and cement countertops. Both rooms were brightly lit, with coastal art scattered around on the walls.

Carlos moved around the space efficiently, pulling down two cups and heating water in a kettle on the gas stove that hissed to life when he pressed a knob beneath the burners.

"I hope you like tea?" he asked Bay, cocking a brow at her in a way that brought heat to her cheeks. She couldn't help grinning.

"I guess now I know where Scott gets it," she muttered under her breath, then answered. "Sure, tea is good."

While Carlos made their tea, Bay sat at the table, trying to keep her knees from knocking as she waited. They made small talk about Bay's family, the weather, and what she thought of New York. Her nervousness over the enormity of their upcoming conversation eased a bit under the warmth of Carlos's easy chatter. Bay wondered as they talked if he had any idea that his son had a short-lived, though heartfelt, romance with her mother…one that led him to New Hope, and likely to fathering a child with Janice Murphy.

"So," Carlos said when he sat down. "I can't imagine that you came all the way to Brooklyn to try my hot tea, Miss LaFleur."

The scent of peppermint warmed Bay as she sipped at the tea. She relaxed a little further into her seat.

"Please, call me Bay. I was actually hoping to find out some information about your son, Marco? I'd like to get in touch with him, but I didn't have any luck finding contact information for him online. I was able to find you, though."

When she mentioned his son, he shook his head and sat his cup of tea down. Bay's heart sank. "I'm afraid that's not possible, Bay. My son didn't make it home from his last deployment in Somalia. He was in the service, you see. Army, Special Forces." He bent over his cup, as if he might read something different in the leaves today. "I never thought we had any business over there, but was proud of his service, regardless. He was passionate about it. I guess I just…"

Bay reached out and covered one of Carlos's hands with her own. It took her some time to force back her own tears before she could speak. What a bitter irony it was to learn that Scott was so much like the father he wouldn't get a chance to know, that he'd even followed in Marco's footsteps. It would have been amazing for them to meet, to share stories and marvel at their similarities together. She'd held out so much hope that she might reunite Scott with his father. But it was too late. "I'm so sorry for your loss," she whispered.

Mr. Ramirez's smile returned but didn't quite make it to his eyes. He patted her hand with his free one. "Thank you for that. It's been a long time, though. We lost him in 'ninety-three. His mother passed four years later." He let out a sigh. "She never really recovered, you know? He was our only child."

"I'm really so sorry," Bay said. It brought on a fresh wave of sadness, imagining that Scott's grandfather had been alone for all this time. To think that he could have found some comfort in a relationship with Scott, that Scott could have found some common ground with his grandfather, was almost enough to make her run from the room and all the way to South Carolina. She fought a surge of anger at her parents for not acting when they suspected the Ramirezes might be Scott's family. It made her want to pound her fists on the table. How could she explain it now? She counted to ten and steadied her breathing before she spoke again. "It must have been hard, losing them both."

"It was almost unbearable for a time, but I have a sister here—in this same building now, actually—and the joy of being an uncle and great-uncle to many wonderful young people. Time heals, Bay. Miraculously, somehow, it does."

She nodded, pulling her hands away and placing them on top of the folder she brought with her. "I'm sorry I won't have the chance to meet your son."

"Why were you trying to find him? I can't imagine many folks around New Hope even remember us, we lived there for such a short time. I suppose your mother would, though. She knew him as well as anyone there would have."

"Well, Mr. Ramirez," Bay started tentatively, "I've got quite a story to tell you, if you'll hear me out."

Mr. Ramirez raised an eyebrow and settled back in his seat. "I love a good story."

Bay took a deep breath and blew it out. "There's a man I grew up with in New Hope. His name is Scott Murphy. The Murphys lived across the way from Blossom Hill?"

He nodded. "I remember, yes. Good people, wild daughter."

Bay shifted in her seat. "Janice, yes. Janice is Scott's mother."

"Oh. She settled down, then?"

"No, not exactly. She had Scott—well, I mean, she wasn't married or anything when she had him. And when we were still little, she left him with his grandmother and took off to California. No one knew who his father was—which is why he was raised a Murphy."

"Okay," Mr. Ramirez said, his brow furrowed. "So, this all happened long after my family left town?"

"It did," Bay said. "But, Mr. Ramirez, did you know that Marco—your son—he came back to New Hope once?"

"He did? When?"

"It was in 1982, when Mama was pregnant with me and my twin sister."

He grinned. "Twin girls, what a blessing. Do you have any

other siblings?"

"An older brother, Ethan," Bay answered, trying to stay on point. "So, Marco came through town in 1982." Bay opened the folder and studied the notes she'd made after her heart to heart with her mama.

"Marco went back to New Hope?"

Bay nodded. "He did. And he sent letters to my mother. I haven't seen those, but she gave me the gist. I've tried to document what I know so I wouldn't fumble around with it when I got here. This sums it up." She slid the notes over to Carlos and waited as he put on his reading glasses, then carefully read through the timeline and notes she'd made detailing Violet's relationship with Marco, and the contact they'd had after.

When he finished, Carlos wiped at his eyes, pressing his fingers beneath the frames of his glasses. "I had no idea."

"I don't think anybody knew except the two of them. Not until much later, anyway."

"Bay, are you here because you think your brother might have been my son's child?"

She shook her head. "No, sir, Ethan is definitely my father's son. I asked the same question myself when Mama first told me her story, but she's certain that's not the case. I do suspect your son might have had a child who grew up in New Hope, though. And I think that child was—is—Scott Murphy."

"But he was involved with Violet. Did he not go to see her?"

"Yes, he did, and…"

"She was a mother already, and pregnant with twins," he whispered.

"Here's where the story is a little more uncertain, because I'm filling in the blanks. And I was hoping your son could help with that. Janice Murphy was working at a local bar at the time Marco stopped over in New Hope. She didn't say who Scott's father might be, and—well, it sounds like you had an idea about Janice. I guess nobody felt it would do any good to press the issue."

"You think my son took up with her while he was there? That he had some kind of fling with her and then left?" Carlos raised his hands in exasperation.

Bay's face burned beneath Mr. Ramirez's hardened gaze. She hadn't meant any insult, but she could understand why he wouldn't want to think of his son as the kind of guy who had one-night-stands with barmaids. "I think maybe he was lonely, and a little hurt after seeing my parents with Ethan, and my mother pregnant again. And he went to a bar, and met a pretty waitress…things like that happen."

"Forgive me, Bay, but you've lost me here. How did you come up with this theory?"

Bay opened the folder again and took out the picture from The Owl's Roost. "We were watching some old footage from a football game. Marco was there, and…well, that smile of his, it took my breath. There was so much of Scott in it. And then I found this picture hanging up at our local coffee shop in New Hope."

"Ah, Marco's senior football team photo. Glory days." He rested his cheek against his hand as he studied the old photo.

Bay pulled another photo from the folder. "And this one is Scott's senior football picture."

She turned it and slid it in front of Mr. Ramirez. He glanced down at it, then sighed.

"It's…" Bay waited as he laid the photo of Marco beside Scott's and studied them side by side.

"You see it, right?" Bay said, since he seemed at a loss for words. "When I saw the picture, I had to at least find out who this guy was. That's when I started trying to find out more about your son, because I thought maybe he might be the key to finding Scott's family."

"How did you find out about Janice and Marco? Did she tell you?"

Bay lowered her eyes. "She did. I realize her word might not be worth much, but from what she told me, I feel pretty certain they had a…thing, when Marco came to New Hope. Knowing he'd been in town when Mama was pregnant with me and Lillie, and Scott's about five month's younger than us—well, the timing works out."

Mr. Ramirez took off his reading glasses and rubbed his eyes. "But still, there's no certainty."

"No, there isn't, but now that Scott's home from Afghanistan, we could find out for certain, if you'd be willing"

"Afghanistan?" Mr. Ramirez asked. "Why was he there?"

"He's in the army, Mr. Ramirez," Bay answered, reaching for

his hand again. "Special Forces."

Mr. Ramirez laughed then. He squeezed her hand before pushing his chair from the table. "This is too much. It's too much." He walked over to the window overlooking the little park behind the building, and a wistfulness settled around him as he considered what he'd heard.

"When I talked to Janice, she confirmed that your son might be Scott's father. But she said she couldn't be sure."

"Did no one else suspect? He looks so much like Marco."

Bay didn't know how to tell him that her parents had suspected, except to tell him straight and hope he'd understand the circumstances. At least he'd kept his back mostly to her. It would be harder to look him in the eye and explain it.

"It dawned on my Mama at one point that Scott strongly resembled Marco. I don't think it occurred to my dad or anyone else because your family moved so long ago…no one would have thought of it. Mama was going to write to him, to ask about Janice, but…"

"Huh," Mr. Ramirez came over to the table and stood behind his chair, squeezing the top wooden slat of its back with both hands. "But what? Why didn't she try to find us?" His voice edged up with anger, forcing Bay further back in her chair.

"Something happened," Bay said, closing her eyes and squeezing the bridge of her nose, fighting against the headache that was beginning to throb behind her eyes. "And it wasn't until 'ninety-four. August eighth, actually. The day that my parents realized there might be a connection between your son and Scott was the same day my sister, Lillie, died."

"Oh, no," Mr. Ramirez said, dropping into his chair. "Oh, Bay, I'm so sorry."

"Thank you," she whispered, looking up at him. The stress of the day, the converging of these tragic stories, finally caught up with her, and Bay couldn't hold her tears in anymore. "We were at the beach, and my parents—well, I guess they argued, trying to sort out what in the world to do. The three of us—me and Scott and Lillie—we slipped out to go for a swim."

She wiped at her eyes while he got up and grabbed a tissue box from an end table in the living room. He took one for himself before handing it to her.

"There was a strong undercurrent that night, stronger than Lillie. We lost her. So, after, I guess it didn't come to mind again for a while." She shrugged. "I don't know why, Mr. Ramirez. I don't know if it was some weird kind of denial, or inability to cope with anything else, but they let it go, or stuffed it down. We were Scott's family. He was ours. And I want you to know, we love him. All of us."

"You and Scott, you're close?" he asked, the obvious question there in his eyes.

"We are, but things are complicated right now. I let him down, Mr. Ramirez. I was hoping…well, maybe if I could help him find the family he wants so badly, maybe it could help him heal."

Mr. Ramirez picked at the corner of his tissue. "It was too late, anyway, by the time your mother realized," he whispered. "Marco was already gone, the year before."

Bay nodded. "It was. But it isn't too late for you now. You may have a grandson, Mr. Ramirez. And if you do, he desperately needs you."

"You said he's home from Afghanistan? He's safe? Was he injured?"

"He is, he's home in New Hope," Bay said. "And safe, yes. But…did you hear on the news about the Special Forces soldier who'd been held by the Taliban? He was rescued the week before Christmas?"

"Scott Murphy," Mr. Ramirez whispered. "His name was Scott Murphy. It just now clicked that he was the one…and to think…"

Mr. Ramirez let his tears fall unchecked.

"I'm sorry it's so much to take in all at once," Bay said. "But like I said, it isn't too late for you and Scott, if we're right and you are family. It's something he wants so much, to know who his father was, where he came from."

"For so long, I've grieved," Mr. Ramirez said after a moment. "Life's gone on, and I've tried to go on, but the grief is always there. But this…it's more than I've ever hoped for, to have a piece of Marco back, to have a grandson of my own."

Bay leaned in closer and took his hand across the table again. "I think you owe it to yourself to find out if you do."

"When do we leave?"

"Well, I have to go from here to Nashville for a couple of days, and then I'll go straight to New Hope. Thing is, I didn't tell anyone I was coming here first."

"Your parents don't know you found me?"

"No, not yet. And then there's one bigger issue that we should maybe sort out before you head into New Hope."

"What's that?"

"Scott. He's got no idea."

Mr. Ramirez took another tissue and wiped his face. "So, you're asking me to wait?"

"I know that's not fair of me, but if you can give me a few days…"

He gave her a quick nod. "I'll get things together. Maybe it's good to process this. It truly is a lot for an old man to take in."

Bay stood and he walked her to the door. "I'll be in touch with you soon," she said as he hugged her one more time.

"Please do, as soon as you can." He squeezed her hand. "Thank you, Bay."

She smiled at him. "No, thank you."

And as she walked down New York Boulevard with another piece of the puzzle in place, she didn't fight the new hope swelling in her heart.

CHAPTER 18

"Let me make sure I understand you."

Bay stared across the sleek glass coffee table at Brandt Thoreau. He was sitting on a low-slung white leather sofa that he seemed entirely too large for, sipping a glass of sweet tea while he took her in with a twinkle in his eye that reminded her of Mel. She couldn't help thinking he'd fit in better at her parents' kitchen table than in the upscale, modern high-rise offices of Thoreau Records, with his worn cowboy boots and jeans, the plaid shirt worn unbuttoned over a plain white tee shirt. You'd think he had ridden right up to the high-rise on a horse that morning. His handsome face was tanned, even in the middle of winter. Brandt looked like the kind of man who was constantly thinking about getting outside when he was stuck inside.

Bay sat up straighter, her hands crossed on her knee, and wished she'd worn something more casual than the suit she bought the day before to mark the occasion, which wasn't turning out to be quite the occasion she'd hoped. "You want to buy my song, for someone else to record? To hell with me, but you'll take my music…that's your offer?"

They'd been at it for an hour already, discussing the appeal of the song she wrote for Scott, what she'd done previously, what she wanted to do with her career, and what Brandt wanted from her. Which was just her song. Maybe more music, if she had more hits in her, but it wouldn't be her recording them, performing.

He wanted her to give her songs away.

He threw back his head and laughed, and Bay marveled at the way the sound of it reverberated around them as if the room had been designed and scaled to make his every attribute seem larger than life. "Really, Bay? You've been around long enough to know better than that. Listen, I realize this might not be the career path you envisioned. I have to wonder, though, if you've considered what it would mean to hold out for the big recording contract…the hours in the studio, the touring, months on the road. It's grueling."

"I get how it works. Like you said, I've been around long enough to know, in the trenches, trying to work any and every legitimate angle I could find to get a foot in the door at somewhere like Thoreau. But it never occurred to me that I might only be taken on as a songwriter." Bay took a deep breath, considering.

"Well, I hope you'll give it some real thought now," he said, taking a more serious tone. "I feel like I can shoot straight with you, Bay. I've done my homework. I always do. As a performer, you're talented, but inconsistent, and inconsistent won't cut it. As a writer, you're as damn consistent as I've seen. Every original I've heard from you is solid. I understand all the upheaval you've had this last year, but in my opinion, that makes this an even better option for you. Takes some of the pressure off, and it pays the bills—quite well, as a matter of fact."

She ran a hand through her hair and straightened, awkwardly crossing her legs at the ankle. "Scott coming home the way he did…it changes things. The last year has changed me in ways I couldn't have imagined."

"In ways that make writing songs for a label rather than for yourself a little more palatable?"

Bay held her hands up in front of her. "I'm still thinking."

Brandt rubbed his chin. "There's something else I'd like your help with, Bay, a special project I'm working on."

"And that is?"

"Did you know that I'm a veteran? Served four years in the Marine Corps. Didn't see any action myself, but my dad served during Vietnam. So, you and I have a little more common ground than I was aware of before."

"Oh," Bay said, sitting up straighter. "I didn't know. Does that have something to do with this project?"

"Yes, it does," Brandt said, nodding. "I've been working on setting up a nonprofit, one to serve veterans struggling with re-entry to civilian life. Did you know that veterans with untreated PTSD have a much higher rate of homelessness, marital failures, and medical issues than the rest of the population?"

Bay nodded. "It's infuriating."

"I agree. And I'd like to do something about that. I think maybe you could help me. And maybe, in time, Scott could help us, too."

Bay felt warm from the inside out as she processed Brandt's offer. Something inside her clicked into place, and it was all she could do to keep her seat. This—this was what she had been looking for, without even knowing it. She wanted very much to do something for Scott, for his brothers and sisters in uniform, and this was an opportunity to contribute through her music. She didn't need to hear more.

"When do I start?"

"Now, yesterday. I want you to bring in whatever else you've written, and I'll get you together with a couple of coaches to get you started, not that you need much in the way of coaching. But I want you to feel like a part of the team."

Bay tapped her fingers on the table, considering. "I need to hustle home and get some things straight first. Can we start after the new year?"

Brandt scowled. "You have a lot of work to do, Bay, and I expect the work to happen before the celebrating starts."

"I know, and the work will be getting done. As a matter of fact, I knocked out another song in the last couple days that's as good as *When You Come Home Again*, maybe better."

Brandt perked up. "Well, let me hear it."

She shook her head. "Not yet. I need to smooth it out a little."

He rolled his eyes. "You're gonna be the devil to get along with, aren't you?"

"Probably." Bay bit her bottom lip. "But I won't disappoint you. I'll work harder than you ask me to, and be better than you expect, but I need the next couple days. Then I'm all yours. Well, mostly. I—I don't know if I can be here in Nashville full time."

He tipped his head and studied her. "We'll work around it, if the next few months go like I think they will. Prove me right about you, Bay."

"Yes, sir," she said as he stood. She got up and shook his hand.

"Call in soon as you get back to town, and talk to Marla. She'll let you know when to be where."

They said their goodbyes, and Bay waited at Marla's desk when the woman took her phone, demanded the security code, and began programming numbers. She gave Bay a time to call in and an email address where she could send any questions she had in the meantime. Finally, Bay made her way to the hotel where they were putting her up, right on the same block. Bay changed quickly, sprawled across the bed and called Mel to fill him in on the day's events.

"Well?" he asked, answering on the first ring.

"Well," Bay echoed, "it doesn't look like I'll be the next big name in country music."

"Oh, baby, I—well, there are other labels, right? This guy obviously doesn't know his—"

"But," Bay broke in before Mel could get more agitated. "He did make me one hell of an offer, just not as a singer."

"What kind of offer are we talking about here?"

"He hired me as a songwriter, Daddy. I'm gonna be writing songs for Thoreau Records."

"And that means you'll be staying there in Nashville, then, even though you're giving up the performing side of it? Bay, are you sure about this?" Mel asked, his tone one of disbelief. He'd have never expected Bay to walk away from the stage, she realized, even after everything that had happened.

Bay scrambled for the right words to say. Her family didn't know about her trip to see Carlos yet, and that she was exploring options that would make it possible for her to be home in New Hope, at least part time. They didn't know she'd decided that her family—Scott included—would be her priority from now on. She couldn't let on about Carlos, not now, or her tentative plans. She didn't want to risk disappointing anyone if things didn't work out the way she was hoping.

"You still there?" Mel finally asked.

"I'm here, Daddy." She picked at a loose string on the bed spread. "I'm sorting things out. I know this isn't what I had planned, what I'd hoped for, but—things change, you know?"

"Ha! Do I ever," Mel answered.

Bay blew out a breath and rolled over to stare at the ceiling. "I think this is the right thing to do. I hope."

"Well, I want what's best for you, baby girl," he said. "But I do expect you to take care of me in my old age."

"Deal," she said, and then laughed. "Thanks, Daddy. Hey, is Mama there?"

Mel hesitated a beat too long.

"Daddy?"

"She's—well, she can't talk right now."

"What you mean is she doesn't want to talk to me."

"Give her a little time, sugar," Mel said, his voice a whisper. "She's just a little upset that you left in such a rush that she didn't get to say goodbye. And she doesn't know how to work that fool coffee pot."

Bay snorted at his attempt at humor. "Tell her I'll be back before she's had time to get used to me being gone again. I promise I'll be back soon, okay?"

"I'm holding you to it," Mel said.

Bay said goodbye, hung up the phone and tossed it on the bed. She took a deep, steadying breath and studied her reflection in the mirror. A few of her Nashville-based friends were meeting up with her for dinner, and they'd all be ready to toast her and listen to every detail of what had happened at Thoreau Records that day. They'd spend the night expressing equal amounts of excitement, pride, and envy, and she would come back to the hotel feeling somewhere between drunk and loved. But at that moment, all she felt was confused, and sad that she had to keep secrets from her family, and from Scott, when she was finally feeling close to them again.

Bay sat down on the bed and wondered at the odds of her eventual success or failure as a songwriter, not a performer. There was no way to know, really, how her work beyond Scott's song would be received. So many years had passed as she struggled, and with every year she knew the odds of failure ticked higher while the odds of success ticked lower, but it still hurt, thinking she might never reach her childhood dream of being a star. The music industry wanted its stars young, even in Nashville, and talent did little to secure a position in the ranks of the elite. Bay never once doubted her talent, but she did doubt her ability to "play the game," as Brandt put it.

And then there were the things she might be giving up to chase that dream any longer. Now that Scott was home, now that she'd mended some fences with her mama, Bay recognized what she could lose if she chose to stay in Nashville, to insist on performing. She thought over her last conversation with Scott, the uncertainty he was feeling. Maybe they shared the same sense of uncertainty, the fear that if they let go of each other again, it would be forever this time.

She jumped when her phone rang and felt around for it. Scott's name flashed on the screen. She waited three rings and then answered.

"That was quick," she said. "Daddy must have called soon as we got off the phone."

"What do you mean?" he asked.

Bay hesitated. "You haven't talked to him?"

"No, why?" he asked, impatience ringing in his voice.

"I was up here meeting with Brandt Thoreau, about—"

"Oh, yeah, I heard that might be happening. Congratulations."

She waited for him to continue, but he didn't. "Scott, why did you call?"

He cleared his throat and hesitated another beat. She could almost hear him trying to put his words in order. "I wanted to apologize for coming over the way I did after Christmas, for mixing things up again the way I did. I was a little out of sorts. I'm sorry if I misled you."

"Misled me?"

"All that talk about building a house, starting a family, you and I both know that's not what you want. I didn't want to leave that hanging out there with everything you've got going on right now, you know?"

Bay let his words settle before responding. "So, I guess Emerson's still there?"

"That's beside the point," Scott said. "But, yes, she is staying, at least for a while."

"Well, then, congratulations to you, too. I hope you'll be very happy." Bay fought back her tears, hoping they weren't heavy enough in her voice for him to hear.

"Bay, please, don't be angry. We—"

"I'm not angry with you, Scott." She let her thoughts tumble over each other before she continued. "I guess part of my coming home this Christmas was wanting to make peace with losing you, to accept that you were never coming home to me. And I guess I need to do that, but not in the way I thought I would."

"So, you're ready move on? I guess you were done with New Hope anyway."

"I don't know what moving on really means," she said, "but—" Bay stumbled over her words, trying to figure what it was that he wanted, or needed, to hear. "I guess it's time to let this go—to you let you go. So you can move on, if that's what you need."

She closed her eyes and imagined his face, letting the tears slip down hers.

"Listen, Bay, I want what's best for you. This is your dream—your music, it's what makes you, you. And you can't give that up. I'd never ask you to. Don't give up on your dreams, okay? I believe in you."

Bay could tell by his tone that Scott had rehearsed these lines, had practiced how to tell her to let him go. She could also tell that it was tearing him apart, being caught in the middle.

And she didn't want to hurt him anymore.

"I believe in you, too, Scott. Take care of yourself, okay?"

"You, too. Goodbye, Bay. I—goodbye."

Scott hung up, and Bay clutched the phone to her chest. She sat down on the bed as sobs shook her shoulders. If she let herself, she could accept his call as permission to forget the drama in New Hope, to leave it and him behind. She could let Violet and Mel continue to provide him a sense of family, or maybe tell him about the possibility of knowing his own. Hadn't Scott and Violet given her the okay to walk away from all of it?

She pulled her bag onto the bed, found the folder tucked inside it, and opened it. The folder was now full of information Carlos emailed to Bay, details about the son he so desperately missed. She hoped that he and Scott would have a chance to know each other, to build a connection…a family. A family that Emerson might end up being a part of.

Bay wondered how in just one day, she found herself confronted with the reality that she may have to trade in her old dreams and make way for newer, more modest ones.

She closed the folder and laid it on the hotel room desk, deciding to mail it with a note to Violet the next day. Bay decided she would leave that up to Violet now. She'd planned to go back to New Hope, to share what she had from Carlos with her parents so they could tell Scott together. But Scott didn't want her there now, and the last thing she wanted was to intrude if what he needed to heal, to be whole again, was Emerson. Even if the idea of it broke her heart.

Besides, even if she did the digging, even if she found Carlos, this wasn't her story to tell. This story belonged to her mama, and Bay needed to leave the telling of it to her. She'd have to hope that she was ready now to do the right thing.

Scott had been right in the tree house—home wasn't Blossom Hill, or New Hope. It was them. And if he didn't want them anymore…well, maybe she was homeless after all.

TREASON

Traitors.

Violet sits across from me at the kitchen table. She keeps reaching her hand across, like I might lean in and take it, make her feel better about what she's done. I sit back further in the chair, keep my back to the wall so I can keep eyes on everyone. Mel stands at the counter, staying out of the line of fire. He's so damn good at that. I can't stand to look at him anymore.

And the man to my left, Carlos Ramirez. My grandfather?

I guess I can see myself in him, but he's an old man now. Maybe if I'd known him sooner, met him when there was some fire in his eyes, like the fire he must see in mine. Because I'm burning up on the inside. Again. Right when I was beginning to think there was nothing left in me to ruin.

My grandfather. Maybe. And they knew all this time, or at least suspected. Eighteen years, they knew. It was my right to know, and these people I called family, they kept it from me.

"Did you ever plan to tell me if Bay hadn't been digging?" I stare at Violet hard, make her look me in the eye. She seems resigned to owning it.

"Like I said before, the day I realized there might be a connection was—"

"I know, Lillie. You noticed the resemblance, wrote a letter that Mel tore up. And then that night, Lillie drowned. I understand that wasn't the time. But you need to explain to me after." I glance in Mel's direction. "Would you like to help explain? Since you've known for as long as she has?"

Mel turns his gaze to the ceiling. Violet takes off her glasses and dabs at her eyes with the edges of her fingers. I tap my knuckles against the wooden top of the table and wait.

Violet tries. "I don't know when I even thought of it again, to be honest. It was so long before I could think straight at all, Scott. You were there. Here."

Control is a tricky thing. You have it one second, and the next you don't. Flip the wrong switch, and everything explodes, the whole world thrown into chaos.

It can be as fast as the flip of a switch.

My fist comes down hard on the table. "Tell me how it never crossed your mind again, that you might have an idea who my father was. How you looked at me every day, and it didn't cross your mind. Please."

I don't mean to yell. Or maybe I do. The one thing I've been trying so hard to hold onto—control—I've lost it.

"Scott, son, you need to calm down."

Mel takes a slow step closer to the table, his hands up in front of him. I laugh. What does he think he's gonna do?

What does he think I'm gonna do?

"Son? Don't you ever call me that again." I stand up and kick the chair behind me so that it bangs against the wall. I kick it again. My insides are boiling from the heat of my anger, and bile pushes up my throat. I could kill them both with my bare hands. Easily.

I have to get out of this house before somebody gets hurt. Somebody besides me.

As I jog the steps I know he's behind me—Carlos. I should talk to him. I know it. But I have to get away from Mel and Violet, from Blossom Hill, right now. Before I lose my mind.

"Running won't help, Scott," he calls, giving up on keeping up with me. I stop in the driveway and turn to him.

"Staying here won't help, either, Carlos," I say, since we're on a first name basis. "Not with them."

He walks toward me, his hands in his pockets. The kindness in his eyes takes the wind out of me, eases the burning in my gut, if only a little. I guess we've both suffered the same loss, at different times, in different ways.

"I get that. If I only knew the part of the story you've heard, I'd feel the same way."

"What is it I don't know? They had an idea of who my father was—who my family was. All they had to do was tell me."

Carlos shakes his head. "Life is never so simple, believe me. Tell you or don't tell you...what? That maybe you looked like someone they once knew? Give you that hope and take the chance that it would get taken away again? Maybe they could have made a different choice. I don't know. But I believe that the LaFleurs have tried to do their best by you. And that they truly love you like family. And family...well, our families are the people who hurt us the most sometimes. That's why we learn to forgive, to move forward."

I let out the breath I've been holding in. "So, my grandpa is a guru or something?"

Carlos shrugs, almost smiles. "Not quite. But I understand what a blow this is for you, to find out who your father is—or likely is—and learn in the same breath that you'll never have a chance to know him. Unfortunately, unless your mother had come forward with some information much sooner than Violet had an inkling...well, it was too late already. Marco was already lost to us."

"But I could have gotten to know you," I say, fighting the sting in my own eyes as his well with tears. He reaches a hand out and lays it on my shoulder.

"It's not too late for that, now, is it?"

I shake my head. "It's just—all this time. It would have been nice to know, you know?"

"Let's not spend too much time mourning the years gone by, son. It won't bring them back, and it won't bring Marco back. God," he says, letting the tears spill down his cheeks, "he would be so proud of you."

My shoulders shake and I let myself fall into the hug he offers. My grandfather. My blood and bones. Whatever tests we have done won't tell me more than I can already feel in my soul when I look at him. This man, he's my family.

All I know is that, right now, I'm spent, and I need something to hold on to. Or someone who will hold onto me. And he's here, and it feels like maybe my dad is hanging out somewhere with Lillie, watching out for me. Watching out for us all.

I don't know how long we prop each other up in the driveway. I finally pull away and wipe my face with the back of my arm. "So, where do we go from here, Pops?"

Carlos laughs. "Onward? I think we go on."

"I haven't been able to figure it out since I got home, the going on part. I don't…it's like part of me is here, the physical part of me. The rest…How do I recover the pieces of me that I left over there?"

He walks past me down the drive, waves for me to come with him. "I don't know, but if you'll let me, maybe we can figure it out together."

"But…does that mean you're staying?"

"Of course, I'm staying. Do you think I'd leave my only grandson alone here to get through this himself? Bay, she told me that you needed me. And besides, it's what your father would want. I packed plenty to get me through a few months. Violet was gracious enough to offer me their guest room, but if it's all the same, I'd like to stay where you are." Carlos studies my face, squinting against the sun. "You look just like him, Scott, you know."

"Actually, I don't know," I say, shaking my head.

He turns and starts walking again. "Well, I guess it's time you get to know him. I'll do my best to introduce you."

CHAPTER 19

April 21st

Dear Mama,

Have you ever been to the mountains in April? It's beautiful up here—everything's blooming. I'm up at this little cabin writing, and thinking. The time's been good for me. Maybe I'm blossoming in my own way, like Scott asked me to.

You've been on my mind a lot while I've been here, and the story you told me at Christmas. Mama, I want you to know this: you don't have to be perfect, and you not being perfect didn't cause you to lose Lillie, or anything else. People make mistakes, even when they're trying to do the right thing. Hell, I've made it a way of life. But you've got to let go of it. You've got way too much to celebrate in your life to live in a constant state of regret. I see now, how all the times I felt you were being cold, you were being careful. Don't be so careful anymore. Especially with me. I promise, you're not gonna lose me.

Did you know it can take years for an oyster to make a pearl? And the longer it takes, the more valuable the pearl will be when it's harvested, fully formed. I guess I need a little extra time before I'm ready to join the Pearl Girls club. Give me a little time, though, and hold on to that pearl you've got tucked away for me.

I'll grow into it someday. I will.

Watch out for Scott for me, okay? I think about him every day. And don't tell anybody, but I miss him every minute. Every time my heart beats. I wonder what's left between us sometimes, why it doesn't seem possible that we could be over. I guess, deep down, I know the answer to that. After all the memories we've made, the laughing and the crying, the heartbreak—after all we've been through together and apart, what's left between us is love. Maybe someday he'll remember that, too.

Does he know yet? I hope you don't feel like I just dropped everything in your lap and left a mess for you to clean up…but sometimes I wonder. It's just that it wasn't my story to tell. And I'm learning that, sometimes, I shouldn't just roll right over things, you know? You deserve a chance to close that loop, to have some closure.

Don't you go missing me, now. Keep the radio on. You never know when they'll be playing my song…even if I'm not the one singing it.

With love,

Bay Laurel

"LIBERATION": NIGHT 127

Carlos sits across the counter from me, watching me with eyes that are too much a reflection of my own. He sips his tea, sighs. I give him the hardest stare I can muster.

"You can go back to bed now."

"Rather not," he says. He settles in, keeps his eyes on me.

"I don't hear them anymore."

"Do you want me to check again, before we turn in?"

I lean against the counter, lean over him. "We both know they're not there."

"Yes, we do. There are no bees in the house. No dead child. No one is here but you and your old gramps."

Deep breath. Another. "Tell me a story."

Carlos goes to his room and comes back into the den, where I've moved to sit, shoulders straight, hands resting on my knees, in Grandma Aggie's favorite chair. He returns and makes himself comfortable on the sofa. There's a letter in his hands, from my father, from one deployment or another. He slides his reading glasses up before he begins, clears his throat.

I close my eyes and listen, let the voice of my grandfather—my *grandfather*—take me to Iraq, 1991...and for a few moments, I am by my father's side. When I was there, was he somehow with me, like Lillie in Afghanistan? I can't help but wonder...maybe he's been with me all along. That little voice in my ear, guiding me through the worst dangers. Encouraging me in my darkest days. Pushing me forward when I was close to giving up. Suddenly I can feel him all around me. Because, of course. He's always been with me.

But this is the only introduction we'll get, a secondhand telling of his stories, so eerily similar to my own. Carlos tells me all the time how very much I'm like my father. It's a loss we share now, a bond.

"Read it again," I say when he finishes.

He starts over. Again and again, he does this for me at night. I've tried to make him leave, to tell him he doesn't need to be here. He refuses to go, says he's lost a son, won't lose a grandson, too.

My grandfather has brought my father home to me, through his memories, and these letters he saved. When I try to thank him, he shakes his head and thanks me for bringing his son home to him, too.

Somehow, we are healing each other. Bay's parting gift to me, a homecoming.

God, I miss her. But I can't ask her to see me through this. I'm honoring this gift from her the best way I can. I'm letting her go.

CHAPTER 20

Bay arrived early to the Fourth of July party at Blossom Hill, but she didn't figure it would matter much since she wasn't invited, exactly. The call she'd gotten from Leigh Anne the week before was cryptic at best, and her first instinct was to blow it off. But Leigh Anne never called her, ever, and for her to be the first person to reach out to Bay from home in months...well, something was up.

She pulled her rental car into the drive and bumped her way up the lane. It was right before lunch, about the time when guests would start arriving to set up picnics and games on the front lawn, unfurling blankets to save their favorite spots before the men put on the fireworks show. Bay parked near the barn and leaned against the car, waiting.

"Do you remember, that last Fourth of July on Edisto?" Lillie asked her.

Bay stared down at the dirty bare feet crossed beside her, the familiar butterflies dancing around Lillie's legs. "I do. It was the one time Mama and Daddy let us go down to the marina on our own."

"That was the first time you and Scott kissed."

Bay looked at Lillie, wide-eyed. "How did you know?"

"I wasn't completely dumb, Bay," Lillie said, rolling her eyes. "Besides, when he pulled you around the side of the dockside restaurant I couldn't help peeking."

"It took me totally by surprise," Bay said. She remembered every detail of that kiss, how nervous she was when Scott took her hand, his fingers gentle on her face, the way he tasted…mango and honey. She smiled at the thought of it. "I kept thinking he didn't realize he'd grabbed the wrong sister."

"Silly Bay," Lillie said. "It was always you. And it always will be."

"I've wondered since the first time I saw you here, Lillie…why don't I see you at Edisto?"

Lillie closed her eyes. "Because, as much as we all love Edisto, we eventually come home, to Blossom Hill. This is home to my soul, on this side. And now it's almost time."

Bay watched as one of Lillie's butterflies drifted close to her, then disappeared. "Time for what?"

"You know how I told you once that things keep repeating until you get them right, until you learn your lesson?"

"I remember," Bay said, nodding.

"Everything is coming full circle now. You'll see…but you have to open yourself to it, Bay. Let this be the last time you and Scott have to find your way back home to each other."

☆ ☽ ☆

"Bay, is that you?" Leigh Anne stood on the front porch, her hand shading her eyes.

Bay lifted her hand and waved. "Hey, Leigh."

They met in the middle and shared an awkward hug. "How was your trip?"

"It was fine, but the airport was a madhouse. Can you tell me now why I'm here?"

Leigh Anne sighed as they walked up onto the porch. She pulled Bay to the corner and looked around, making sure no one was in earshot. "You're here because Scott needs you here, but he'd never admit it in a million years. Now he's not here, and you are, so my little plan is shot to shit."

"Where is he?"

The screen door swung open, and Violet stepped out. When she saw Bay and Leigh on the porch, she let out a whoop.

"Bay Laurel LaFleur, what in the name of all things holy took you so long?" Violet flew at Bay and flung her arms around her. "We've been waiting for you."

Bay scrunched her face, turning from Leigh to Violet. "I thought nobody knew I was coming."

"I didn't, but I've been waiting since you left," Violet, said, then looked to Leigh. "What, did you?"

"Okay," Leigh started, "so I know we all agreed not to interfere, but somebody had to call her, or her stubborn ass would have never come home from Nashville. And now she's here. So y'all need to talk."

Leigh Anne scurried across the porch and into the house under Violet's icy stare.

"Really, sometimes I don't know with her," Violet said, still watching the door after it slammed.

"Mama, what's going on?"

Violet turned to Bay and took her face in her hands. "How are you, honey? Are you okay? How is Nashville?"

"I'm fine, I'm okay, Nashville's fine. Why did Leigh call me? And if you needed me, why didn't you call me?"

Violet let her breath out in a huff. "Let's sit down a minute, shall we?" She took a rocker, and Bay took the one beside her. "When you left right after Christmas, Bay, I was livid with you. I guess we all felt like the writing was on the wall, that if you had an opportunity to get out of here, you'd take it."

"But that wasn't what I was doing at all."

"Yes, dear, I know that now." Violet rolled her eyes. "When I got that package in the mail from you, Lord, I almost left for Nashville that instant to bring you home. You can thank your daddy for stopping me. I felt awful for refusing to speak to you when you'd called to tell us your news. I'm so sorry I reacted that way. I should have been excited for you, supportive for once. But I was so hurt that you left the way you did. If I'd known at the time why you had, or that you were planning on coming home before you made any decision…"

Bay threw up her hands. "So why didn't you call me when you realized it, Mama? Or after I wrote to you?"

"Mel and I had a long talk about it. We went through everything you sent us from Carlos, and we realized how foolish we'd been, both of us. Scott deserved to know who his father was, and here we'd been all these years sitting on it." She put a hand to Bay's cheek. "If we'd been brave enough to do what you did, Bay, when you went to New York…if we'd been brave enough to do that years ago, when we first realized the possibility, Scott and Carlos would have had so many more years together, but at least they have each other now. And Scott has a great aunt, and cousins."

"Wait, wait, wait," Bay said in a rush. She stood up and moved to face Violet. "They had the tests done? It's confirmed?"

"It sure is." Carlos stepped up onto the porch, grinning at Bay. "Hello again, Bay. It's so nice to see you home."

Bay stared and him, her mouth hanging open. "You're here?"

He laughed. "I came as soon as Violet called me, back in January. I've been staying over at Scott's since. We needed each other, you see." He approached her, then wrapped her in a hug. "Thank you so much, Bay, for giving me my grandson. I can't tell you what it means to me."

"Wh—what's happening here?" Bay stammered as Mel and Will joined them on the porch, coming over to hug her, too. "I'm having a little trouble catching up. Are y'all mad at me or not? And if you're not," she said, holding Mel by the shoulders, "why the hell hasn't anybody called me about this? And if you are…well, then what's wrong with y'all?"

Violet laughed. "Okay, Bay Laurel, let me try to summarize for you. Mel and I talked it over, and we decided that you'd done the right thing when none of the rest of us could figure out how. You just did it. So, we had to follow through and get Carlos here, and tell Scott what we knew."

"And let me tell you," Will said, "Scott wasn't happy with them, or anybody, really. Not one bit. He wouldn't even talk to me until Carlos worked on him a while, and I didn't have anything to do with this mess."

"And I'm so grateful to Carlos here for helping us all work through that, because Lord knows we didn't intend…well, we didn't intend to do any harm," Violet said. "We all—your daddy and Scott and me—we talked about whether we should call, see about getting you home, after things settled a bit. But Scott insisted we let you be. We'd all told you to stay in Nashville. So, he told us we all needed to let you go do what you needed to do, and let you decide when, and whether, you wanted to come home. He needed some time, too, to...well, he's been dealing with his own feelings, I guess. It's been a rough patch for him, but he's some better. And after everything that happened, we all thought maybe it was best to give you some space." Violet reached for Bay's hand and squeezed it. "Scott was right, we all need to respect your choices. And we're so proud of you. I hope you know that."

Bay squeezed Violet's hand back. "Thank you, Mama. And Scott was right, I needed to decide what's best for me. I'm glad Leigh Anne called me, but I was on my way home soon anyway. You should know that."

"You were already planning to come home?" Violet put her hands on her hips.

Bay nodded. "I've had a lot of time for thinking, and the writing..."

Mel put an arm around her. "It wasn't going well?"

"No, actually, it's been fantastic. It's the best stuff I've ever written."

"I don't understand, then," Violet said. "If it's the best you've ever written and it's going that well, why would you want to leave Nashville now?"

"After everything that happened when Scott came home, I buried myself in the music, you know? I let myself get lost in it and create. All the love and the heartache and the pain, I bled it out. And it's great stuff. It helped me figure some things out. I can't keep running away because I'm afraid things won't work out the way I want them to. Truth is, if I can't get over being so damned scared of what I really want, then I'll never know. So, I'm here, and I'll be staying, soon as I get all the details worked out. I'll catch y'all up later, though. Now, where is Scott? With Emerson somewhere?"

Violet looked up at Mel, and he nodded at Carlos.

"He's down at Edisto, alone," Carlos finally answered. "Emerson was gone before I came down. All I know about that is what he told me, which was that she didn't belong here. He's been spending a lot of time on The Witch Hazel. And he didn't want to be around a crowd of people today."

"We gave him the boat," Mel said. "He wanted it, and none of us used it."

"He's down there alone?" Bay asked.

"Yes, he is. He's been spending a lot of time alone, keeping to himself," Will answered.

"We're worried about him, Bay," Violet said.

"He seems better most of the time," Carlos added. "But he doesn't talk to anybody much. We all know he's going through a hard time, but he's made up his mind to handle it on his own terms. None of us can get through. I help as much as I can, but…"

Bay nodded her head, bent to kiss her mama's cheek, then kissed Mel's and Carlos's. "I'll be back," she said, making her way down the steps.

"Where are you going?" Violet asked, following her.

"I'm going to get Scott," Bay said. She looked at them before she got in the car. "He's been saving me my whole life. He really is my hero, you know. But now it's my turn to do the saving. It's time he left Afghanistan behind him. Maybe we can't fix it, but we can see him through it. He's coming back home, with me."

CHAPTER 21

The marina was bustling with activity when Bay pulled in, making it difficult to find a place to park and avoid running over anyone. It was late afternoon on July 4th, and there would be a party and fireworks later. She grabbed her overnight bag and Sally from the back of the car, locked it, and made her way to the docks. A warm breeze cut through the smell of salt water, festival food, and the lingering warmth of the day. Although Bay wasn't entirely sure Scott would be on the boat for tonight, it was more likely than him being at the house or out at a club. But maybe he had a party to go to, or a date, or maybe he'd gone somewhere else altogether. About the time she stepped up to the boat slip, it occurred to her that she hadn't really thought this through, but then she heard music from below and smiled to herself as she made her way aboard.

Breathe in. Breathe out.

"Scott," she called through the open hatch. "Are you down there?" She heard a loud thump, then heard him swear, and tried not to laugh. "Are you alright?"

"Bay?" He came into view, peering up at her while rubbing his left elbow, eyebrows drawn together either in pain or confusion. "What are you doing here?"

"July 4th. I thought I'd catch the fireworks."

He wiped a hand across his forehead. "Happy Fourth. Now get

the hell off my boat."

Bay buckled a little under his harsh gaze, but she willed herself to stand her ground. "You haven't returned my calls."

"I've been busy," he said with a smirk. "And I figured you were, too."

Bay crossed her arms and snarled her response. "Well, I was making time to talk to you, and I did come all the way here to see you. So, I guess that makes one of us too busy for the other one. Although from what I hear you're not very busy at all."

Scott came up the steps to the deck and stood in front of her, hands on his hips, green eyes flaring. "I didn't know what to make of it, you calling me, and I didn't know what you'd have to say, or whether I'd want to hear it. And I figured if it was important…"

"I'd come home? Well, I did."

"Because you wanted to, or because you didn't have a choice?"

Bay reached out a hand and shoved his shoulder. "Why are you being such a pain in the ass?"

Scott gave her a gentle push with one finger in response. "I'm not the pain in the ass in this equation, not by a long shot."

"Scott—don't." Bay hated how her voice twisted with pent-up emotion, but she didn't want to fight. She sat down hard on the side of the boat and covered her eyes with her hands, pushing against them to try and hold in her tears. Scott's arm brushed hers as he sat down beside her, and he bumped her knee with his. "Hey, no crying on my boat. It's a rule."

Leaning into him, Bay worked at steadying her breathing and managed to hold the tears in. "Sorry," she said, "I seem to be doing that a lot lately, and it's really not my thing."

"Okay," Scott set, letting out a long, slow breath. "Okay, let's start this over. I need to thank you, Bay. I know what you did, finding out about my father, and eventually finding my grandfather. It means more than you know. But I didn't want to use that as an excuse to reach out to you, because I knew I'd try to hold on."

Bay took Scott's hand. "Would that have been such a bad thing?"

"I know it's been a busy time for you, with the new gig and all, adjusting to being a bigshot around Nashville. I've been busy trying to adjust here, myself."

She narrowed her eyes at him. "Who said I'm a bigshot, or that that's all that's been on my mind?"

"Well, it appears to me—"

"Why does everybody assume I'm all about me all the time?" Bay bounced to her feet and walked the short length of the boat before spinning on him. "You don't even know half of what's been going on in my head, or a quarter, really, since the last time we talked. A lot *has* happened, but not what you think."

"Okay, okay." Scott held his hands up in front of him, squinting against the setting sun. "Tell me what's happened, then. What's got you so fired up?"

"Well, for one, I've had my head down writing. And writing is hard, but it's also cleansing. I couldn't write one line when you were gone, then it all came pouring out. And thank the Lord, because it helps me work things out. This time around, what I've worked out looks a lot different than what I thought it would."

"How so?" he asked.

"As it turns out, while I am an excellent writer of songs, I'm not really into the 'mover and shaker' thing. And Brandt doesn't mind me working outside of the office. So, I'm making some adjustments to my living arrangements, now that I've settled in at Thoreau." She watched as surprise registered on his face and couldn't hold back a smile at the way his eyes sparked.

"What does that mean?" he said as she sat down again. Bay edged in close to him as the sun dropped lower. "Are you actually cold?" he asked.

"Yeah, a little."

He laughed and ran down for a blanket, wrapping it around her shoulders when he came back.

"What that means is, I'm a songwriter. Just a songwriter. And songs can be written anywhere," she said. He sat down and turned toward her.

"Am I happy about this, or not happy about this?"

"I think happy," Bay answered, nodding. "Definitely happy."

"You know, I heard there's a position open for a music teacher at the elementary school in New Hope, if you were looking for an old new place to live or anything." He took her hand, his eyes full of expectation as he studied her. The hope in his eyes warmed her from the inside out, and she moved closer to him.

"There was, I heard."

Scott shook his head and let it drop forward, staring at his feet. "I guess somebody already got hired, then."

"You're right, somebody did. Me."

He looked up at her, eyes wide. "You?"

"Me," she said, grinning at him. "They didn't have a whole lot of applicants, and I figured it'd be a good way to settle in, working at the school. Plus, I'll have time to write, and time to work on a little project for us, a partnership."

"Project?"

"I'm working on ideas for a nonprofit, a re-entry program for wounded soldiers that includes a support system for their families."

"You—you're doing that?" Scott whispered, his voice thick.

Bay shrugged, trying to downplay it. "I can't take much credit. It's Brandt's idea, and he's got his people handling most of the research and planning. Anyway, I'm gonna be working on fundraising and sponsorships soon. It'll help to be a little closer to Fayetteville, so we can work face to face with the folks at Bragg sometimes rather than on video calls."

Scott ran a hand through his hair, which was getting longer than he'd kept it since high school. "All this time, I thought you must be so pissed at me, pushing you away, and you've gone and done something…wonderful. You never cease to amaze me, Bay."

She laughed. "Like I said, it's Brandt's brain child. I'm only helping out. It's been good for me, though. It means something to me. Because of what you mean to me. It's more than that, though. It's…more. If you get me."

"So…you're coming home?"

"I'm coming home," Bay beamed at him. "And you're coming with me."

"This is—I—"

Bay took his hands between hers. "Scott, I understand that you're struggling. I think I've felt your struggling in my soul all this time. Whatever you have to go through, to get through, we're doing it together from now on."

Scott moved her hands between his. "I don't know if you'll feel that way once you know the truth, Bay."

"What's the truth?"

"I see things, hear things…I wake up and I'm back there, chained to a wall. Flashbacks. Then things that aren't flashbacks, more like bad dreams, in the daytime. I can't be in a crowd. All I want is to forget, to move on with my life, but all I do is remember."

"Do you remember the first time you kissed me?"

He smiled. "July Fourth, eighteen years ago today."

Bay leaned in to kiss him, and then let her head drop to his shoulder. "Full circle," she whispered.

"What?" He asked, wrapping an arm around her protectively.

"Full circle…all these years we've been on this journey, and we're right here where it started."

"Hmmm…"

"When you're getting lost in the dark memories, I'll lead you back to the light. We'll make new ones, better ones. I'm sorry I left you before. It won't happen again."

Bay held quiet to let him think, enjoying the warmth of his arm around her, the feel of his strong shoulder against her cheek. "Are we starting again, Bay Blue?"

"Is that what you want?" she whispered.

Scott pressed his lips against her hair. "You know it's what I want, but are you sure this is what you want? You can still go back to Nashville. If you're giving up your life there because you don't think you can make that work and us work, too…"

She turned to him, but his face was unreadable as night fell around them. "I've had plenty of time to think this through, Scott. And I even wrote a song to tell you how I feel about it."

"Really, now?"

"Yes, really." She broke away and pulled Sally from her case.

"Another song for me?"

"For us," Bay said, smiling at him. She strummed her guitar, and hummed quietly for a few minutes. "You wanna hear it first?"

"Oh, this is the virgin voyage for your new tune?" he asked, eyebrows raised. Bay couldn't help but laugh.

"You could say. I was waiting because I wanted you to hear it first." She continued to play the tune as he watched her, and then finally began to sing.

She played a few extra bars at the end before setting Sally

aside. "It's not really done yet, but that's what I got so far." She found herself shifting beneath his steady gaze, wishing she'd held off a little longer on sharing the song when he didn't respond right away.

"Bay," he said after a moment, "what a beautiful, beautiful creature you are."

She smiled and let her eyes meet his. "Yeah, but how did you like the song?"

"I've known you forever and a day, and still, you surprise me."

"Good. Now, next time you decide to write something, make it about me," Bay said, laughing.

He crossed the short distance between them and pulled her to her feet, his eyes locked on hers. When he bent to kiss her, letting his lips barely brush against hers at first, it felt to her like a prelude and an ending all at once. She pulled away from him and took his face in her hands, struck again by how unreadable he could be.

"What is it?" she asked, rubbing her thumb over his bottom lip.

"I love you, Bay Laurel LaFleur. I've loved you my whole life, even when you thought I didn't. Even when I didn't want to. And I will love you for the rest of my life, but I promise you, I'll love you better than before. Like you said with your song, let's do something new…let's do this right."

"I love you, too, Sergeant First Class Scott Jackson Murphy."

"Oh, yeah, something else that's new…can you deal with being Mrs. Ramirez?" Because I'm a Ramirez. Scott Jackson Murphy Ramirez."

"Wow," Bay, laughed. "Was that a proposal, then?"

Scott scrunched up his face and peered up at the sky. "I do believe it was. But wait." He dropped down on one knee and took her hands in his. "Marry me, Bay. Be my wife. You and me."

"Yes," Bay, answered, beaming at him. "But then the answer has always been yes, hasn't it?"

Scott laughed. "I'm starving," he said, taking her hands and kissing them both before pulling her toward the pier. "Let's go load up on junk food before the fireworks start."

"And make out behind the restaurant," Bay added.

"Right," Scott said, smiling at her. "Full circle."

☆☽☆

Bay woke up first the next day. Unable to sleep through the sunrise on the water, she slid from beneath Scott's arm and out of the sleeping bag they'd curled up in the night before. After finishing off their hot dogs, funnel cakes, and a great bottle of champagne, they'd fallen asleep on deck soon after the fireworks show ended in drowsy, companionable contentment. For the first time in months, she'd woken up comfortable, at home in her own skin.

"When do you have to head out?"

"Soon," she answered. "My flight leaves this afternoon."

"Do you have to go?" he asked.

"I do, but not for long." She gazed out past the other boats in the marina at the calm inlet waters, trying to soak up the peace surrounding her. Scott pulled the blanket from her shoulders and wrapped it around his, then pulled her into his arms.

"And you're coming to New Hope as soon as possible?"

She laid her head on his shoulder. "As soon as possible, absolutely. You can come with me, you know."

"Okay. I'd like that."

"Really?" She turned in his arms so she could see his face. "You've never been much for it, and I only have to go for a couple of weeks."

"Really, I want to come. I want us to start on this something new together immediately." He turned to press a kiss against her forehead.

Bay sat down and pulled the blanket around her. "You're not afraid of jumping right into this?" She looked out over the water, unable to face the truth she might see in his eyes, regardless of his words.

"Honest answer?" he asked.

"Of course." She felt him watching her, but still didn't turn to meet his eyes.

"I've been waiting to jump right into this since the first time I kissed you behind the dockside restaurant. I'm sure, Bay."

Bay laughed. "I think I have. But I haven't been so crazy about myself, so I couldn't accept that you of all people could be."

Scott sighed. "Me of all people? What do you mean?"

"That you're the person I love best in the world, and the best person I know in the world, and it's almost too good to be true that you love me, too."

Scott got to his feet and reached for her, then held her close against him, letting moments pass. "So, I've been really studying up on the sailing thing."

"Yeah?"

"Yeah. When you're sailing, and you're on the right course relative to the wind, do you know what you do?"

"No, I do not. Enlighten me."

"You let go and haul."

She laughed. "Like haul ass?"

"No, not exactly," he answered, laughing along with her. "More like you trim the sails and steady your course."

"So, what you're telling me is we are finally, forever on track?"

"Yes, that is exactly what I'm telling you. Let's do this, Bay. You and me, together. I can't even believe after all that's happened that I'm home, that I have all the people I love with me, except you. I need to come home to you, Bay. I need you to come home to me."

"You don't think I'm sure of how I feel, or that I'll stay?" she asked him, her voice barely hovering above a whisper.

"Are you sure? This whole thing I'm dealing with…I'm a mess. Are you sure you want this?"

Bay nodded her head. "Yes. I want this more than anything, Scott. I want you more than anything. Now, let's go to Nashville and pack up my stuff. Let go and haul, all that."

Scott laughed. "You should put that in a song."

"Hmmm… it could work," she grinned at him as she gathered up her things.

"Okay, then. Let's go home," he said.

Bay smiled in response, knowing full well in her heart they were already, finally there.

LIBERATION: WEDDING NIGHT

I don't count days or nights anymore. I'm just grateful for them, however many come and go. Everything that counts in this world I have here with me, either in New Hope, or in my heart.

Afghanistan is a dream to me now, or a nightmare. I never want to go back there, not in my real life or in my mind. But sometimes I'm drawn back. I've learned to allow myself to hurt. In the end, there's no way around it. But I've also learned that love is there to liberate you from that hurt, if you let it. Bay's given me that gift. Her love is the key that unlocks the hurt, so I can escape it. She can't fix it, but she stands by me. She sees me through it. When the darkness comes—and it still comes—she reminds me that there's light, that there's balance. Even when the bees come, Bay tells me that bees are necessary for flowers, and they're necessary for butterflies, and…well. She reminds me to make the best of it all.

This is my home, my tribe, my family. This is the way of life I pledged to defend when I enlisted, and I did my best. Now I'm gonna do my best to live it. It's the best example I can set for my family. Seeing the things I've seen, I promise you, other ways of life pale in comparison. They can keep their war, the shale-slick mountains, and their desert storms. My boots are on the ground for the last time, planted here in my own little corner of Blossom Hill. I've left it for foreign soil for the last time.

When Lillie appears, I'm almost afraid, but then she smiles and speaks to me for the first time since she's been on the other side.

"I knew you'd make it home. I knew you were strong enough."

It takes a few seconds for me to find my voice, and when it comes, it's heavy with emotion. "I wouldn't have been strong enough without you."

"I don't believe that for a second, but I'm glad I finished my mission."

"Finished your mission?"

Lillie nods. "You and Bay, you made it back home. Tonight's the night. Time for me to say goodbye...but I couldn't go without bringing you a gift on your wedding night."

"Lillie, don't—"

Before I can finish, she opens her palms and butterflies swirl in the air. I'm falling back into a memory, a familiar one...Lillie's brought me back here before. The football field, fifth grade, the rec league and alumni scrimmage at halftime. It's a third down play, and I'm under center at quarterback. I take the snap and find Will near the sideline, hurl a pass to him the second before an alumni player grabs my flag.

"Great arm," the man behind me says.

I turn and look up at him with a grin *"Thanks."*

He's smiling back, and this time I see it. I couldn't have seen it then, but I know—I remember—I felt it. He's bending to talk to me, and I want to reach out, to touch his face. His eyes...they're so much like mine.

"Your dad out here?" he asks, looking around the field.

I shake my head. *"No, he's not around."*

"Well, his loss," he says, nudging me. *"You got family in the stands?"*

I point to Bay. *"Her."*

"Your sister?" he says, waving up to her.

"Nah," I smile. *"That's my girl."*

"Wow," he says, laughing. *"She's a keeper. Nice to meet you...I didn't get your name?"*

"It's Scott."

"Nice to meet you, Scott," he says, shaking my hand. *"I'm Marco. See ya down the road?"*

I nod.

When the memory fades, I'm left breathless with the knowledge that once upon a time, for the briefest moment, I talked to him. I shook my father's hand.

And he saw what I see in Bay. She's definitely a keeper.

"See ya down the road," I whisper.

Lillie waves and spins around, sending her butterflies up in the air. "We'll be waiting," she says before she fades away.

I understand now that she wouldn't rest until we got to where we belong, me and Bay, with both our families made whole again, in spite of our losses. And where we belong is right here, together. For always.

It's good to be home.

CHAPTER 22

Bay Laurel LaFleur knew something about last times. Her life had been full of them, after all. Tonight would be the last time she'd stand in the window of her childhood bedroom as a LaFleur, gazing down through the dark to the front lawn of Blossom Hill. It was bittersweet, she thought, taking in the winter landscape lit with fairy lights, a wonderland spread before her, a goodbye and a welcome home all at once.

It was her wedding night. These were the last moments of her single life, the last before she officially became Mrs. Scott Jackson Murphy Ramirez. She almost couldn't have been happier. Almost.

"It has to be here somewhere," Bay said, throwing her hands up.

"When did you say you saw it last?" Leigh asked from where she stood, plundering through one of Bay's dresser drawers.

"Monday or Tuesday. I took it off and put it right there like I always do before my shower," Bay answered, pointing at the little glass dish on the dresser. "And when I came back to get it, it was gone."

"I don't see it anywhere over here," Reva said, standing up from where she'd been kneeling to look under the bed. She put her hands on her hips. "I've checked every inch of this carpet."

Amelia let out her breath in a huff. "And I've been through both of your nightstands. Nothing."

"Well, we can't start the ceremony until we find it. I won't get married without it." Bay crossed her arms over her chest.

"Good thing you won't have to." Violet breezed in the door wearing a peaceful smile and a flowing forest green dress. In her hands she held a blue velvet box like many others Bay had seen before, from The Palmetto Tree.

"Mama, I told you I didn't want—"

Violet held up a hand. "I know what you said, and I heard you loud and clear. Which is why I took a few liberties."

"Liberties? What do you mean?" Bay asked.

"For the record, I cleared my idea with Scott before I had this made. He agreed this was the perfect piece for you," Violet said, tracing the emblem on the top of the box with a finger.

Bay took a step toward her mama and cocked an eyebrow. "Oh, he did, did he? Y'all both know I wear Lillie's butterfly every day, and that dumb ring that itches me." She put a hand to her chest, at least grateful that the red spot had faded where the ring irritated her skin.

Violet nodded, her smile still firmly in place. "Well, it won't be itching you anymore. I may know you better than you think, Bay Laurel."

"You do know how to pique my curiosity," Bay said, reaching to open the box as Violet held it for her.

Bay's heart skipped as she took in the necklace Violet had made for her. "Oh, Mama…"

"No tears," Violet said, even as her own eyes glistened. "Nothing else would do, now, would it?"

Careful of the delicate new chain, Bay lifted Lillie's butterfly from its velvet bed. It sparkled in the soft light of the room, its original shine restored. One perfect pearl had been set in each wing, and the pearl from the promise ring Scott had given Bay was placed at the center of the butterfly's body.

"It's perfect," Bay whispered.

"One for you, and one for Lillie, and at the heart of it, the one from Scott." Violet stepped around Bay to hook the clasp around her neck. "Bay Laurel, it is my honor to welcome you the ranks of The Pearl Girls tonight, finally. With this gift, we recognize the importance of remembering where you came from as you step forward into your future. May it be as expansive as the ocean from which most pearls come, and as enduring as the love that brought you and Scott back home to each other."

"Ladies," Mel called from the hall. "If we don't get this show on the road soon, we'll have to pay the minister extra."

"We're coming," Violet called, her voice breaking.

"I'll be just a minute," Bay said to Violet, squeezing her hands as the other women filed out. "I just need a minute to…"

Violet nodded. "I know."

☆ ☽ ☆

"Tonight's not an ending, so much as it's a beginning."

Bay turned to see Lillie standing there, her pale blue eyes studying her, taking in the beautiful lacework of the wedding gown Violet and Leigh Anne had been unanimous on.

"You are absolutely perfect," Lillie said, smiling.

"Thank you, Lillie. I was wondering if you were going to show up tonight."

"Of course I wouldn't miss this, Bay. I've been waiting for this day as long as you have."

"Oh, Lillie…" Bay's eyes filled with tears, and she fanned at her face.

Lillie giggled at her. "Don't you dare ruin that mascara. Leigh Anne will combust, as mama would say."

"That she would," Bay said, laughing. "I feel…I miss you more today is all."

"You never have to miss me, Bay Blue, ever. I'm right here, a heartbeat away."

"But—"

"I love what Mama did with my necklace. Our necklace, how it's meant to be."

Bay ran a finger over her butterfly and smiled at her sister. "I nearly turned the house upside down looking for this necklace when it was at the jeweler's. I never suspected Mama would find a way to add our pearls on to this old thing, but I'm so glad she did. It makes me feel close to you, wearing it."

Lillie closed her eyes and smiled, too. "See, I'm always right there. Everything's come full circle. And it's time for me to go now. Like I said, I've been waiting for this day, too."

"I'm not ready."

"Oh, you're ready, Bay." Lillie opened her eyes. "There's one little secret left to uncover…"

Bay took a deep breath. "Please, no more surprise family members." She glanced out the window, smiling over the little cluster of Ramirezes that had descended on Blossom Hill for the wedding, along with Janice Murphy, who'd surprised herself and Scott by finding the courage to make the trip. "I don't know how many more we can house."

Lillie gave her a knowing grin. "I think you and Scott have room at your house for one more by summer."

"One more?"

"Maybe you could name her Lillie. That'd be sweet."

Bay's eyes went wide, and she pressed her hand to her stomach.

Lillie twirled toward the door, sending butterflies up into the air. "I do know some things a little ahead of schedule," she said. "Love you forever, and forever."

"Love you with all my heart," Bay whispered as she watched Lillie fade away.

A knock at the door brought her back to the moment, to the ceremony that was just getting underway. Mel and Violet came in to escort her downstairs together. Violet handed Bay her bouquet, special ordered cream-petaled daylilies with burgundy throats. And pearl blossoms, of course. They stepped onto the front porch to watch Leigh Anne and the girls make their way down to the newly constructed gazebo, erected for the occasion. As Bay stepped down to the grass between her parents, butterflies swarmed the bouquet in her hands and her face lit.

"What in the world—butterflies in December?" Mel whispered, bending to get a glimpse of Violet.

"It's Lillie, saying hello," Bay whispered. "She wanted to escort me down the aisle, too, I guess."

Bay winked at Violet, whose eyes flooded with tears. "Hello, my Lillie love," she whispered into the air. "I feel you, too, tonight."

The three of them collected themselves and made their way toward Scott, who was the most handsome man Bay had ever seen in his Army dress uniform. His grandfather stood beside him, beaming, and Ethan and Will smiled down at her. Bay was overwhelmed at the volume of the love humming in the air around them. It carried her forward on a wave of joy toward the only future she had ever wanted, one she would share with Scott.

Their ceremony was one of laughter and tears. They wiped each other's eyes as they exchanged their vows, giggled at Scotts trembling hands when he slid the slim gold band onto Bay's finger, and shared their first kiss as Sergeant and Mrs. Ramirez to a heady round of applause.

The Ramirezes danced their first dance in the decorated barn, and Bay whispered to her new husband the news that he would also be a father soon, another first already in the making. Later, she grinned at her daddy as he made the first toast with sparkling cider, and laughed when Will whispered in her ear that she was too old for him anyway, and screamed as Scott shoved the first piece of wedding cake in her face. Scott shed tears as he stood with an arm around his mother's shoulders, watching his wife dance with his grandfather, whom he may have never known if not for her. Bay cried more tears of her own as she watched her parents sway cheek to cheek across the dance floor, the distance and secrets between them finally gone.

As they walked hand in hand after the wedding, down the lane to their new home, Bay laid her head on Scott's shoulder. On the front porch, he picked her up to carry her through the threshold.

"So, are you happy to have spent your last night as a single woman, Mrs. Ramirez?"

Bay threw her head back and laughed. "You know what? I'm ecstatic. Now, Sergeant Ramirez, can we get started on my first night as a married woman?"

So, on that first night in the home they built together, on the first night of their always and forever, Bay Laurel Ramirez stopped counting her lasts and started looking forward to all the firsts waiting for them. They were together, they were strong.

And it was really, really good to be home.

THE END

☆ ☽ ☆

☆ ☽ ☆ ABOUT THE AUTHOR ☆ ☽ ☆

Gina Heron is a native of South Carolina, where she currently lives in her hometown with her son and daughter and ferocious Maltese, Kobe. She has a degree in English Literature from Francis Marion University. She's had a long career in the software development industry and continues to work in research & development for a local firm. She also provides productivity coaching for individuals and small businesses.

Gina loves hearing from friends and readers at www.ginaheron.com.

Made in the USA
Middletown, DE
07 December 2018